The **Huron River**

The Huron River

Voices from the Watershed

Edited by John Knott and Keith Taylor

Ann Arbor

The University of Michigan Press

Copyright © by the University of Michigan 2000
All rights reserved
Published in the United States of America by
The University of Michigan Press
Manufactured in the United States of America
⊚ Printed on acid-free paper

2009   2008   2007   2006   6   5   4   3

A CIP catalog record for this book is available from the British Library.

Library of Congress Cataloging-in-Publication Data

The Huron River : voices from the watershed / edited by John
  Knott and Keith Taylor.
       p.   cm.
    ISBN 0-472-09729-6 (acid-free paper)—ISBN 0-472-06729-X
  (pbk. : acid-free paper)
       1. American literature—Michigan—Huron River Watershed
  (Oakland County–Monroe County) 2. Huron River Watershed (Oakland
  County–Monroe County, Mich.)—Literary collections. 3. Michigan—
  Literary collections. I. Knott, John Ray, 1937–   II. Taylor, Keith, 1952–
  PS571.M5 H87   2000
  810.8'097743—dc21   00-08549

ISBN 978-0-472-09729-6 (acid-free paper)
ISBN 978-0-472-06729-9 (pbk. : acid-free paper)

Acknowledgments

We ARE GRATEFUL TO the staff of the Huron River Watershed Council for their strong support. Former director Paul Rentschler endorsed the project in its early stages and contributed an essay. Current director Laura Rubin has been consistently supportive, as have Kris Olsson and Joan Martin, who cheerfully responded to many inquiries. Others who offered advice or help include Robert Marans, who represents Washtenaw County on the Huron-Clinton Metroparks Board of Commissioners; Dave Moilanen, spokesperson for the Metroparks Authority; Stephen Horn, supervising naturalist at Indian Springs Metropark; and Gerald Wykes, supervising curator at the Lake Erie Marshlands Museum and Nature Center, who contributed an essay and helped with illustrations; Paul Seelbach, biologist with the Fisheries Division of the Michigan Department of Natural Resources; Lana Pollack, president of the Michigan Environmental Council; Janis Bobrin, Washtenaw County drain commissioner; Jane Johnson, Donna Johnston, and JoAnn Peraino of the staff of the Department of English at the University of Michigan; and James Crowley, lecturer in the Department of English at the University of Michigan. Anne Frantilla of the Bentley Historical Library provided important help in identifying photographs and historical sources in the Bentley collections. Brian Dunnigan of the William L. Clements Library helpfully identified maps and other historical materials. We are particularly grateful to our editor at the University of Michigan Press, Mary Erwin, who has provided encouragement and good advice at every turn.

The Office of the President, the Office of the Provost, and the Office of the Vice President for Government Relations of the University of Michigan, along with the Mosaic Foundation of Rita and Peter Heydon, provided crucial financial support.

We are grateful to the Bentley Historical Library for permission to quote material from the Harlow Whittemore Papers and to reproduce photographs, a drawing by Jasper Cropsey, and one of the Gardner S. Williams Survey Maps of the Huron River Valley from its collections; to the William L. Clements Library for permission to reprint the 1796 map by Patrick McNiff; to the Fisheries Division of the Michigan Department of Natural Resources for permission to reprint maps of the watershed; to the Huron River Watershed Council for permission to reprint "Clamming on the Huron" by Gerald Wykes and "Huron Hex Hatch" (from *The Ripple Effect*) by Paul Seelbach; and to Past Tents Press for permission to reprint "Little or Nothing" by Ken Mikolowski.

Contents

A watershed is a marvelous thing to consider: this process of rain falling, streams flowing, and oceans evaporating causes every molecule of water on earth to make the complete trip once every two million years. The surface is carved into watersheds—a kind of familial branching, a chart of relationship, and a definition of place. The watershed is the first and last nation whose boundaries, though subtly shifting, are unarguable. Races of birds, subspecies of trees, and types of hats or rain gear often go by the watershed. For the watershed, cities and dams are ephemeral and of no more account than a boulder that falls in the river or a landslide that temporarily alters the channel. The water will always be there, and it will always find its way down. As constrained and polluted as the Los Angeles River is at the moment, it can also be said that in the larger picture that river is alive and well under the city streets, running in giant culverts. It may be amused by such diversions. But we who live in terms of centuries rather than millions of years must hold the watershed and its communities together, so our children might enjoy the clear water and fresh life of this landscape we have chosen. From the tiniest rivulet at the crest of a ridge to the main trunk of a river approaching the lowlands, the river is all one place and all one land.

—Gary Snyder, from *"Coming into the Watershed"* (A Place in Space)

Introduction

WATERSHEDS ARE THE OLDEST and most durable markers of place. Yet we are less likely to know the boundaries of our watershed (the area drained by a particular river) than we are the political boundaries (township, city, county, state) that determine who collects the taxes and provides the services that we depend upon in our everyday lives. Watershed boundaries affect our lives by defining our natural environment, not only its topography but its soils, its plant and animal life, and to some extent its weather. The water that sustains most of us is the water that flows through the watershed, in our case that of the streams that empty into the Huron River. The river gives many of us our drinking water and carries away our wastewater and the runoff from storms. It has influenced the history and design of many of our towns and villages. It offers us opportunities for play.

The ways we have used the river have changed dramatically in the relatively brief period of European settlement in the watershed. It is no longer the significant transportation route that it was for the early settlers and the native peoples who lived in the watershed or traveled through it for millennia before the settlers arrived. The mills that mushroomed along the river in the nineteenth century to take advantage of water power have come and gone; the future of at least some of the twentieth-century dams that reshaped portions of the river is uncertain. With the increase in population and the acceleration of development, the character of the river and the natural life it supports have changed. The river and the ways we live with it will surely continue to change, but, as the words of Gary Snyder that serve as an epigraph to this book suggest, in the longer view the watershed will outlast our adaptations of it: "The water will always be there, and it will always find its way down."

As rivers go, the Huron is neither spectacular nor famous. It drains a relatively modest watershed of 908 square miles and flows 125 (or 130 or 136, depending on who you talk to) miles from its origins in the Huron Swamp and Big Lake to the marshes where it joins Lake Erie at Pointe Mouillée. The

Huron has followed its present course for about twelve thousand years, since the last retreat of the glaciers, but the early European settlers found a river that looked different from the Huron we know: generally narrower and deeper, clearer, more shaded by forested banks. Bays and pools in the river and adjacent marshes and bogs nourished vegetation that supported more diverse aquatic life than one can find today. As agriculture and settlement spread through the watershed, and wetlands were drained, the flow of the river became much more variable, with increased spring flooding disrupting spawning patterns of fish and lower flows in the summer warming water temperature. Flooding and erosion broadened the river's channel and increased sedimentation. Despite the degradation of habitat and the loss of some species of fish and other aquatic life, the Huron today is a relatively healthy river, generally regarded as the best in southeast Michigan. The April 1995 Huron River Assessment of the Michigan Department of Natural Resources describes the condition of the river and traces the distribution throughout the river system of ninety-nine species of fish, many of them native to the Huron.

Dams and lake-level controls have deepened glacially formed lakes along the course of the Huron and have created new man-made lakes (including Kent Lake, Ford Lake, and Belleville Lake). In its course through five counties in southeast Michigan (Oakland, Livingston, Washtenaw, Wayne, and Monroe) the Huron changes from a small, relatively high quality stream above Kent Lake to a sluggish and conspicuously more polluted river by the time it reaches its mouth at Lake Erie. The upper Huron flows through marshy country and lakes above Kent Lake. Between Kent Lake Dam and Delhi, a stretch designated as "country-scenic" under the Michigan Natural Rivers Act, the Huron offers excellent canoeing and some of the best small-mouth bass fishing in the Midwest. In the middle Huron, the area of greatest population density, dams in the Ann Arbor and Ypsilanti areas (Barton, Argo, Geddes, Superior, Peninsula, Ford) broaden the river and create opportunities for boaters and others who take advantage of city and county parks. Below Belleville Lake the lower Huron slows as the terrain flattens in the ancient Maumee lake plain.

Most people know the Huron River today as a place for recreation (boating, fishing, swimming in its lakes, picnicking or perhaps jogging or bird-watching in one of the many parks that give access to the river). A growing population enjoys the chain of metroparks (Indian Springs, Kensington, and Huron Meadows on the upper Huron; Hudson Mills, Dexter-Huron, and Delhi near Dexter on the middle Huron; Lower Huron, Willow, Oak-woods, and Lake Erie on the lower Huron) and state recreation areas (Pontiac Lake, Proud Lake, Island Lake) as well as numerous city and county parks along the course of the river. The present pattern of intensive recreational use of the Huron and the lakes that form part of its course is, however, a relatively recent phenomenon in the history of the river. The essay written by John O'Shea for this book, "The Huron River Past," sketches the long tenure of native peoples along the Huron. As he notes, this history is visible today through the traces found by archaeologists. These reveal overlapping periods of hunting, foraging, and cultivation dependent on the river and its environs. The coming of Europeans and the influx of settlers in the early nineteenth century displaced the tribes living here at the time and rapidly transformed a natural environment that to that point had evolved slowly over millennia with comparatively little alteration by its inhabitants. As the written records of that period suggest, the new preoccupations were claiming land, building log houses and settlements, and clearing the forest to establish permanent farms.

The earliest settlers made their way from Detroit up the Huron by flatboat as far as French Landing (Belleville) or Snow's Landing (Rawsonville), striking out overland when they had to with a wagon and a team of oxen on roads that were primitive to nonexistent. Many established mills at places where the drop in the river or a tributary creek was sufficient to make use of water power to mill lumber or grind grain, building earthen or rock dams and millraces to channel the water. Mills were in operation at Snow's Landing by 1824, Ann Arbor by 1825, Milford by 1832, Brighton by 1833, and Commerce by 1837. The mill era reached its peak in the late nineteenth century, with large paper, woolen, and flour mills at Ypsilanti and a flourishing economy based upon mills at Delhi. The Huron remained important to the commerce of the area through the nineteenth and early twentieth centuries. Freight moved by boat on the lower Huron; ice was cut from the river and stored in icehouses before the days of electric refrigeration; there was even a small clamming industry, described in the essay by Gerald Wykes, "Clamming on the Huron," in the first quarter of the twentieth century.

Between 1912 and 1925 Detroit Edison, after acquiring the necessary land and water rights, established a series of dams on the Huron for the purpose of generating hydroelectric power. These were built on the stretch of the river with the steepest gradient, from just above Ann Arbor (Barton Dam) to just below Belleville, where the dam constructed at French Landing in 1925 created Belleville Lake. Seven dams turned what had been a winding river with a few small dams, such as the one that created Geddes Pond in 1826, into a virtually continuous series of impoundments. One effect of dam construction was to block the spawning runs of sturgeon, muskellunge, herring, and whitefish from Lake Erie. In "Special Report on the Huron," published by the *Ann Arbor News* in October 1992, biologist Paul Seelbach describes these as "big runs, walk-across-the-back runs." By fragmenting the river the hydroelectric dams further reduced the diversity of aquatic life. At the same time they increased recreational opportunities on the river by creating new ponds and lakes. When Detroit Edison found that it no longer made economic sense to make the dams part of its power grid, municipalities had the opportunity to acquire them along with large tracts of land bordering the river. A purchase in 1963 made possible Ann Arbor's still expanding network of riverfront parks and bike paths.

One of the major changes along the Huron in the middle and late twentieth century has been the emergence of metroparks with facilities that include beaches, picnic areas, boat launches, nature centers, golf courses, and water parks. Since the ratification in 1940 of legislation creating the Huron-Clinton Metropolitan Authority (HCMA) by the voters of the five counties affected, the HCMA has developed one of the outstanding regional park systems in the country, with close to twenty-four thousand acres of land in thirteen parks along the Huron and Clinton Rivers. As the HCMA continues to interpret its mandate to provide recreational opportunities and maintain parkland, for an expanding regional population, controversies over what kinds of recreation should be favored are likely to grow. Do we need more golf courses and water parks or more effort to preserve the natural features of the parks? How can the preferences of those who drive to the parks from elsewhere in the region be reconciled with those of local users of particular metroparks? Whatever their recreational preferences, park users are likely to share a common desire to see the quality of the rivers nurtured and thus to welcome signs that the rivers' health is improving.

A significant development in recent years has been the sharp increase in efforts to monitor and improve the quality of the Huron, with the Huron River Watershed Council, a coalition of local governments and residents of the watershed, playing a leading role. Working with biologists from the Fisheries Division of the Department of Natural Resources and from the University of Michigan, and with the support of county drain commissioners who serve the more than sixty communities along the river, the Watershed Council has developed an extensive program of monitoring streams in the watershed, enlisting volunteers to sample aquatic life as a gauge of water quality. In addition to conducting ecological research the Watershed Council promotes planning for intelligent growth and community education on the sources of pollution. Its Adopt-a-Stream program has prompted the development of creek groups throughout much of the watershed dedicated to improving the quality of local streams.

The quality of the Huron River itself has improved significantly since the enactment of the federal Clean Water Act in 1972 and the regulation of industrial and other identifiable sources of pollution. We no longer have pipes pouring untreated waste into the river. As growth continues to spread in the watershed, however, so do impervious surfaces (roads, parking lots, building sites) that increase contaminated runoff into the river. Runoff from agricultural areas and lawns carrying fertilizers and pesticides adds to this non-point-source pollution. At the same time community awareness of the threats to the Huron posed by development is increasing and with it volunteer efforts to preserve the quality of the river for the future. Huron River Days, combining cleanup efforts with educational activities, have become annual events in Ann Arbor and Milford.

If much of the activity along the Huron River today mirrors the dramatic changes in our culture in the last two hundred years, some things have not changed. The water is still there, still finding its way down. People still take to the river in boats, although today's canoes are made of fiberglass or aluminum rather than birch bark and kayakers now play in the rapids at Delhi. Some people still fish for their supper in the Huron, while others practice their fly-fishing skills. The river valley still nourishes abundant natural life, although some of the species the early settlers and their predecessors knew have retreated (wolves, bears, bobcats) or become extinct (passenger pigeons). If the river looks different now, broken up by dams and subject to greater fluctuations with the loss of wetlands and woods and open spaces that formerly moderated its flow, it remains a constant in our landscape, changing with the seasons and showing a remarkable capacity to renew itself.

The idea for a book that would collect imaginative responses to the Huron River and its watershed grew out of a specific event, a visit to the Ann Arbor area in March 1998 by the Orion Society's Forgotten Language Tour, a group of six writers sponsored by a coalition of community groups and the University of Michigan. The writers met with representatives of these groups on several occasions. On the last of these, the Huron River Watershed Council hosted a potluck dinner at which they met with members of the community involved in some way with protecting the quality of the river and its tributary streams. The writers, including a couple involved in efforts to publicize and protect western rivers (Annick Smith and William Kittredge of Montana), talked about the kinds of contributions writers can make by telling stories of an area and giving people new ways of imagining the places where they live. All of them (including essayists Scott Russell Sanders of Indiana and Stephanie Mills of Michigan and poets Pattiann Rogers and Alison Hawthorne Deming of Colorado) demonstrated the value of writing about place, through their comments and through public readings of their own work.

Recent discussions about place and its importance, and the flourishing literature of place, are very different from older discussions of setting or regional literature, what used to be called the literature of "local color." The knowledge of a place—its natural history, its history, and the relationship between the two—can influence the creative response of writers and also that of artists working in other media. As the travels around the country of the Forgotten Language Tour and other efforts by writers have shown, awareness of and concern for place among an area's artists can influence the political will to protect its natural features.

We were aware of references to the Huron in the works of some writers who had spent time in Ann Arbor, including Marge Piercy and Nancy Willard, whose novel *Sister Water* plays on symbolic meanings of the river. We also knew that the Huron had been maligned by the protagonist of Jim Harrison's 1976 novel *Farmer,* who complains about having to spend six weeks in Ann Arbor, "a town he loathed on sight with its smelly, polluted Huron River." We figured that the remark reflected Harrison's northern Michigan attitudes and that anyway his character's perception of the Huron was out of date. Shorter works by Charles Baxter and Thomas Lynch, both of whom live and work in the watershed, impressed us as outstanding examples of imaginative responses to the Huron River. We have included both these works, Baxter's short story "A Late Sunday Afternoon by the Huron" and Lynch's essay "Mary and Wilbur," and they have served as touchstones for some of our contributors.

Almost everyone we queried about contributing to this project answered with interest, some commenting that they had thought about the river or that they had work in progress that might be appropriate. Their responses take the form of stories, poems, drawings, and essays ranging from personal reminiscence to reflections on the human or natural history of the place. We enlisted some contributors with a specialized knowledge of the area—biologists, naturalists, and an archaeologist—to give a richer sense of the physical and cultural environment. We have supplemented these contemporary responses with maps, photographs, and quotations (voices from the past) to give a sense of historical context. Several of our contributors explore the history of a particular part of the watershed, usually with an eye to its relevance to current issues and habits of living. Some focus on the experience of canoeing or other kinds of boating, some on the rich natural life along the river, particularly on the opportunities for birding. Others portray human dramas that reflect and comment upon the places in which they unfold.

Taken together, these responses from writers and artists constitute a kind of imaginative mapping. Any such mapping can only begin to suggest the nature of a particular place and the human interactions that give it a history, but we hope that the efforts of the contributors to this book will increase awareness and appreciation of the Huron River and its watershed and that they will suggest some of the ways they have affected and continue to affect the lives of those who have chosen to live and work here.

John Knott
Keith Taylor
Ann Arbor, September 1999

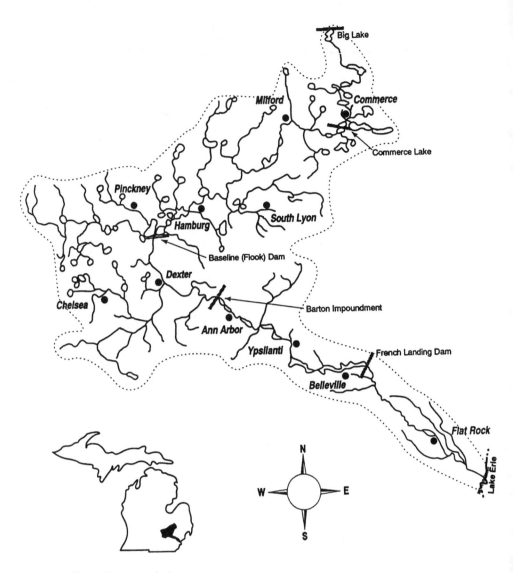

Huron River watershed

PAUL RENTSCHLER

Belonging to the Watershed

AFTER A HURRIED DINNER with my family and a quick drive along country roads, I pull into the parking lot. Mayflies and caddis flies, born in the river, circle the streetlamp as I pull a slide projector and a box of pamphlets and newsletters from the car and walk to the town hall. It's a familiar scene. Over the last ten years, working for the Huron River Watershed Council, I've become familiar with a number of town halls and school and church cafeterias. I've eaten a lot of Rotary dinners. Lugging my slide projector from place to place, giving slide shows about the Huron River, I realize that people are looking for their connection to the river. They wish to know where they live in relation to the watershed boundaries, how long the river is, which towns the river flows through and connects, if the water is safe to drink and swim in. So, in my attempt to save a river, I talk. In these talks I use maps, diagrams, and charts. I cite statistics and show photographs of the river's beauty. This is meant as a kind of incantation, an attempt to invoke, and incite, a sense of connection to the river system.

The river does connect us. It connects a half million people and sixty-three communities. It connects us geographically, historically, connects us by our common use and need of its waters. The best way I know to describe those connections is to describe the places and workings of the river itself, from headwaters to mouth.

The river begins near Andersonville in Springfield Township, in the rolling glacial moraines of western Oakland County, as water inconspicuously bubbling out of the ground. A little bit here. A little bit there. Barely discernible, the water adds to itself, water from the last spring rain mixing with water stored in the soil for a hundred years, to form and sustain the Huron Swamp. The river is not the dominant feature in the landscape here. The oak, maple, and beech forest; the blooming of wildflowers; the sounds of woodpeckers drilling for food are what one notices most. But the water begins to pool, filling Big Lake. It coalesces into a small stream, so small here one can step across it. The river springs from the black soil like the skunk cabbage and marsh marigold and begins its journey to Lake Erie, the St. Lawrence River, and the sea.

The Huron Swamp is the headwaters, the birthplace, of the Huron River's main stem (it is also the headwaters to the Clinton and Shiawassee Rivers). But the river has similar origins across a vast area in parts of Oakland, Livingston, Ingham, Jackson, Washtenaw, Wayne, and Monroe Counties. Like the tall oaks of the swamp, most of a river system is made up of the branches. The river's main stem stretches approximately 130 miles, yet it's fed by an additional 370 miles of tributary streams, each of these beginning with an upwelling and joining of water like that which occurs in the Huron Swamp.

The river flows through the lakes region of Oakland County: Pontiac Lake, Oxbow Lake, Cedar Island Lake, Commerce Lake, Proud Lake. Between Proud Lake and the village of Milford, north of the city of Wixom, the river winds through a wide valley. The river channel is sandy bottomed and rimmed by broad marshes. Although the river is generally too warm for trout to reproduce on their own, trout are stocked in this area. Each April, anglers shoulder together fishing for them. The first month of the season is limited to catch and release, and each fish is caught a number of times before it can finally be kept and taken home for a meal. Downstream from Milford, where the river pours over the dam that holds back Kent Lake, its beauty receives official recognition. The next 27.5 miles of river are designated by the state of Michigan as a scenic river, the only river in southeast Michigan with such status and its accompanying restrictions. These limit the number of homes that can be built along the river and require that they be set back from the river. The result is a more scenic riverfront but also a false sense of security. From the river here, one does not realize the magnitude of new development affecting the upper watershed.

Flowing out of Kent Lake, the river enters and cuts across the southeast corner of Livingston County. Here the forest canopy closes in on the river, the slope of the land flattens, and the surrounding woods hold the spring floods. The river's banks are a tangle of tree roots. The river meanders back and forth upon itself. Fallen trees stretch almost from bank to bank and serve as an avenue for mink crossing the river. The mink don't really need to walk across the river. They're able swimmers, catching fish and dining on mussels.

The river again enters a chain of kettle lakes: Strawberry, Zukey, Baseline. These were carved by tremendous chunks of ice calved from the retreating glaciers over ten thousand years ago. Between the lakes, the river's bottom is now strewn with gravel, cobble-sized stones, and larger boulders. Patches of broken mussel shells sparkle in the sun and catch one's eye. The dried "skins" of dragonfly nymphs cling to boulders above the water's surface. Having spent most of their lives in the river, the dragonflies emerge, transform to adults, and then patrol the river in search of prey and mates.

Flowing into the river from the west at the downstream end of the chain of lakes, Portage Lake bears the outflow of the Pinckney recreation area and its vast wetlands and numerous lakes. Leaving the main river at this point and moving upstream through Portage Lake, along Portage Creek to the village of Stockbridge, one would reach the place where, geologically, east meets west. Here, at the top of the Huron drainage, one crosses over into the Grand River watershed. With a short portage from Portage Creek to a tributary of the Grand River, Native Americans and early European settlers used this route to cross Michigan's Lower Peninsula from Lake Erie on the east to Lake Michigan on the west.

Below Portage Lake the river main stem changes course. Flowing largely southwest to this point, it now turns and flows southeast toward Lake Erie. Still bordered by forest, the river becomes too wide for fallen trees to span the channel. The trees now serve as landing pads for little green and great blue herons. The little green herons stay put as canoes move past, hoping if they don't move they won't be seen. The great blue herons launch into the air as canoes approach, fly downstream, and land in another tree. They repeat this as the canoes again approach, playing a form of leapfrog down the river.

In the water below one sees the brown and black saddles on the backs of northern hognose suckers swimming in schools in the gravel shoals near Bell Road, their vacuum-hose snouts scouring the bottoms for mayflies, caddis flies, and stone flies. Their name belies the fact that they are dependent upon clean water and clean gravel stream bottoms. They are a dominant fish in the Huron, an indication that the river system is still healthy. Burrowing mayflies also inhabit the stream bottom. Their stout forearms, designed for digging in the sand, make them look like weight lifters. In August, they emerge and gather in swarms above the river; a short-lived orgy of mating and reproduction for the mayflies, a feeding orgy for smallmouth bass.

Mill Creek, the Huron's largest tributary, enters below the village of Dexter. Once an expansive, shallow system of marshes and tamarack swamps, the Mill Creek system has changed dramatically since European settlement. Silts, loam, and sands washed away from the terminal face of melting glaciers settled in the Mill Creek valley, forming the finest agricultural soils in the watershed. Thousands of years later, many of these wetlands were drained to make way for farms. Stream channels were dredged to carry the water away faster. Where water once warmed in shallow marshlands, it now flows through these deepened channels— many of which have been cut to a level below the water table. The result is a system that now supports fish species that prefer cooler water but also delivers more water and sediment to the river main stem. Northern pike once swam up Mill Creek from the Huron to spawn in the valley's wetlands, but in the 1800s a dam and sawmill were built on Mill Creek at Dexter, blocking their upstream migration. Around the country, after more than a century of intensive dam building, biologists, anglers, and politicians are beginning to reverse history with the demolition of some of these dams. Dexter Village leaders and state fisheries biologists are part of this movement, considering removing the Dexter dam and restoring the connection to the larger river system.

The upstream wetland complexes—the Waterloo area at the upstream end of the Mill Creek valley, the Pinckney recreation area in the upper reaches of Portage Creek, the chains of lakes, the broad floodplains and the glacial moraines of the upper Huron—are the linchpins of the Huron River system. They store the floodwaters and the rich silt they carry. They also provide groundwater to the stream, helping balance the system against feast and famine, too much water in the spring rainy season or too little during late summer droughts.

These spaces, which make the watershed a functioning ecosystem, are put at risk by the heavy assault of new homes, parking lots, and shopping malls, the cumulative effect of new and old development taken together. The risk is heightened by the loss of our connection to this place. The building boom begun following World War II has yet to slow. New and old watershed settlers alike build in the filled wetlands, placing their homes within the river's floodplain without an understanding of how rivers move on the landscape over time or of seasonal cycles of flood and drought. When the spring rains bring the river within inches of their front doors, or when low water in late summer leaves them unable to put boats in the water, those who do not understand these river rhythms call for the river to be walled in or dredged.

After Dexter the river flows on to Ann Arbor. Above Ann Arbor the state scenic river designation ends, and one can see and feel the impact of human activity in the modification of the river. This is the watershed's population center, with over half of the one-half million people who live in the Huron River watershed living in Ann Arbor, Ypsilanti, and the surrounding townships. Here the river is impounded behind dams that create a series of seven artificial lakes between Ann Arbor and Belleville. The river is used for industry and for the disposal of treated municipal wastewater.

Actually, towns throughout the river basin use the river for wastewater treatment. A friend who lobbies on behalf of rivers throughout the country once told me that as a student at the University of Michigan she had been shocked to learn that by the time the river reaches Ann Arbor, "it's passed through nine sets of kidneys." An unsettling but apt image for our dependence upon wastewater treatment plants.

Jay Stielstra's song "The Huron River" in this volume refers to the Huron as a "working river." It certainly is put to work here, where 140,000 people get much of their drinking water just upstream from Ann Arbor. The water is piped to our homes, emerging from faucets and showerheads, filling our toilets, then flowing through another set of pipes to the wastewater treatment plant downstream from the city. Dams in Ann Arbor, Ypsilanti Township, and Van Buren Township channel the river through turbines to generate electricity. Despite being worked hard, this stretch of river remains beautiful. Paddling through Ann Arbor and Ypsilanti, one is amazed by the scenic beauty that remains, much of it in parklands. Except for areas where homeless people unfurl their bedrolls along the wooded stream banks, spending their nights where the river valley holds a bit of the day's heat, it doesn't feel like the middle of a city.

Below Ypsilanti, the river descends from glacial moraine to the flats of ancient lake plains, the bed of the glacial ancestors of Lake Erie. Inundated now by Ford and Belleville Lakes, impounded behind dams for recreation and the generation of electricity, this area once afforded a much different kind of recreation and another kind of power.

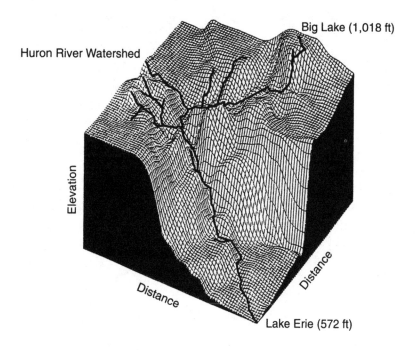

Huron River, rate of descent

When a river tumbles down steep slopes and suddenly levels out upon a plain, it is filled with pent up energy. To dissipate that energy, the river moves laterally, meandering, winding back and forth, increasing its length to counteract the loss in slope. This is exactly what the Huron River underlying Ford and Belleville Lakes did. Maps from the early 1900s, prior to the construction of these dams, show a river of serpentine meanders and cut and abandoned oxbows snaking across a broad valley. The maps themselves are so beautiful I wish that I could have seen the actual place. I imagine it teeming with waterfowl. Downstream from Belleville Lake, at Lower Huron Metropark, is the last substantial piece of the bottomland hardwood forest that bordered these meanders and oxbow lakes. There one can find more species of trees and shrubs than in all of Europe. Redbuds bring drama to the

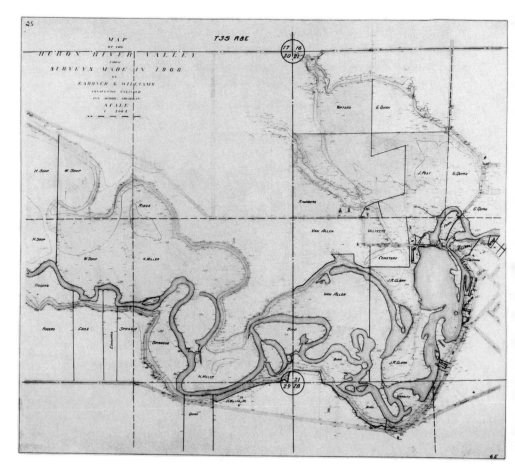

Huron River before Belleville Lake, Gardner S. Williams Survey Map, 1908

riverbanks in May. Giant sycamores mark the lateral shifting of the river's course over the centuries. Ephemeral vernal pools up on the floodplains are raucous with the spring songs of wood frogs.

The advance and retreat of glaciers in this area created geographic connections completely different from those we know today. One of the glacial precursors to Lake Erie, Lake Maumee, at its highest stage met the Huron in northwestern Ypsilanti. Its water surface was some 230–40 feet higher than current Lake Erie levels. Approximately thirteen thousand to fourteen thousand years ago, Lake Maumee alternately found an outlet southwest near Fort Wayne, Indiana, and north near Imlay City. At these times, when the American mastodon and the stag moose roamed its swamps, waters of the Huron flowed not east to the Atlantic but west across the Lower Peninsula to what would become Lake Michigan and from there into the early Illinois and Mississippi River systems.

Lake Maumee receded long ago. The current Huron River watershed narrows below Belleville Lake, dropping further toward Lake Erie. At Rockwood, South Rockwood, and Flat Rock the river flows over an outcropping of bedrock, from which these cities get their names. At Flat Rock, the river flows through its last dam. In all, the river and its tributaries are slowed and impounded by ninety-six dams, one for nearly every five miles of stream. Placed wherever the gradient of the river channel was greatest, they have eliminated almost all of the whitewater habitat the river once had, replacing it with slower lakelike waters, and a different fish community as well.

As the river flows, the dam at Flat Rock is the last. From the standpoint of fish that historically moved from the Great Lakes up the river to spawn in its marshes, in its gravels, or on the bedrock at Flat Rock, this dam is the first barrier to migration. Until only a couple of years ago, fish would be stopped here, approximately twelve miles from Lake Erie. Now, however, local anglers and the Department of Natural Resources have built a ladder, a series of stair-step pools that allow fish to bypass the dam. The pools are not large enough to allow the larger fish like lake sturgeon, which may have once spawned in the Huron, to navigate the ladder. Perhaps the genetic memory of this river is long gone from the remaining lake sturgeon population anyway. The fact that some species now can move farther up the river system, extending its connection to the lake, makes us realize that we can remedy some of the problems that we have unintentionally caused.

Below Flat Rock one can feel the proximity of the lake. The river widens and slows further. The Huron once ended in a vast delta of marshes, formed in a process of give-and-take with the lake. As the river approaches the same elevation as Lake Erie, it slows, and the sediment it carries falls out of suspension. These sediments built the delta. Each year, Lake Erie washed away at the sediments, and the river would annually replace what had been lost to storm and wave action. The repeated damming of the river reduced the flow of sediments, and the delta marshes were ultimately carried away by the lake. Today, however, marshes have been re-created, held in place by dikes at the Pointe Mouillée wildlife refuge, once again providing vital habitat for resident and migrating shorebirds, waterfowl, and raptors.

As I give this talk or write this narrative, hoping to provide a sense of connection, I realize that I can't. The facts and figures, the dire predictions, the images of the river's beauty and of our utilitarian modifications of it don't demonstrate connection so much as dependence. Codependency actually. We use and need the river to support our lives and lifestyles. The river depends upon us to make the right decisions, to protect its integrity as a physical and living system. The type of connection I hope to foster is one based on familiarity, intimacy, a knowledge of the passage of seasons, a sense of place—both of geography and of our place within the river system and its processes, a sense of belonging.

In an essay entitled "Place in American Culture," Paul Shepard writes that "Belonging is the pivot of life, the point at which selfhood becomes possible— not just belonging in general, but in particular. One belongs to a universe of order and purpose that must initially be realized as a particular community of certain species in a terrain of unique geography." I wish to deepen and strengthen my own sense of belonging to this place. After studying the river system as a whole for more than a decade, I'm in awe of the fisherman who knows one riffle intimately, who knows on a still August evening, though they may be miles away, that the Ephoron hatch is on. I'm in awe of the scullers who know the vagaries of wind on water where they row daily. I'm in awe of the woman who knows, and marks on her calendar, when the redwing blackbirds will return to her marsh.

When I was a boy, my father and I canoed from our home, in the river's headwaters, through a chain of lakes and the small channels that connected them, to the Huron's main stem. Between the lakes, the channels were in places only inches deep, and we carried the canoe as much as we paddled. In those channels, we carried the canoe over concrete blocks, abandoned Christmas trees, between chain-link fences lining both banks. Small as the stream was, I wondered why the people whose houses we skirted had turned their backs to the stream, how they were so disconnected from the river that they could use it for disposing of their refuse. If we are to know our place in the workings of the river system, we need to store up memories of time spent with the river. We must learn once again to belong to the watershed.

JAY STIELSTRA

The Huron River

1. The Huron runs through Livingston and four more counties. She
2. She's pretty up near Dexter close by the cider mill where

never stops 'till past Flat Rock at the Great Lake Erie. Some
you can buy a rusty glass in the early autumn chill. She

places she is dirty. Some places she is clean. She
rapid runs at Delhi, at Barton she goes slow.

is just what she's told to be by people and machines
Then on to Ann Arbor where the ivory towers glow.

She flows to Ypsilanti where you seldom see canoes She

winds around Frog Island where you sometimes hear the blues. They

fish her well at Bellville, 'n from the last dam to the Lake. In the

mallard marsh at Mouillée she feeds her hens and drakes. She's

not the Mississippi, she's not the Rio Grande, she's

just a working river in the south of Michigan

The Huron River . . . was called Cos-scut-e-nong Sebee *or
Burnt District river, meaning the plains or oak openings, lands or
country. . . . [It] is a beautiful, transparent stream, passing alternatively
through rich bottoms, openings, plains, and sloping woodlands,
covered with heavy timber.*

History of Washtenaw County, Michigan, *1881*

JOHN M. O'SHEA

The Huron River Past

FROM ALMOST ANYWHERE you view the river, it is the hand of modern development that catches the eye. The dams and highways, railroad bridges and sprawling parks corset the river and give it shape. But the dominance of the modern world is an illusion. The erratic advance and grudging retreat of the great ice sheets shaped the land we see. The hills and ridges are the piled debris left behind as the ice withdrew twelve millennia ago. The rush of icy meltwater that flowed from beneath the ice formed the first river and set in motion the cycle of erosion and aggradation that made the river and the hills appear as they do today.

To talk about the river, and how it figured in the lives of earlier peoples, we must look to archaeology, for it is to archaeology that the study of culture in the past has been entrusted. Yet like a gift bestowed by an ambivalent god the archaeologist's vision is incomplete.

The Pawnee tell a story about a young girl who was too ill to travel when the village set out on the summer bison hunt. She was left behind, alone in her earth lodge. When the fever finally broke and the girl awoke, she found herself not alone but surrounded by the bustle of village life. She could hear the sounds and voices plainly but could not see any people. Over time, she was able to see the dust raised by the people's feet and later their moccasins and then their lower legs. But before she could see more, a voice cried, "The people are returning," and the spirit villagers departed, leaving the girl. When the villagers returned, they found the girl despondent for her departed spirit family, a family none of the villagers could see.

Archaeologists are like the young girl. With time and practice, we learn to see the traces of past peoples. We see the dust from their feet, the trash from their meals, their tools and ornaments, but we can never see the people. Yet, where archaeologists see these traces, most see nothing at all.

This inability to see the people makes the present task difficult, and unlike the young girl, we cannot hear the past peoples. Until the time of written records, I cannot even tell you the name the people called themselves. Yet, because we can see their traces, it is possible to say a great deal about how past peoples lived and the role the Huron River played in their lives.

Over the past twelve thousand years there have been four distinct patterns of life along the river. These patterns are partly chronological, in that one follows another in time. But they also reflect different ways in which the people used the river and its lands. It is from these patterns that we can glimpse how these earlier people lived and possibly also imagine how they viewed the world that surrounded them.

The first of these patterns is that of the ancient hunters. The hunters were the first to occupy the land, and it was a harsh land. Across a landscape of tundra and parkland they pursued the migrating herds of caribou, mastodon, and other large mammals. They traveled light and covered great distances in their pursuit. The territories they moved in were large, much larger than those used by later peoples. We can follow their movements by the stones they used for the manufacture of tools, which can be traced to distant quarries.

Because the ancient hunters moved frequently and in small bands, the traces they left are faint and difficult to find. Occasionally we encounter their camps. In these camps we see the finely made spear points and scrapers that are the hallmark of the time. The elaborately finished fluted points made by the first hunters evidence an artistry that is undiminished by the ages. But there is no mistaking the serious purpose of these finely finished tools. The time spent in these camps was for rearming. Many of the points found here are broken, discarded as the weapons were repaired for the next foray. The cutting and scraping tools reflect the successes of the hunt and the processing of meat, bone, and hides. Their uses are told by the distinctive wear gloss left on the surface of the tools. The forms of these tools resemble those of tools made by other Ice Age hunters around the globe.

Yet for all the austere beauty of the stone tools, one is struck by what cannot be seen. Neither the hide robes nor the finely polished wood spear shafts survive. Even the animal bone is dissolved away by the acid soils. Beyond the base camps, the traces of the ancient hunters are even fainter. Here on the middle Huron, their presence is attested only by the occasional find of an isolated spear point, a calling card left by the hunters as they followed their game along the river valley. To the ancient hunters, the Huron River was a map for traversing their wide domain and an ambuscade for their quarry.

Though imperceptibly to the living, the world of the ancient hunters was changing. The climate was warming. The great ice sheets continued their retreat, and the Great Lakes filled with the meltwater. The plant and animal

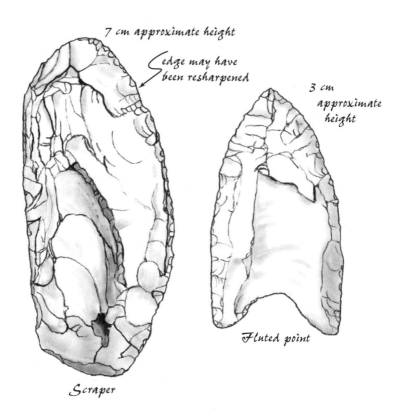

7 cm approximate height

edge may have been resharpened

3 cm approximate height

Fluted point

Scraper

communities also changed. The region was becoming more temperate and richer, and the lifeways that developed took full advantage of the new abundance.

This second pattern, termed the Archaic by archaeologists, is characterized by the harvesting of a broad array of plants and animals as each becomes abundant through the cycle of seasons. These included important new plant foods, such as nuts and small seeds. The territories of these foragers shrunk even as their populations grew. The foragers were drawing more from a smaller territory by exploiting it more intensively. This change was gradual and occurred in step with the still changing climate. By about five thousand years ago, conditions stabilized and have remained essentially unchanged to modern times. This was the time of the florescence of the foragers, and their sites are numerous and varied.

With the foragers came a pattern of settlement and land use in the middle Huron that would persist to the time of European contact. This pattern consisted of base camps surrounded by a halo of small and ephemeral activity sites. The base camps were used repeatedly and show the traces of a wide range of activities, from food preparation and storage to tool manufacture and occasionally the burial of the dead. They were sited carefully, in locations that were dry with good visibility and easy access to water and the season's resources.

The smaller sites are scattered all over the landscape and often were used only once. A site might be a spot where a group of hunters processed their kill or a place where a family collecting blueberries or acorns spent the night. At one small campsite in north Ann Arbor, we found a large glacial boulder with a scatter of fresh chert flakes around one side of it. It appears someone once sat on the boulder facing a small fire, flaked a stone tool, and then left. The site was never again visited or disturbed. The flakes lay just as they had fallen from the maker's hand, three millennia ago.

The foragers moved with the seasons, and the river and its adjacent wetlands were a frequent stop, offering migratory waterfowl in the spring and autumn; fish, clams, and aquatic tubers in warm weather; and beaver in winter. The surrounding uplands held acorns in the autumn and deer yearround. To the foragers, the Huron Valley was a basket filled with each season's abundance.

Sometime during this period, the foragers began to take a more active role in tending the plants they harvested. Their efforts were modest at first, encouraging particular weeds that grew in the rubbish heaps of their camps or shaking out seeds in damp areas to create predictable stands of desired plants. Agriculture did not develop here as a revolution.

The first domestic plants to be used developed from local weeds. While they were domestic plants, they were still exploited following the logic of the foragers. They were one more seasonally available food among many. But the foragers were paying more attention to plant foods and particularly to the processing of small starchy seeds and nuts. Grinding stones are a common tool in the base camps, as is an important new material, pottery.

Throughout much of the world, the origin of pottery tends to be associated with the processing of plant foods and the development of agriculture. The earliest pottery found here was thick and coarsely made and may only have served as a portable storage pit. Soon, though (at least as time is reckoned by archaeologists), the pottery became finer, with thin walls and a variety of vessel forms and decoration. Agriculture and ceramics mark the beginning of the time period termed the Woodland, and it is this tradition that persists up to the coming of the Europeans in the Huron Valley.

Across the Midwest, the Woodland period is a time of major cultural development and florescence. It is the time of the Mound Builders and of expanding regional contacts and exchange. We see traces of these developments here on the Huron but with little evidence of any fundamental change in the relationship between the river and the people.

Later, new plants from the tropics joined these locally domesticated plants. The earliest of these, the bottle gourd, was not a plant food at all but was dried and used as a container. It was maize, squash, and later beans that set in motion the changes that produced the river's third pattern. These tropical cultigens transformed the relationship between domestic plants and people, and changed the broad-spectrum foragers into farmers.

By about A.D. 1000, domestic plants had ceased to be just one resource among many and were now relied upon as a staple. This farming required fields to be cleared and tended and the harvests to be protected and stored. Seasonal patterns of movement around the river changed. So did the location of settlements. Now, access to fields and stores determined the location of villages. The upland forests were difficult to clear, and the soils did not maintain their fertility and were vulnerable to drought and wind. The soils of the river bottomlands were easily worked and remained fertile. So it was to the river bottoms that the people entrusted their fields.

Most traces from these fields and settlements disappeared as the floodplain was developed and as the river itself wandered within its valley. But occasionally we still see glimpses. When the low riverside near Fuller Pool in Ann Arbor was leveled for soccer fields, the graders revealed large clusters of deep pits, many with layers of fire cracked rock used in stone boiling and roasting. The settlement was back on higher ground under Fuller Road, while the pits marked the area of cultivation and food processing. We mapped and drew as many of the pits as we could, even as the graders continued their work. It is likely that most of the river's bottomlands were cultivated at one time or another as the farmers shifted their fields to ensure fertility.

Farther down the Huron, the late Woodland period saw the formation of great villages and huge fields, but on the middle Huron developments were more modest. The farmers never abandoned hunting and gathering, but these activities were now scheduled around the agricultural calendar. Isotope studies suggest that people obtained roughly a fifth of their diet from maize. They still hunted in the uplands and gathered on the river margins. Yet their fields held them like an anchor. They stayed closer to home and were more predictable in their movements. To the village farmers, the Huron River was a field grown rich in maize.

The final pattern I can describe should be the clearest, since it is the most recent and since it is the one time period where written sources supplement what has to now been an archaeological story. This is the time of European contact. It should be the clearest, but it is not.

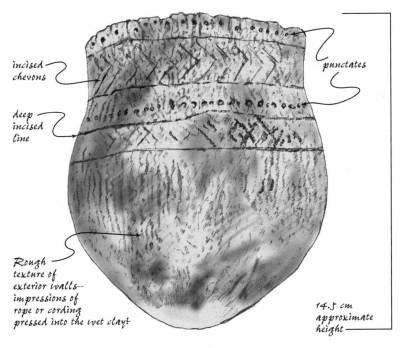

incised
chevons

punctates

deep
incised
line

Rough
texture of
exterior walls—
impressions of
rope or cording
pressed into the wet clay?

14.5 cm
approximate
height

Wayne Ware

Long before the first Europeans reached the Huron River, the impact of their arrival was felt. The metal tools, guns, and diseases brought by the Europeans to their New World produced a cascade of wars, population movement, and cultural upheaval that reverberated far ahead of their actual appearance. Written accounts, even those of the first explorers to the region, are hopelessly out of date. They record the view after the tidal wave of change has passed. The whole of southeastern Michigan was already ceded by the Treaty of Detroit in 1807. In 1810 we see villages with increasingly mixed ethnic populations, Potawatomi and Ojibwa villages along the upper Huron, Shawnee villages and small Wyandot reservations near the river's mouth on Lake Erie. Earlier there had been Sauk, Fox, Kickapoo, and Mascouten. But by 1824, when Ann Arbor was founded, the era of autonomous native settlement on the Huron River had already come to an end.

So what of these people and the Huron River? They were uprooted and on the move. The Huron River to them was a highway. Their trails were well worn and were dutifully mapped by the surveyors who came to plat the land. Some were so well known that they had names. The Potawatomi Trail began near the mouth of the Huron River and followed the river on its north bank up through Ypsilanti and Ann Arbor. A second trail paralleled it on the river's south bank.

We use many of these trails today, although we rarely think of them as such. Dexter Road follows the path that led to the Grand River Trail. Route 12 follows another well-worn trail that led from the lakes near Clinton and Tecumseh up to the River Rouge.

In some ways, we know more about the trails than we do about the people. We see the dust but not their faces. In the diaries and other written accounts left by the settlers, the Indians are almost spectral. An entry will note that the Indians camped nearby or were seen moving along the trail. They appear as visitors from another world, and neither side seems eager to engage the other. When contacts are made, they almost always produce misunderstandings. The Indians move silently at the periphery of vision, and through the written accounts we see them already in sepia tones. The change was on the land, and they could do nothing but change with it.

This is not a vanishing Indian tale, because the people did not vanish. They are still here and are capable of speaking for themselves with great eloquence. But the pattern of life on the Huron was irreversibly broken.

So what are the ancient voices from the watershed? What did the Huron River mean to the ancient peoples? It was an ambuscade, a full basket, a ripening field, and a highway. But more than anything, I suspect, it was an anchor. It was the constant to which their knowledge of the physical world, both near and far, was affixed. The river was a given. The settlers brought a different vision. The world was mutable and could be shaped to suit their needs. The forests could be cleared, the uplands could be planted, and the river itself could be changed. As you look out over the river today, you can see that both visions are true.

M. de La Salle continued his journey without hindrance until the 4th of April [1680], when two of his men, worn out, fell sick, and were unable to walk, so that it became necessary to look for some river flowing into Lake Erie, and build a canoe. Finding a suitable stream [probably the Huron], he felled on its bank a species of elm-tree called by the Iroquois Carondagate, from which the bark can always be peeled,—but at this season only with much difficulty by the constant application of boiling water, great care being needed not to crack the bark. The canoe being soon finished, they all embarked, but navigation was soon interrupted. Trees which had been brought down by the floods or had fallen on the bed of the stream, barred the passage to the canoe, and forced them frequently to debark; moreover, the course of the river was so circuitous that in five days they found they had not got on as far as they were accustomed to go on foot in a single day. So, as the sick men began to feel better, they abandoned the canoe, and in a few days reached in safety the bank of the Detroit, through which Lake Huron pours into lake Erie, and which is here quite uniformly a league in width.

La Salle, Relation of the Discoveries, 1679–81

The night of the second of April [1680] was excessively cold. Their clothes were hard frozen, and they were forced to kindle a fire to thaw and dry them. Scarcely had the light begun to glimmer through the gloom of evening, than it was greeted from the distance by mingled yells; and a troop of Mascoutin warriors rushed towards them. They were stopped by a deep stream, a hundred paces from the bivouac of the French, and La Salle went forward to meet them. No sooner did they see him, and learn that he was a Frenchman, than they cried that they were friends and brothers, who had mistaken him and his men for Iroquois; and, abandoning their hostile purpose, they peacefully withdrew. . . . Two days after this adventure, two of the men fell ill from fatigue and exposure, and sustained themselves with difficulty till they reached the banks of a river, probably the Huron. Here, while the sick men rested, their companions made a canoe. There were no birch-trees; and they were forced to use elm bark, which at that early season would not slip freely from the wood until they loosened it with hot water. Their canoe being made, they embarked in it, and for a time floated prosperously down the stream, when at length the way was barred by a matted barricade of trees fallen across the water. The sick men could now walk again; and, pushing eastward through the forest, the party soon reached the banks of the Detroit.

Francis Parkman, Discovery of the Great West

MICHAEL A. KIELB

Walking through Time and Space: A Natural History, of Sorts

How do you summarize the natural history of a place? Every site, or group of sites, in this case the watershed of the Huron River, is so much more than its components at any particular time. It depends upon when you look. To appreciate the watershed fully you must walk or paddle through it—from the headwaters to the outflow—from January to December and also consider how it has evolved over many years.

The watershed is composed primarily of nonliving material: water, sands, gravel, rocks. The living, or biotic, portion of the watershed is where the great complexity arises. From bacteria and viruses to fungi and plants and on to an array of animal life, the biota of the watershed is diverse and complex. Each living thing relies on something else and is in turn relied upon by other living things. Without the tiniest of microscopic soil bacteria the largest of trees would die, as would all other forms of life. So, in thinking about the life within the watershed, imagine it as a complex pile of sticks. If one is removed, all the others shift. Some collapse and roll away into extinction. Others fall to where they do not belong, and some do not appear to move. But they all do, from the tiniest grain of sand tumbling down the length of the river to the largest tree.

JANUARY

On a cold winter's morning the tall trees at Indian Springs Metropark can be a shelter from the relentless north winds. From these seemingly modest origins in Oakland County the Huron River will ultimately flow through five counties in southeastern Michigan until it reaches Lake Erie.

The wet beech-maple woods are home to a wide variety of animals and plants. While the variety of plants essentially doesn't change across the seasons (although the ability to find or identify them varies greatly), the variety of animals does change, sometimes dramatically.

Several birds have expanded their ranges locally and are now found consistently. Among these, several can be found at all times of the year, while others are found primarily in the spring and summer. The loud drumming and raucous calls of the pileated woodpecker now emanate from the dense woods throughout the year. It is hard to miss, or misidentify, a pileated woodpecker, which is the size of a crow. The presettlement woods of the Huron River watershed once were home to these woodpeckers, but with logging and the removal of the large trees and tracts of woods the woodpecker disappeared. The early 1980s brought quiet rumors of pileateds. By the 1990s the rumors had become annual sightings. From the headwaters at Indian Springs down to the southwestern edge of the watershed at the Sharon Hollow Preserve, this once rare woodpecker is now sporadically seen. The ecosystem and habitat have matured, and the birds have returned.

With the return of the pileated woodpecker came two other species, diurnal raptors, birds of prey. The red-shouldered hawk had once been a common nesting bird in southern Michigan. It was a species of dense, close-canopied woods and bottomlands. In the 1940s it was still quite common in the watershed. Then came DDT, intense farming, and cutting of many woods to expand farmlands. The birds' numbers began to dwindle, from ten to twenty pairs per township to one or two pairs then singles. Finally, by the late 1970s, the red-shouldered hawk was essentially a hanger-on, with very few pairs scattered through the area. By the 1980s it was gone. Then, as with the woodpecker, the red-shoulder began to have a small resurgence. Birds were appearing consistently year-round in areas where woods had matured and the canopy was filling in with mature trees. Now, while nesting has not been reestablished, birds are seen regularly throughout the northern and western portions of the region.

A final species, the broad-winged hawk, had been a rare nesting species in the watershed through the late 1800s. With logging and the removal of most larger woods, the hawk disappeared. Very few nestings were documented from the turn of the century to the 1970s. Like the pileated woodpecker and the red-shouldered hawk, this bird began to appear in greater numbers during the nesting season. Although still a rare occurrence, broad-wings do nest in scattered locales throughout the watershed. Recently, nests have been discovered from the headwaters down to Ann Arbor, where fledged birds have been sighted soaring during the Art Fair in mid-July.

FEBRUARY

Long before the trees and other plants spring to life some birds begin to nest. Traveling along the Huron River, and the roads crisscrossing adjacent land, the astute observer notices large piles of sticks and twigs in some of the taller trees. These are the old nests of hawks and crows.

In February the loud booming calls of the great horned owl can be heard echoing throughout the watershed. This nocturnal predator sits atop the food chain. Nothing, with the exception of man, is safe from the nighttime marauding of this hunter. Skunks, raccoons, opossums, squirrels, mice, birds, cats, and other owls all become its prey.

The great horned owl does not build a nest. This owl appropriates one, usually from a hawk or crow, and it is in February that we first see owls sitting quietly upon these nests. Females incubate eggs and small young while the males hunt. Male owls are great providers, feeding their mate and the young for over a month during Michigan's coldest season.

Two other nocturnal predators start defending territories at this time of year. The calls of the barred owl and eastern screech owl permeate the forests and floodplains throughout the area.

Barred owls are denizens of the rich bottomlands, close-canopied forests, and floodplain forests that once dominated the watershed. As these habitats disappeared, so did the owls. The eight-hoot calls of the barred owl are now only rarely heard in the northern and western portions of the watershed, but as the forests mature more of these dark-eyed owls are being found. Unlike the great horned, this owl is a cavity nester, requiring old trees with large holes for nesting. The barred owl is sensitive to both predation and territorial eviction by its larger cousin the great horned owl. Then again, sometimes the remains of a screech owl appear in the midden of this owl.

It is in February and early March that bald eagles repair and rebuild old nests. The story of the eagle within the watershed is long, complex, and interesting. A hundred or so years ago the bald eagle could be seen hunting for fish and other carrion along the Huron River, especially in Monroe and Wayne Counties. Then with the expansion of humans, more than 80 percent of the wetlands disappeared. With this loss of habitat the species declined.

Then came DDT. With DDT sprayed across the length and breadth of the watershed, crops flourished, but insect populations were wiped out. Indeed, some insects, like the giant lacewing, a predator who fed on many of the species targeted by DDT, have apparently become extinct. Robins dropped dead in Lansing, and southwestern Detroit was sprayed indiscriminately while thousands of children played outdoors. DDT became part of the food chain, and it was concentrated as insect-eating animals ate dead and dying, contaminated insects. These animals were in turn eaten by predators and by omnivores, animals that eat plants and animals. In the upper level predators, DDT reached toxic levels. Since bald eagles would just as soon eat something dead on the shore of a lake as catch something fresh, they suffered tremendous problems as a result of DDT. The effect on the adult eagles ultimately added to the population decline in the region, but an insidious effect went unnoticed for years. Eagle eggs were cracking under the weight of the adults. DDE, a metabolite of DDT, was weakening and thinning the eggshells. By the late 1960s, the bald eagle had vanished as a nesting species from the region.

By the late 1980s, about ten years after DDT was banned, eagles were once again starting to nest at the outflow of the Huron. Once again, eagles were seen cruising up and downstream throughout the watershed, searching for fish. By the year 1999, the breeding population in Monroe County had reached five pairs.

MARCH

When the small ponds start to thaw, and the earth warms ever so slowly, the salamanders and newts start to become active. They emerge from their homes under stones, in protected crevices, and in rotten logs. Quietly these cold-blooded amphibians make their way to barely thawed spring pools, and, on warming spring nights, they mate. Leaving behind masses of fertilized eggs, soon to become swimming little larvae, the adults feed and return to their hidden existence, with most rarely seen by human eyes.

The first days of March, especially during a year with a late spring, can be cold, windy, and snowy. Many of the smaller lakes and ponds will still be frozen. It is at this time that the Huron can play host to a large variety of winter ducks. These usually include common goldeneye and common merganser, among the large overwintering flock of mallards and Canada geese. Mixed in with the mallards are a few of their close relative, the black duck.

Small numbers of other ducks will be mingled with the more common species. These usually include a small number of wood ducks and hooded mergansers and sometimes something as unusual as an American wigeon, a northern shoveler, or a teal.

As March progresses the species composition changes with it. Many if not all of the winter ducks disappear, and the once uncommon or rare winter species start to appear in large numbers. Diving ducks, such as redhead and canvasback, start to arrive, stopping over at larger lakes in the watershed on their way to northern breeding grounds. Dabblers, such as wigeon, shovelers, and both green-winged and blue-winged teal, are now common in large numbers, not only on small ponds and lakes but also on flooded farm fields where they spend their days feeding from the bottom of these small, ephemeral ponds.

Sometimes I let my mind wander back and forth in time as I roam along the river. What will it be like in ten, twenty, or fifty years? I know it will change, having watched the changes over the last twenty years, but I also wonder what it was like fifty, a hundred, or more years ago. My mind wanders back beyond 1900, the 1880s, the Civil War, Michigan statehood. I finally reach 1810. Michigan is little more than a territory, and the Huron River watershed is a healthy, thriving assortment of ecosystems.

It's an early April morning, and the sun has not risen. I have set up a blind in the open oak savannah west of Ann Arbor, closer to Manchester. In the predawn darkness I can hear booms and pounding feet. Soon cackles join the soundscape. In the first streams of light I see forms in the distance. The spring dance of the prairie chicken. They cannot see me in my blind. The males stomp on the ground, booming out their mating calls, the females cackling like chickens. The males begin to kick at one another, taking their jousts to wing. The females watch and wait. They choose to reward only the winners. Those who are most fit, physically, behaviorally, pass on their genes, expressing their genetic fitness.

The greater prairie chicken is a creature of the prairie and savannah. As Europeans moved west across the continent the bird slowly gave way, losing ground, habitat. As croplands and oak-hickory forests replaced native prairies across the expanding nation, the habitat of the prairie chicken shrank. Forced onto smaller and smaller patches of prairie, the species was soon disappearing throughout its once expansive range. The bird also suffered because it was good eating. As with their relatives, the grouse, prairie chickens were considered excellent game birds. Unlike the ruffed grouse, prairie chickens formed breeding leks in the spring. Here the males would strut, call their low-pitched, far reaching booms, and fight with other males in mock battle to see who would get to mate with the greater number of female chickens. As I watch from my blind, I realize how easy it would be to fire off a few shots with a shotgun and take home a bag full of these "chickens." Unfortunately, by the early 1900s the open savannah habitat in southern Michigan was rapidly disappearing, and the last prairie chicken was seen in the watershed well over a half-century ago in 1940. The species disappeared from the entire state in the late 1970s.

The sun is rapidly lighting the scene. Once only silhouettes on the horizon, the males are easy to identify with their reddish-orange cheek pouches and erect head feathers. The females are totally drab in comparison, better suited for sitting unnoticed on a ground nest in the prairie.

As I think about the prairie chickens and the far more numerous passenger pigeons, also once present in the watershed but extinct in the wild by the late nineteenth century, my mind wanders ahead to the future. Will the millions of blackbirds be here in 2050? What of the neotropical warblers, the robins? And on and on. We think of these birds as common, too common to keep track of. But in the late 1500s the passenger pigeon, Carolina parakeet, and heath hen (the eastern race of the prairie chicken) were so common as to define the North American avifauna.

MAY

A walk on a May morning through the mesic woods or floodplain along the Huron River or its tributaries yields a wealth of spring ephemerals. These are the stunning spring wildflowers that carpet the forest floor before the days get too long and warm. Mayapple, trillium, wild ginger, adder's tongue, and bloodroot begin to burst through the decaying leaves that offered them protection throughout the winter months. Fresh green foliage in the dappled shade of leafless trees and shrubs.

For some people interested in natural history the spring wildflowers are the apex; for others they are the beginning, marking the onset of the return of the neotropical migrant birds from Central and South America. Thrushes, warblers, vireos, wrens, and more are all returning to their northern breeding grounds after spending months on their tropical wintering grounds. Then by the end of the month insects start to emerge in numbers, giving the flower and bird lovers something else to study.

On a late May morning when the trails along the river are swathed in foggy mists one of nature's rare events happens along the Huron River, the immigration of the hellgrammites. Hellgrammites, the aquatic larvae of the dobsonfly, are creatures out of someone's worst nightmare. These black larvae are over two inches long and closely resemble the dinner-scene creature in the movie *Alien*. As I walked along the river trail in Nichols Arboretum, dozens of these bizarre creatures were making their way from the riverbank, across the road, into the debris and leaf litter of the hillside. These neuropterans, named for the network of veins in the wings of the adults, were leaving their aquatic homes, searching out safe sites to pupate and undergo metamorphosis, becoming adult dobsonflies. I quit counting at twenty-seven and decided to collect one for my wife, Susan. I made a little tent out of a journal sheet. Slowly I coaxed a hellgrammite into the paper cage and gently placed the creature in my breast pocket. Birds along the river were few that cool, damp morning, but the insects were great.

Susan was delighted with her hellgrammite and placed it in a terrarium. Within twenty-four hours it had disappeared. I was sad. How often does a husband give a present to his wife, only to have it disappear after her initial glee? We thought it had died and decayed, its smelly body becoming part of the terrarium's humus. It was a month later that an adult male dobsonfly emerged, himself a ferocious relict of some bygone epoch.

During May, the arrival of migrant birds waxes and wanes with the passage of warm fronts from the south and their collision with lingering cold fronts from the north. The best mornings are often the ugliest, weatherwise. Cool, sometimes damp, and with light north winds. All this following a warm front. To be a successful bird-watcher you have to study weather patterns. Warm and light southerly winds at bedtime, changing to cool northerly winds by 2 A.M., and the morning will reward you with a plethora of migrant birds, especially warblers.

Species diversity among the warblers increases throughout the month, from three or four the first few days, to twenty, or as many as thirty by May 15. But don't let the number of species be a measure of when to search out warblers. Some species come early; others come late. A visit every day in May will yield the greatest satisfaction. The better days will be overwhelming; the slower days will allow better views of each individual bird. Regardless, every day will have its own flavor. Early birds will be searching for food among the spring ephemerals. Later migrating species will be dodging in and out of the leaves. In the spring there are fewer migrants than in the fall, but all of the migrants are in breeding plumage, and the males are singing distinct songs, both aids in identification.

By the time May draws to a close the days are longer, the air is warmer, and the trees are fully leafed. The time for birds is passing, and the insects start to dominate the landscape.

JUNE

As the middle of June rolls along, the kids are out of school, and the best way to experience the Huron is from a canoe. Starting north of Delhi Metropark and slowly making our way downstream to the rapids and riffles at the park we find a wide variety of species otherwise rarely seen.

Surely the most interesting animals are the aquatic ones. Fish of a variety of sizes and shapes can be seen through the clear waters. Carp are easily identified and also an array of small bluegill and pumpkinseed. As we move slowly and quietly through the water it becomes obvious that a number of different reptiles are basking on logs just above the surface of the water or sometimes just below. A brown water snake undulates across the river, leaving a wake in the still water, while on a log at the water's edge two garter snakes are coiled, absorbing the sun's warmth.

In the middle of the river, at a deeper spot, you notice the nostrils of a turtle, close behind the slimy green domed shell. It is a floating snapping turtle, on the lookout for an easy dinner. Near the opposite shore you see a whole string of small turtles, each with its head either resting on the shell of another or pointing up into the sun. Midland painted turtles, the common pond and stream turtle in southern Michigan. First one and then the others notice you, and "plop, plop, plop" one after the other all drop down into the safety of the river.

Sitting back and floating on you watch the bottom of the shallows, looking for other animals that might be interesting. Then you see them, along the muddy bottom: the large, rounded shells, brownish-green, with bright vermilion dots along the edge. With their long noses pointed up toward the water's surface they are easily identified. You start counting—three, four, five, in a loose group, all placidly sitting on the muddy bottom—spiny soft-shelled turtles. Your paddle disturbs one, and it startles off, raising a cloud of fine silt that obscures your view of the others. As the muck settles, they are all gone, hidden somewhere else in the river's depths.

Continuing down the river you find footprints in the muddy bank. From what, you wonder? Raccoons, probably. But then again, maybe mink. The watershed is home to a healthy population of mink. These large weasels are most often seen at dawn or dusk, since they are crepuscular creatures. Unfortunately, over the last few years I have seen as many mink as road kill as I have alive along the river and its tributaries.

Before reaching Delhi, you see a small cattail marsh, the home of a colony of red-winged blackbirds. The redwing is the small generic blackbird that everyone seems to ignore. It is one of the most abundant birds in North America but also one of the most interesting birds behaviorally. Redwings form nesting colonies in stands of cattails. A pond measuring fifty by a hundred feet encircled with cattails can probably support thirty to forty pairs of these intriguing blackbirds.

In their marshy colony nesting territories are packed in densely. Neighbors sometimes nest within eight or ten feet of each other. Sometimes particularly successful males, high on the dominance hierarchy, will have two females, each with an active nest. Imagine forty to fifty nests, all active simultaneously. Every male defending his territory from other males and from nonblackbird intruders. Every female working on nest upkeep and feeding the young. Every young bird, usually three to four per nest, begging loudly to be fed. A red-winged blackbird colony is a sight to behold and to hear.

JULY

By this time many of the birds are secretively conducting the late stages of family life. There is little song, and that is mostly restricted to early in the day or at dusk. In traversing the watershed in the heat of July it is easy to turn your attention to the insects and plants.

An interesting group of nonflowering plants dotting the shores of the Huron is the *Equisetum,* more commonly known as scouring rush or horsetail. Two species are commonly found in the watershed, field horsetail (*Equisetum arvense*) and swamp horsetail (*E. fluviatile*). Their close proximity has resulted in a third member of the group, the hybrid shore horsetail (*E. litorale*). While hybridization in plants is neither rare nor unexpected, this is an interesting situation. Identifying the three is easily accomplished by taking a specimen and making a cut through a stem. Field horsetail has a very thick-walled stem with rough prominent ridges; swamp horsetail has a very thin-walled stem with ridges that are barely perceptible; and shore horsetail is almost exactly intermediate between the two. The stem walls of shore horsetail are medium thick, with ridges that are noticeable but not predominating.

AUGUST

In the late summer of 1996 a student brought some specimens of dragonflies into the University of Michigan Museum of Zoology's Insect Division for identification. Since I was working on the dragonfly collection at the time, it naturally fell to me to identify the specimens. They were common dragonflies, found not only throughout southeastern Michigan but also throughout most of the eastern United States. We had plenty of time to talk about the other dragonflies he had encountered at his study site, the university's E. S. George Reserve in southwestern Livingston County. In the course of the conversation he casually mentioned that both green darner and comet darner occurred at the site. I was quick to correct him, telling him that he most likely was misidentifying female green darners as comets. He quickly responded, no, they were indeed comet darners. Here we had a dilemma. Not only did comet darners not occur in Michigan, their closest viable populations were hundreds of miles east of here. There was no record, or specimen, from the state. It turned out that these students studying the tadpole response to predators had uncovered a species of dragonfly that was totally unknown in the region prior to this time.

By late August fields and marshes are alive with dragonflies. Long, sleek, black and blue darners darting from twig to sky snatching insect delicacies. Compact red meadow hawks, another dragonfly, now number in the hundreds in many fields, each gorging on insects we consider pests: mosquitoes, gnats, and flies.

SEPTEMBER

September is the month when most bird-watchers turn their attention to the arrival of the birds of autumn. As in the spring, the floodplain forests along the Huron River and its tributaries will be filled to capacity with migrant passerines. It is after the breeding season, and for every pair of birds that headed north there are four or five birds heading south. More birds, more bird-watchers, right? Wrong!

The father of bird-watching, Roger Tory Peterson, gave the masses the book that enabled them to go out and look at birds. Before that book, most people used Audubon's method of identification. He viewed birds through the sights of a shotgun. But Peterson also gave us the ultimate excuse *not* to go out looking for warblers in the fall. Conditions in the fall are often more difficult for bird-watching. There are always more leaves, and many are of the multicolored eastern hardwood tree varieties, but the deathblow to fall warbler watching was the title of several plates in the *Peterson Field Guide to Eastern Birds:* "Confusing Fall Warblers." If Roger Tory Peterson considered these birds to be confusing, how could *we* possibly identify them?

Many bird-watchers will not even try to identify a warbler in fall plumage. As I walk along the river, I see the trees dripping with small flocks. We might have a group of fifteen birds, three bay-breasted warblers, a black-and-white, a male black-throated blue, and oops, they've moved on. So, let's move on with them. Here is one aspect of bird-watching that we may be losing as a bird-watching species: the thrill of the chase. It's not the outcome that's important but the pursuit. And a walk along the river on a fall day is gorgeous in its own right.

Fast forward to the end of the river, the outflow, at Point Mouillée State Game Area. Actually, stop a little farther north, at Lake Erie Metropark, just over the Wayne County border, north of Monroe County. Erie Metropark has become one of the premier hawk-watching sites in North America. Hundreds of thousands of hawks, falcons, eagles, vultures, and harriers pass over the southern portion of the Huron River watershed as they stream south from Canada to southern wintering grounds. While diurnal raptors pass through this area every day from late August until late December, the greatest passages are on days with northwesterly winds, especially a day or so after a cold front has passed. On these days the sky can be filled with thousands of individual raptors of up to fifteen species.

Nearly the entire population of several species nesting in Canada migrates along this route. The first to appear is the broad-winged hawk. On days with north winds, following a cold front after around September 9, the onslaught starts. Over a period of several days, and sometimes of up to two weeks, hundreds of thousands of this one species pass over the eastern portion of the watershed. Single days of over 100,000 occur annually.

The next species that passes in toto is the red-shouldered hawk. This species has a small population in Canada, probably numbering 400–500 pairs. Thus, when 800–1,200 birds pass over in late October and early November this represents a significant portion of Canada's red-shoulders. The next to pass is the turkey vulture. Over the last fifteen years, the passage of vultures has grown from 3,000–5,000 to over 30,000 annually. Turkey vultures have continued to expand their nesting range farther and farther to the north each year, and their numbers are also growing locally.

Finally, and most spectacularly, we see the passage of the golden eagles. While numbers rarely top 125–150 for the season, this represents a significant proportion of the population in eastern Canada. These spectacular eagles wander as far as the western edge of the watershed, where they sometimes spend the winter feeding on geese and ducks. The rest continue on into the southern Great Lakes states or onto the Great Plains.

The migration of blue jays can be even more spectacular than the movement of raptors. The morning sky will be filled with tens of thousands of these little blue bullets, passing in flocks of tens, hundreds, and thousands, all headed for feeders along the Huron River. It is during late September and early October that flocks descend on well-stocked feeders, leaving them empty. Blue jays spend many fall days planting seeds and nuts, hidden caches for those tough winter months.

As I travel down through the Huron-Clinton metropark system heading toward the outflow of the Huron River I keep encountering passage migrants, birds headed south for the winter: late warblers, sparrows, finches, ducks, and hawks. This passage is far more than a trip to warmer climes; it represents a maturation, a passage of lives. Close to 80 percent of the birds that have fledged this year will never live to see the next breeding season. Once a bird reaches adulthood it has a 50 percent chance, or greater, to live to see the next summer.

How many times have I heard, "That's my robin; she nests under that sill every summer" or "Yup, my barn swallows are back, nesting in the same place they did last year." We see birds in *our* yards, *our* woods, *our* parks, whatever, and they become *ours*. But how do we know that they are ours, when birds have such a tenuous existence from year to year? How do we *know* the bird nesting under the eaves is the same one that was there last year? Most of the time we don't.

There are two species we see nearly every day throughout the year, and another common summer resident, that were not commonly found in southern Michigan a little over a hundred years ago. The cardinal, mourning dove, and turkey vulture have all invaded the state since the Civil War. It is interesting that these species have all steadily expanded northward during a period when the mean temperature has been increasing annually. They have been able to take advantage of a regional event that went unnoticed by humans for over one hundred years.

Throughout October and into November, turkey vultures migrate from the Great Lakes, heading for warmer southern feeding grounds. The sky can be filled with hundreds, if not thousands, of vultures—swirling black eddies in the sky, largely unnoticed from below. These are the birds that take us into November.

NOVEMBER

Bird-watching close to the mouth of the Huron River just south of the Wayne County line, at Point Mouillée State Game Area in Monroe County, can be extremely rewarding in October and November. Hawks spiral high into the invisible warm currents of air overhead. But before the hawks start crossing the mouth of the Detroit River, before the sun has warmed the coastal marshes, come the ducks. If not for the ducks, the state game areas and many federal wildlife refuges would not exist. Duck hunters pay for the habitat in the form of hunting permits. They use it for three months, and bird-watchers use it for free the rest of the year.

As I sat there one early morning years ago, the glow on the horizon hadn't started to show before the first shots were fired. How did they do it? How could they identify a duck in an almost blue-black sky, speeding by at sixty miles per hour? I couldn't even assign them a genus, let alone a species, and I was using 10 × 40 field glasses. I would ponder that question not only for minutes that day but for years thereafter. I think the answer lies in what I tell people who are amazed when an experienced hawk watcher identifies a hawk a mile away, well before the doubter could ever hope to find it floating among the islands of clouds. Experience is an amazing teacher.

Flock after flock sped by, dodging the gauntlet of hunters. Peaceful silence sporadically broken by shotgun fire. Then quiet.

A large flight of mostly small ducks appeared on the horizon. Teal, wood ducks, and what else, I couldn't tell. Then I heard the shots. It was like a distant cannon barrage with single shots, many in unison, and the echoes off the nearby trees. The ducks darted and dodged the pellets. Most accelerated and gained altitude. Small groups split off, leaving flock mates they had traveled with for hundreds of miles. They used every evasive maneuver they could to avoid their predators.

The sun had broken the horizon, and I could see a small group of green-winged teal tearing through the sky way too low, well below the others. Another barrage ensued. Two teal fell below the others, gliding, no longer flapping. The shooting stopped. One duck seemed to collapse, wings flailing in the sky. It tumbled down, hitting the water and bouncing once. His wounded companion glided farther, wings stiff, before crashing into the river below. Two less teal, culled from the southbound hoard.

On my way home, somewhere along the lower reaches of the Huron, I stopped and took a walk along the river. Here one of autumn's surprises waited for me. In the bleakness of the overcast sky I saw them. The spindly yellow flowers covering the naked stems of these shrublike trees quickly identified *Hamamelis virginiana*. Witch hazel, neither a witch nor a hazel, bears the last flowers of the year this far north. Trees had lost their leaves; amphibians and reptiles were hidden away in burrows; most adult insects had died; birds were headed south; and this one tree's flowers were splayed across the dark branches of these wonderful trees along the banks of the Huron River.

Back in Ann Arbor, the sun was starting to descend on the western horizon, and I had one final stop to make before returning to the warmth of home. For years we have noticed the buildup and passage of crows around Ann Arbor. It was a few years ago, sometime in the mid-1990s, that a graduate student at the Museum of Zoology started studying these large black birds. Cindy Simms discovered that crows were forming a large roost at the

Forest Hill Cemetery at Observatory and Geddes Road on the edge of the University of Michigan's central campus. A crow roost is a place where hundreds or even thousands of crows come together to spend the night, seeking warmth and protection.

I stood there, along Geddes, watching the western sky, still lighter than the darkening eastern view. The crows were arriving, gliding in at heights of a hundred to several hundred feet and then descending into the cemetery. Their calls were starting to fill the air behind me. And the sky in front of me was starting to fill rapidly. Since it was first discovered, this roost, the largest in the watershed, has grown to nearly ten thousand birds. At their peak they were appearing at over a thousand birds a minute! As I wandered into the cemetery the uproar was deafening, with every imaginable sound a crow could make. Then, as if alerted by some special signal, the whole mass took to wing and swirled into the sky, forming a huge black mass against the ever darkening sky. They circled overhead for a minute or so, then streamed off, a black river of birds, to Angell Hall. It was there that they would spend the night.

DECEMBER

A quick walk along the river, remembering to get home with plenty of time for wrapping Christmas gifts. The crab apples abound, with overwintering robins feeding within the warm shelter of the river by the tens, the hundreds, and, in exceptional years, the thousands. If you could paint a thermal portrait of the watershed on a winter's day, the hot spots would be adjacent to the open water of the river. Two, three, maybe five degrees warmer than the surrounding areas and offering wonderful surprises.

Birds that normally spend winter in the deep south appear along the river, robins of course but many more, attracted by the warmth, the insects, and the wealth of berries. A yellow-rumped warbler feeds furiously on poison ivy berries, gulping down one after another. A winter wren skulks in a thicket. Hermit thrushes dash from thicket to berries and back again. And the rarest, turkey vultures. Roosting quietly in the trees along the river, these lingering scavengers await death. All of these birds in the cold of winter seek out the warmth of the river as I race home, seeking the warmth of my family.

KEITH TAYLOR

Back Home

MEMORIAL DAY. Warm and humid. Gray, with several rain showers and one good thunderstorm. My wife and daughter and I have traveled across Detroit from the west side to the east side, stopping at various cemeteries to lay flowers on the graves of my wife's forebears.

After we've found the last grave and have pulled back the grass growing over the stone, we head north and west, moving up past 8 Mile Road into the northern suburbs, west through the wealthier subdivisions built on wooded hills, until north and west of Pontiac, after moving around several small lakes, we come to Indian Springs Metropark and the Huron Swamp. Somewhere on our drive through all the interconnected cities we passed a forgotten height of land between river systems. Now we are at the headwaters of the Huron River, back home in our own watershed.

On our drive into the park we cross a bridge over a small stream, not four or five feet wide. I stop in the middle of the road. "Look, it's the Huron," I say. My daughter seems uninterested; my wife is worried about getting hit by the car behind us.

When we walk out into the wet forest behind the Nature Center, I stop by every swampish pool or trickle of water. "Look," I say. "It's the river. You could dam it up with your hand." They slap at mosquitoes and keep walking.

At the end of the trail we follow a short side spur through some old fields overgrown in lush green grasses, up a small hill. My wife and I stop to watch bobolinks chase each other over the field, then drop down into the nests they've hidden in the grass. The males are particularly vivid in their fresh breeding plumage, their breasts glossy black and their backs imprinted with a complicated pattern of white and yellow. I tell her something I remember reading, that bobolinks have a healthy population of around three million individuals, that all of them winter in northern Argentina then come all the way back here to nest in the spring.

"Three million doesn't seem like very many," my wife says. "Not compared to us, anyway."

When we get to the top of the hill, we find my daughter gazing off to the southwest. Even though she is a child who has seen the ostentatious scenery of mountains and oceans, she can still say here, "Wow. Look. It's really cool."

We follow her gaze. Beneath the gray sky, a slight and gentle valley, shrouded in a humid haze and surrounded by the new but full growth on the trees, heads off to the southwest. We know that cities and their developments are all around us, but we can't see anything from here except one road. There are no houses or businesses or freeways. We are looking down the valley of our river, the Huron, where it flows back toward home.

KEITH TAYLOR

Before the Freeze

IT WAS THE FIRST WEEKEND of December, but I had worked up a good sweat by the time I finished tying the canoe on top of the car. One of the neighbors came by and said, "Can you believe it? Canoeing in December!" We made a couple of jokes and shook our heads about global warming. My wife and daughter came out wearing short-sleeved shirts.

We wanted to try the Proud Lake area up east of Milford, but we stopped in town and talked with Tom Lynch for quite a while before we got out on the water. By the time we were there, the sky had darkened and the wind had picked up. Still, we'd driven thirty miles, so we thought we deserved a good paddle.

Just as we got out on Proud Lake itself a warm drizzle began. We weren't too worried about that and paddled off down the valley toward Milford. The trees were bare except for a few brown oak leaves clinging tenaciously to the

upper branches. The landscape had the dull gray look it gets just before the first snows. The rain got stronger, its drops striking the water hard enough to create small splashes and tiny symmetrical ripples. We turned back.

The wind quickly whipped up whitecaps on the lake, and we tried to keep in close to shore as we paddled back toward the car. Almost as if someone had turned off the warm water faucet and turned on the cold, the rain changed to something like needles of sleet, piercing our clothes and hurting the backs of our hands. I was worried, but suddenly, for no reason I could see, my wife started laughing. Then my daughter started laughing. And, finally, so did I. And we paddled quickly back to our car, soaked and cold and laughing the whole way.

The rain changed to snow that night. Two weeks later the river was frozen solid.

THOMAS LYNCH

Mary and Wilbur

LIKE ALL GREAT CITIES, ours is divided by water. Dublin has its Liffey, London, its Thames. Milford has the Huron River. The Mighty Huron is what knowing locals call it—afloat in the high tide of hyperbole. It is a river that, from its headwaters in Proud Lake, five miles east of town, to the dam at the west end of the village, never works up much of a commotion nor more than one hundred feet of width, except where it fattens in Central Park into what we call the Mill Pond. Of course it flows on westward through Ann Arbor and Ypsilanti and down into Lake Erie, and it begins to look like a real river downstream. You can find it on maps. But here, near its headwaters, it's more of a stream. It is reasonably clean, good for canoers and carp fishermen and raft races. Once a year there's a Duck Race sponsored by the Rotary Club and a good sucker run in early April. Where the train tracks cross over the river at Main Street, there's a trestle they call the Arch and diving from it is against the law—a prohibition largely ignored by local boys for a hundred and fifty years now.

The river divides the south side from the north. It divides the car dealers and liquor stores and light manufacturing shops on the south side from the trendy restaurants, banks, boutiques, and booksellers of the north. The south side has its Southern Baptists, North Main, its Presbyterians. Brakes and mufflers are procured on the south side, diamonds and divorce attorneys on the north.

And as the village is divided by the Mighty Huron so too the souls and psyches of its inhabitants. When it snows we look like Currier and Ives—a Main Street on which neighbors stop to talk, know the merchants they do their business with, nodding and waving their ways between storefronts, grinning for no apparent reason. There's a skating rink in Central Park all winter, and volley ball and tennis in fair weather. And a permanent installation of playground equipment: merry-go-rounds and jungle-gyms. And east and west of Main, old neighborhoods of wooden homes built around the turn of the last century. Each comes with a history well researched by the Historical Society. Five thousand people live in town and ten thousand in the surrounding township. They occupy their cozy homes, shop locally, support their police and volunteer fire departments, and enjoy the usual parades down Main—on Memorial Day and Fourth of July and Christmas. We have Sidewalk Sales and Old Homes Tours, a Classic Car Show and Milford Memories—a festival in August that brings them in from all over the tri-county area. The past three Januarys we've even had an Ice Spectacular—huge blocks of ice brought in and whittled by chainsaws into likenesses of palm trees and dinosaurs. Folks brave the cold to come and see. There is the general sense that the lives we lead here are busy with the neighborly business of making what twenty years from now we intend to call the Good Old Days.

As past president of the Chamber of Commerce and a Rotarian in good standing, I am delighted to mention our abundant park lands, inland lakes, good schools, and churches, our proximity to hospitals and golf courses, our upmarket home values. And the wide array of services and merchandise locally available at reasonable prices. But as a citizen at large, and the undertaker here, and a witness at the changing of the millennia, I'm obliged, as any witness is, to say what happens.

It's a good place to raise families and to bury them.

We've had terrors on both sides of the river. Two girls were found dead here at the end of one summer—stabbed to death and stuffed into a culvert on the wooded west end of Central Park and, in the same park, two years before, a girl kidnapped, raped, and strangled and buried in a shallow grave out in the township by a serial killer who perpetrated similar evils in townships north and south of here. The men who did these wicked things are all in jail and books are being written about them. There is talk of a movie. None of these facts provide a moment's solace. And there have been boys killed by mischief and misadventure. One was found in pieces on the railroad tracks that run behind the west side of Main Street. Whether accident or homicide or suicide has never been determined. Was he walking home, maybe drunk, and was he hit by the train, or was he killed and placed there, or did he put himself there and wait for the train to come for reasons we can only imagine? There is still talk of drink, recreational drugs, teen vendettas. As there was when the body of a boy was found hung from the branch of a sugar maple in the woods behind his house. Or when a month after Kurt Cobain, lead singer of Nirvana, blew his head off, one of our local boys came home from school to do the same thing with his father's rifle and Kurt's tune "Rape Me" playing on the tape deck and the fire whistle blaring out across town.

That whistle is often the first notice we get of damage here—the signal in these parts of disaster. Men drop what they're doing and come on the run—

volunteer firemen with lights and sirens rigged to their vans and pickups. They have hoses and oxygen, stretchers and tourniquets. They've been trained in CPR and other heroics. And it is the one shrill note of the fire whistle that proclaims a grass fire or heart attack, car crashes or dead bodies. It is the sound of trouble heard all over the township, of damage or the threat of damage to persons or property. Dogs all over town are driven to howling. Every Saturday at noon they test the thing—a kind of secular Angelus we set our watches by. No one takes much notice on Saturdays. It's only a test. No time to have a heart attack or kitchen fire. The Catholics out on the east end of town have restored their carillon that plays at ten and two and six o'clock, old melodies: "Shall We Gather at the River" and "Abide with Me." So our air is filled with a medley of bells and whistles declaring that in the midst of life, we are in death. God is among us and so is the Devil. The river that runs through this town divides us.

So, while we look, in the right light, like a late-century rendition of the Waltons or Lake Wobegon, there is no shortage here of outrage and heartbreak. There seem to be two topographies—both real but vastly different.

My wife and I take walks at night. She sees the architectural detail of Greek Revival homes, Queen Anne's, Federalist, and Victoriana. I see the garage where two teachers, long married and childless, known for their prowess at ballroom dancing and careful fashions, were found asphyxiated in their Oldsmobile. I remember the perfect penmanship of the note they left explaining their fear of age and infirmity. Or my wife sees a well-made garden, bordering the backyard of a house where I remember painting a bedroom overnight in which a man had shot himself, so that his children, grown now, wouldn't have to return to the mess he'd made. Some things won't cover no matter how many coats we apply. She sees good window treatments, the warm light of habitation where, too often, I see vacancy and absence, the darkness where the light went out. We get along.

And for every home made memorable by death, dozens are made memorable by the lives that were led there utterly unscrutinized by the wider world—lives lived out at a pace quickened only by the ordinary triumphs of daily life: good gladiolas, the well-shoveled walk, the mortgage payments made, the kids through college. Or by the ordinary failures: the bad marriage, the broken water main, trouble with the tax man, the sons and daughters who never call. We know our neighbors and our neighbors' business here. It is the blessing and the curse of the small place. It's getting better lately, and getting worse. As new subdivisions sprout all over the township, we have traffic jams and parking problems, and more privacy. It is a "bedroom" community.

Most people work elsewhere. Here is where they come to "get away from it all." People are less curious about one another.

Once there were five bridges over the river. One at Garden Road, at the east end of the township; and one at Mont-Eagle Street—it was also known as Oak Grove Bridge because it provided riverside access to Oak Grove Cemetery. Then one at Huron Street, another at Main, and, finally, one at Peters Road on the west edge of Central Park, just upstream from the dam.

In the early 1970s, the Oak Grove Bridge was declared unsafe for vehicular traffic by the county road commission. Barriers were placed on either side. Bikes and walkers could make it through but cars couldn't. "Bridge Out" is what the signs said. Some months later, the bridge fell into the river, proving, I suppose, beyond all argument, the road commission's point. No one seemed to notice. The only place it went was to the cemetery. There seemed no hurry to repair the bridge. Oak Grove was the elder of two municipal burial grounds in Milford, dating back to the years before the Civil War, when farmers and mill workers first made a town here. Oak Grove had served the township well, taking the dead for a hundred and fifty years—old families our roads are named after, rooted to places, settled in, in ways the highly mobile types of the late twentieth century do not comprehend. Where our ancestors stayed, we move, twenty percent of us every year, from east coast to west coast, from starter homes to dream house, from condos to time shares and retirement villages. The dead and buried remain, for the most part, immobile, eating the dust of new aging generations who have learned to travel light and fast and frequently and put some distance between themselves and their dead. One of the obvious attractions of cremation is that it renders our dead somehow more portable, less "stuck in their ways," more like us, you know, scattered.

But just as Dante had his Lethe and Venice has its Zattere, the slow corteges that crossed the Huron over Oak Grove Bridge, all those years ago, no doubt took note of the evident metaphor—that the dead parent or child or sibling had gone to another shore, another side, changed utterly into townspeople of another dimension.

When the kids were little, we fished off the bridge abutments on summer evenings and watched the bats fly out from the trees in Oak Grove to feast in the buggy air over the river. Sometimes I'd take them there to get rubbings of headstones to match new granite to old designs as elder stragglers of the old families were buried, shipped back home oftentimes from Florida or Arizona or North Carolina. We'd walk among the old trees and monuments trying to imagine the lives they marked. They would ask me questions about the way things worked. It was where I learned the answer "I don't know."

What I did know was that Oak Grove was different from the new cemeteries, where people hustled back to their cars and back to their lives the minute the minister was done with the benediction. At Oak Grove people would remain, trading news of graduations, marriages, grandchildren. They would browse among the neighboring stones of long dead elders with the look on their faces you see in libraries and museums where we study the lives and works of others to learn about ourselves. And the stones had a presence, huge by today's standards. They could not be walked over or mowed over. Likewise, they told, in the eloquent plain chant of the stonecutter, not only the facts but some of the features. Kin was buried with kin. Lots were bought eight graves at a time, or ten. Folks stayed put. Nor has Oak Grove any "chapel" for indoor services—that tidy enterprise whereby the dead are left unburied while the family goes back to their lives, untroubled by inclement weather or harsh realities. A burial at Oak Grove means dirt, a hole in the ground, contending with the "elements."

Among the several duties of a funeral is, of course, the disposal of the dead for the living's sake. And this trip—taken for long years from the corner of Liberty and First Streets, where our funeral home has always been, down Atlantic Street to Mont-Eagle Street, and over the bridge—passed in its three-quarter-mile route, not factories or shops or shopping malls, but homes—brick and clapboard, large and small, but homes. The dead were put, properly, out of our homes but not out of our hearts, out of sight but not out of town.

Thus, Oak Grove always seemed a safe extension, a tiny banishment of the dead from the living, a kindly stone's throw away—a neighborhood of its own, among whose stones the living often spent their Sunday afternoons picnicking among the granite suburbs of grandparents, spinster aunts, ne'er-do-well uncles kept alive in the ordinary talk of the living. Geraniums were planted for "Decoration Day," flags stuck in the graves of old soldiers, grass clipped around headstones all summer, leaves raked and mums planted in the fall, and grave blankets placed before the first snows of winter. The distance between the dead and the living seemed no greater than the river. Neither strange nor embarrassing, the dead were only dead, no less brothers and sisters, parents, children, friends. And death was considered part of the nature of things in a culture where crops failed, cattle starved, and neighbors died. They were waked, eulogized, buried, and grieved. And against forgetfulness, huge stones were hauled in with names and dates on them to proclaim their permanent place in our townscapes. It is this ancient agreement—the remembrance of the dead by the living—that accounts for all burial grounds and most statuary and entire histories.

After Oak Grove Bridge fell into the Mighty Huron, we took a longer, more complicated route through town: First to Commerce, then westbound to Main, then south through the middle of town with its gridlock and onlookers, and over the Main Street Bridge to Oakland Street on the south side. Left on Oakland past the abandoned jelly factory, the long-filled city dump, across the railroad tracks, and into the back entrance of Oak Grove. It wasn't much of an inconvenience except for the terrible repair of Oakland Street, which had badly decomposed from years of inattention. There were pot holes in it small cars could be lost in, and we'd always have to wash our fleet—the hearse and flower car and family car, covered invariably in dust or mud or slush. And there was some difference, though I never heard it said, between crossing the river and crossing the railroad tracks, between marsh banks full of waterfowl and the town dump with old Impalas rotting on their rims, between the backyards bordered with perennials and the factory yard surrounded by chain-link and barbed wire.

Still, no one regarded it as much of a hardship—this rerouting of funerals from a primarily domestic route to a primarily commercial one. And, washing the hearse afterward I'd content myself that it was somehow good for business to take our shiny black parades through town, all flags and flashers and police escorts, letting the locals get a look at how well we directed funerals.

Except for a fellow who wrote a really fine auto parts manual, I was the only published writer alive in town for several years. Then a local Vietnam veteran wrote and published his memoir of that war and there were three of us literary stars in Milford's firmament. But I was the only poet. And like most poets who want to live amiably among their neighbors, I had avoided any temptation to read them my poems. For their part, my townspeople, like the population at large, were pleased to have a poet living among them, in the way we approve of good infrastructure and school systems, so long as we don't have to pay too close of attention. And a poet in the environs is handy if you need a poem for a special occasion—the in-laws' anniversary or the retirement of clergy, or the matriculation of high school students every June. I drew the line on such activities years back when the owner of the local Dairy Queen asked me for something to commemorate the opening of a satellite location by the entrance to the metropark. "No" is what I told him and was resolved to tell any others evermore. No amount of coaxing could change my mind.

Then Mary Jackson called.

Mary lives in Milford half of each year in the house on Canal Street, two blocks from the funeral home, that her parents and her grandparents lived in. The other half of every year she lives and works in Hollywood in the movies and TV and theater. Maybe her most memorable part was of Miss Emily, one of the spinsterly Baldwin sisters on "The Waltons," which was popular in the seventies and early eighties and still can be seen in reruns on cable. Mary was the tiny smiling sister who would spike the punch at Christmastime with their father's recipe and make John-Boy and Susan and Grandpa and Gramma all a little tipsy in a way we approved of in horse-and-buggy days.

When Mary isn't acting or living in Hollywood, she comes home to Milford as she has for years. Friends visit from New York and London and L.A.—theater types of all ages and persuasions who probably think of themselves as "on location" here. It makes Mary seem ageless, which, of course, she is. She takes them to dinner uptown and introduces them to friends and neighbors in her parlor.

All of Mary's people are buried in Oak Grove. There's a bench made of Barre granite, hand cut in Vermont, with JACKSON on it. And a stone with Mary's own name on it—her married name actually, "Mary Jackson Bancroft"—the details of the marriage and its end, unknown to us. But Mary has staked her claim in Oak Grove and has every intention of being buried there.

When word first got to Mary about the collapse of the bridge, she was disturbed. When it became clear that no plan for its repair was in the works, she was quietly outraged. The Village and the Township offices proffered "money problems" in answer to her first inquiries. The county road commission could not promise action. Its budget had been pushed to the limits by boom times in the county. As country roads became major thoroughfares, old farms turned into subdivisions, how could they spend the money "on the dead" when the living needed to get to school and to work and to church and to the shopping mall? How, they argued, convincingly, could a case be made for the dead's convenience, when the living lived with such inconvenience?

Mary came to see me. She said she wanted to make her "arrangements." She brought a list of pallbearers and alternates—stunt doubles she called them. She said I should read a poem—"The Harp-Weaver" by Edna St. Vincent Millay—and that the Methodist minister should do the rest. That she trusted me with the ultimate theater I took as high praise. She said it was a shame about Oak Grove. "The bridge, you know. Something should be done." Then she told me she had made a decision. She steadfastly refused to be buried by way of the back door of Oak Grove. In all her eighty plus years, she explained, she had seen, in her mind's eye, the tasteful little procession leaving the funeral home by First Street, detouring slightly down Canal and right on Houghton, thus passing her house (the hearse pausing briefly according to custom), then left on Atlantic, right at Mont-Eagle, then down to the river, crossing the bridge under the high gate of Oak Grove to rest in the companionable earth there. She would not, she insisted, be a "spectacle," processing down through town while strangers shopped in the dime store or browsed in the sale racks of Arms Brothers or Dancers Fashions.

I am not ashamed to say that for a funeral director, the refusal of one of a town's most cherished and well-heeled citizens to be buried in the ground intended for her, is a threat to be taken seriously. It's the kind of thing that could catch on. I tendered other options for the crossing of the river. Perhaps a barge, Viking style, with the mourners ferried back and forth, a la Dante? "Like Elvis on that ridiculous raft?" she said. "Floating around those man made lagoons in Blue Hawaii?—Never! Not even over my dead body!"

We could drive a little east, I lamely suggested. The Garden Road Bridge was still intact, wonderfully remote—"far from the maddening crowd," I said—but Mary would not hear of it. No detours, no barges, no catapults, no excuses. She was going the way she intended to go, the way her mother and father and her uncles and brothers had gone, over the Oak Grove Cemetery Bridge. It would have to be repaired.

Truth told, Mary Jackson had the wherewithal, no doubt, to write a check and have a new bridge done—still working in her eighties and the royalties still coming in has its rewards. But being a good American, she formed a committee, knowing that the problem was not only one of finance but of perception. She called Wilbur Johnson, her neighbor and old friend. His own darling Milver had suffered the indignity of the Main Street route just months before. Wilbur agreed something had to be done.

Wilbur Johnson knew everyone in town. It was his style. For seventy years he'd worked in the produce section of the local market, proffering welcome to newcomers and old timers over heads of lettuce and ears of sweet corn. The market first owned by his father and then by his brother had changed hands a couple more times since Wilbur's youth. But Wilbur always went with the deal—an emblem of those times when people came away from the market with more than what they'd bought. Once known by Wilbur, you were known. Unafraid of growth and change, he thrived on the lives of those around him from children in shopping carts, their young mothers, husbands sent to market with a list, bag boys, and cashiers. His own life, perfectly settled—he never changed jobs or wives or churches or houses—gave him an appetite for changes in the lives of others. He kept an open ear for the names of newborns and newlyweds, news of setbacks and convalescences, the woeful monologues of the jilted, the divorced, the bereaved. He remembered the names of children, visiting in-laws, friends of friends. He had a good word for everyone and everyone knew him. Nowadays we call this "networking" and the store of information Wilbur kept on the lives of others, a "data base." But Wilbur called it "neighborly"—the attention we pay to each other and each other's lives.

Mary and Wilbur became the co-chairs of the committee. They called some of the other old timers in town—descendants of the Ruggles brothers who founded the town in the early nineteenth century, Armstrongs and Arms, Wilsons and Smiths. Meetings were scheduled, mission statements made, pictures taken. Articles began to appear in the *Milford Times*. An account was opened in the bank. Appeals for matching funds were faxed to county commissioners and state representatives and senators whose staffs sent back well-worded letters full of good wishes and intent that, all the same, managed to thread the needle between Yes or No. They wanted to make it perfectly clear, though what "it" was remained a mystery.

The effort, in the minds of most of us, was noble but doomed to failure. Teenagers and young marrieds never thought about cemeteries, being immortal. Folks in their thirties, busy with starter homes and credit-card debt, could not be counted on for cash. And the baby boomers in their forties planned to be buried in Milford Memorial—a sumptuous and well-kept memorial park with flat markers and easy maintenance—the commemorative equivalent to the lackluster subdivisions that sprouted in the fifties where every house looked like the next and the lawns were well maintained in a purgatory of sameness. Or they planned to be cremated and scattered in some far-off and really meaningful locale—a favorite fishing hole or golf course or shopping mall. Or they simply did not think of it at all, trying to keep, in the parlance of the generation, "their options open." Among fifty-year-olds, trying to maintain the fiction that they were still in "middle age" and would all, accordingly, live to be a hundred, the mention of cemeteries was strictly taboo, conflicting as it did with those old lies about life beginning at fifty and it being such "a great time to be silver!" A bridge to reconnect us to an old cemetery, rarely used for new burials, occupied the nethermost place on the totem-pole of worthy causes. Public and private beneficence seemed better spent on the homeless, the addicted, the battered and disenfranchised; the living not the dead.

So when Mary called to ask me to compose a poem to be read at the dedication ceremonies she saw in the future, I told her, "Yes, yes of course, I'd be honored etc. . . ," breaking my long-standing ban on occasional poems with the thought in mind that she would never get it done. The bridge, the poem, the whole project would lapse, in time, into the rosy realms of well-intentioned but never realized dreams. The good old days, like the lives of

Miss Emily Baldwin and John-Boy Walton, of Mary and Wilbur and the rest of the sepia-colored characters that populate the home towns of our memories, were gone. Gone forever. No money would be spent on metaphor while real needs were so great.

All the same, Wilbur kept talking and Mary kept lobbying and those of us who loved them hadn't the nerve to prepare them for the eventual disappointment. "Keep up the good work," is what we'd say when we saw them. "Something good will surely come of it." To be sure, Mary and Wilbur began to look like ambassadors, emissaries of a time long gone when folks took seriously their connections to the dead, their access to them, their memories. Memories, after all, were what they were peddling—good old days, or so it seemed—when the dead were somehow different from the dead today.

Of course, those days, like the ones we occupy, had no shortage of heartache in them. At the turn of the last century, more than half the deaths recorded were the deaths of children under twelve. The life expectancy was forty-seven years. Men marched off to war and died. Women died in childbirth. Everyone was born with a dose of mortality. In this way they were terribly modern. And the parents of children dead nowadays of AIDS bear more than passing resemblance to the parents of cholera victims a few generations back, or small pox or the flu. And the widowed then, like the widowed now, trade passion for remembrance of passion. But somehow, memories of the dead seemed more accessible, the dead themselves not so estranged.

I often think about this schizophrenia, how we are drawn to the dead and yet abhor them, how grief places them on pedestals and buries them in graves or burns the evidence, how we love and hate them all at once; how the same dead man is both saint and sonovabitch, how "the dead" are frightening but our dead are dear. I think funerals and graveyards seek to mend these fences and bridge these gaps between our fears and fond feelings, between the sickness and the sadness it variously awakens in us, between the weeping and dancing we are driven to at the news of someone's dying. The man who said that all deaths diminish me was talking about the knowledge at the edges of every obit that it was not me and someday will be. Thus graveyards are a way of keeping the dead handy but removed, dear but a little distant, gone but not forgotten.

No doubt the impulse to do this—to get the dead to their own quarters—was, at first, olfactory. The Neanderthal widow, waking to the dead lump of her man, likely figured he was only being quiet or lazy. Was it something he'd eaten? Something she'd said? It might have been hours before she knew something was different. Here was a preoccupation or an indifference she'd never seen before. But not until his flesh started rotting did the idea come to her to bury him because he'd been changed utterly and irretrievably and, if her nose could be trusted, not for the better. Thus the grave is first and foremost a riddance. But this other impulse—to memorialize, to commemorate, to record—has a more subtle motive. I think of Bishop Berkeley's tree, requiring someone to hear it fall. We need our witnesses and archivists to say we lived, we died, we made this difference. Where death means nothing, life is meaningless. It's a grave arithmetic. The cairns and stone piles, the life stories drawn on cave walls, the monuments in graveyards, one and all, are the traces left of the species before us—a space that they've staked out in granite and bronze. And whether a pyramid or Taj Mahal, a great vault in Highgate or a name on The Wall, we let them stand. We visit them. We trace the shapes of their names and dates with our fingers. We say the little epitaphs out loud. "Together forever." "Gone but not forgotten." We try to reassemble their lives from the stingy details, and the exercise teaches us something about how to live.

Is it kindness or wisdom, honor or self-interest?

We remember because we want to be remembered.

Mary Jackson can bring the dead to life. In reminiscences launched over luncheons or teas or walks through Oak Grove, she restores them to us. In her narratives, the dead become perfectly modern, given to the same fits of joy and sorrow as ourselves. As when her Uncle Nick Stephens, in Mary's childhood, came across a stone on the Crawford lot that read: "Behold me now as you pass by. As you are now, so once was I. As I am now soon you will be. Prepare for death and follow me." A good Victorian epitaph, memorable and morbid, a jingle in the stonemason's best script. To which Uncle Nick, never at a loss for words, replied on the spot: "To follow you I won't consent until I know which way you went."

We buried Wilbur Johnson a few years back. He was put in the grave at Oak Grove next to Milver and his name and dates carved into the stone. I see him striding up the steps of my office twenty-five years ago to ask if I was the new funeral director in town. "Well you're a man I'll need to know," is what he said and then he said I could pick him up the following Wednesday and drive him to the Chamber of Commerce luncheon. Wilbur always went more than half way when it came to welcomes. And I can see him, in his last year, arm in arm with Mary Jackson in the ceremonial crossing of Oak Grove Bridge, the new bridge built by their determination, to cut the ribbon and open it to the general public. Bands were assembled, politicos, old soldiers from the VFW, the reverend clergy. It was a bright morning at the end of May—Memorial Day. Townspeople gathered at the river to watch the festivities. A microphone had been rigged up with loudspeakers in the trees. Wilbur thanked all of the committee for their tireless efforts. The Village President said wasn't it a fine thing. The state senator was pleased to have helped with a grant from the Department of Commerce and read off the names of people in Lansing. Then Mary read the poem I'd written when it began to look like she'd actually get it built. And people stood among the stones and listened while Mary's voice rose up over the river and mingled in the air with the echo of Catholic bells tolling and tunes in the Presbyterian steeple and the breeze with the first inkling of June in it working in the fresh buds of winter oaks. The fire whistle was silent. No dogs howled.

Mary has the gift of voices. When she speaks the words, she sounds like one of our own. And the words, when she says them, sound like hers and hers alone.

"At the Opening of Oak Grove Cemetery Bridge"

Before this bridge we took the long way around
up First Street to Commerce, then left at Main,
taking our black processions down through town
among storefronts declaring Dollar Days!
Going Out of Business! Final Mark Downs!
Then pausing for the light at Liberty,
we'd make for the Southside by the Main Street bridge
past used car sales and party stores as if
the dead required one last shopping spree
to finish their unfinished business.
Then eastbound on Oakland by the jelly-works,
the landfill site and unmarked railroad tracks—
by bump and grinding motorcade we'd come
to bury our dead by the river at Oak Grove.

And it is not so much that shoppers gawked
or merchants carried on irreverently.
As many bowed their heads or paused or crossed
themselves against their own mortalities.
It's that bereavement is a cottage industry,
a private enterprise that takes in trade
long years of loving for long years of grief.
The heart cuts bargains in a marketplace
that opens after-hours when the stores are dark

and Christmases and Sundays when the hard
currencies of void and absences
nickel and dime us into nights awake
with soured appetites and shaken faith
and a numb hush fallen on the premises.

Such stillness leaves us moving room by room
rummaging through cupboards and the closetspace
for any remembrance of our dead lovers,
numbering our losses by the noise they made
at home—in basements tinkering with tools
or in steamy bathrooms where they sang in the shower,
in kitchens where they labored over stoves
or gossiped over coffee with the nextdoor neighbor,
in bedrooms where they made their tender moves;
whenever we miss that division of labor
whereby he washed, she dried; she dreams, he snores;
he does the storm window, she does floors;
she nods in the rocker, he dozes on the couch;
he hammers a thumbnail, she says Ouch!

This bridge allows a residential route.
So now we take our dead by tidy homes
with fresh bedlinens hung in the backyards
and lanky boys in driveways shooting hoops
and gardens to turn and lawns for mowing
and young girls sunning in their bright new bodies.
First to Atlantic and down Mont-Eagle
to the marshy north bank of the Huron
where blue heron nest, rock-bass and bluegill
bed in the shallows and life goes on.
And on the other side, the granite rows
of Johnsons, Jacksons, Ruggles, Wilsons, Smiths—
the common names we have in common with
this place, this river and these winteroaks.

And have, likewise in common, our own ends
that bristle in us when we cross this bridge—
the cancer or the cardiac arrest
or lapse of caution that will do us in.
Among these stones we find the binding thread:
old wars, old famines, whole families killed by flues,
a century and then some of our dead
this bridge restores our easy access to.
A river is a decent distance kept.

Peter's Bridge, Milford, c. 1910

A graveyard is an old agreement made
between the living and the living who have died
that says we keep their names and dates alive.
This bridge connects our daily lives to them
and makes them, once our neighbors, neighbors once again.

Daniel Minock

Island and River

Ten people showed up at the Nature Center Parking lot at Kensington Metropark early on a Saturday evening in late April. Half were active members of the local Sierra Club group, and the others were their friends, husbands, or mothers. My plan for this outing was to show them the great blue herons and great horned owls nesting on a nearby island. I knew that others would wander up and join us. The park has plenty of visitors on pleasant evenings, especially on the weekends, and the place we were going has three routes running close together: the main park road, an eight-mile trail around Kent Lake used by bicyclists, roller bladers, and pedestrians, and a two-mile nature trail around Wildwing Lake. I set up my spotting scope on the concrete slab of the overflow basin, where water flows from Wildwing into Kent Lake.

Leading outings for the local Sierra Club group is what I do as an environmentalist: I find out things, usually things about birds, and help others see them.

One of the Sierra Club members there that night, Sue Kelly, makes a very different contribution. Recently, for example, she has been trying to save a three-and-a-half-acre woods near the city of Brighton, surrounded on two sides by I-96 and an exit ramp and on the other two sides by a new shopping center; it had been declared a park under an act initiated by and named after Lady Bird Johnson back in the 1960s. But now the owners of the shopping center thought it would make a good addition to their parking lot. Sue, practically single-handedly, waged a six-month campaign to keep the park from being sold and developed. And, with the help of the Michigan Department of Transportation, she won. The tenacity of developers means that the victory is not necessarily permanent, but for now the Lady Bird Johnson Park remains unpaved, though it is pretty much surrounded by concrete.

It occurred to me this evening that Sue and I are both working with very different kinds of islands in very different ways, but I was too much occupied with the task of leading an outing to finish the thought. I have been watching my island for close to ten years now, ever since, early in the 1990s, I noticed a pair of great blue herons bringing twigs to a high crotch of an oak there. Over the years, more pairs of herons have brought many more twigs, so that now there are dozens of nests in the trees out there. Marvelous, I used to think—still do think—that they should have chosen this spot, so close to the main park road, so visible to walkers on the trail around Wildwing Lake and the bike trail that goes around Kent Lake!

As the group of us approached the shore, I saw one of the herons approach the island with an absurdly tiny twig in its beak.

"Watch this," I said. "Here's how the nests are built."

Since there was a slight southwest wind, the heron circled around the island until it was northeast of it and then, from the downwind position, began to approach one of the nests. When it was just above the nest, it reached out its long legs and clutched a couple of tiny tree-tip twigs in its feet, balancing there, while another heron came rising out of the nest like a cobra out of a snake charmer's vase.

"Listen," I said. "You may get to hear the heron's howl."

There almost certainly was a high, thin call, something like a howl, as the sitting heron stretched its neck, just before it reached for the twig its mate had brought. But there were cars passing just then, so the sound didn't reach us. Instead, we watched the sitting heron take from the bill of its mate the offered twig and begin the slow task of weaving it into the nest.

"That same ritual takes place every time a heron brings a twig."

"Every twig in every nest?" someone asked.

"Herons don't mind doing the same thing over and over," I said and told the story of the Virginia gentleman who liked to hunt ducks while floating down the Shenandoah River. On some days as he moved along, he would surprise a great blue heron, who would lift up from the shallows and, slowly pumping its wings, cycle a little further downriver, to land and again be surprised when the canoe appeared a few minutes later. After three or four repetitions, and the prospect of chasing the heron all day and having it disrupt his hunting, the gentleman would lift his expensive double-barreled shotgun and kill the bird.

Cries of dismay from my listeners. And I saw that the effect of my story was not to illustrate the behavior of herons but to emphasize the impression of refuge that the island gives.

I had watched at another heronry in a swamp. It took immense work, patience, and time to map the location of nests in that heronry. And I only got to see the herons fly away from me. But here at Wildwing Lake I am not an intruder. The birds pay no attention to people. And people can see them clearly, can watch them being herons.

Pleistocene grunts from a pair of birds teetering above one of the highest nests, flapping their wings into each other's outthrust beaks. But mostly what happens out there is not drama but just theater. The movements of the great blues around their nests suggest a practiced, even elegant awkwardness, and the birds in their mating plumage seem to be—in fact, are—in elaborate costume. The slowness of their movements implies an audience. It is Heron Opera out there on Wildwing Island.

When I come out to watch the opera, I find myself in a swirl of other dramas: right at an edge where people come into contact with a startling display of bird life. At least it startles a few. They return: I learn their names: Mark, Nancy, John, Heather, Melanie, Mary. I meet their children, their friends.

But I've been surprised that more people aren't more interested. And so, besides being a student of the herons, I have come to think about those who stop—or don't stop—to look at the herons. And I have also studied myself in this situation.

On this particular Saturday night, just after I had set up the scope, I heard tires slow and an engine idle loudly behind us and then a voice calling: "Excuse me, can you tell me what those big birds are? Are they cranes or hawks?"

Sometimes, especially in the first years, I would respond fully to these drive-up inquiries—go to the open window and politely answer questions and provide information—usually too much information. People stopping in the middle of the road, I've found, don't want to know too much about the habits of great blue herons. At other times, I would pretend not to hear the called-out questions. "If they really want to know," I would say to myself, "they can park their car and walk over here." They never did.

It is not that I expect everyone to be a naturalist or to snatch the opportunity to become one. What surprises me is the tepid interest of many people. Mistaking a ruby for a piece of hard candy, they seem to put the heronry into a category that includes zoo exhibits, nature documentaries, and museum dioramas. It is as if those birds have been carefully placed there, as captives or semicaptives, and so are not as interesting as a bear crossing the road or a white-tailed deer standing in a field or a water snake on a footbridge. It may also be a matter of scale. Although the island is only about a hundred yards offshore, the herons register on the retina about as large as a sparrow in a nearby bush. In contrast I have seen a roller blader fall—one measure of startle—at the sight of a pair of close-by Canada geese with six golden chicks.

When in February 1994 a pair of great horned owls took one of the heron nests left from the previous summer, my interest in Wildwing Island ratcheted up several notches. Though I was still interested in the herons, continued to map their nests and count the young and observe their behavior, in truth it was the owls that drew me back night after night to stand and gaze. Great blue herons are common birds in the Huron River watershed—seen standing motionless in the shallows of ponds and streams or flying with slow wingbeats high overhead. Great horned owls are much less easily seen. They are fierce, dignified, and solitary. They carry with them always a little wilderness, a little silence, a little night.

The Sierra Club theory is that people who see more and know more of the natural world will care more, which will translate into letters to legislators, attendance at meetings, donations to environmental groups, and pro-environment votes, and—though the process is beginning to sound both too simple and too complicated—bring about a human society that will allow the birds I am looking at to thrive. If indeed I believed in the simple equation that more exposure to nature creates more environmental awareness, I would have told everyone who lingered near my spotting scope about that owl.

I did tell many people, in fact; but I found myself withholding the information methodically from all those who called to me from the road: "What are those big birds out there?" "Herons," I would say, continuing to look at an owl in my spotting scope. And I did not push the information at those who walked by without stopping. Lately I have also found myself not telling those who for reasons that are not always clear to me I decide aren't interested, though some who I think might be interested clearly are not.

Actually, the activists did not seem as interested in the owl as I might have expected them to be. Nevertheless, I told them, and the passersby who had swelled the group, the owl history of Wildwing Island—that the pair in 1994 raised one young owl; that owls came again in 1995 and 1996 but left in the middle of March, probably because the eggs did not hatch. Then in 1998, last year, a pair raised two owlets.

The owls arrive early in February, before the herons are back, and take over the best nest. Up until this year, I had noted minimal conflict between the species. But late in March, when the number of herons began to increase, and possibly when the owlets (two again this year) were not much bigger than frogs, the adult owl began to clear the island of herons every evening. It was hard work and took a number of flights from the owl, straight at a heron, who would roar in alarm and launch itself like a schooner weighing anchor, drifting out of control until its wings caught the air. Eventually there were too many herons to chase away, or perhaps the adult owl saw that her young were too big for a heron to swallow, so that show came to an end.

Now the owlets were two-thirds the size of the adult and were beginning to take leaps from nest to adjacent twigs and back again. Someone asked me how many herons there were.

"Well, there are forty-five working nests, including the owls', so that means eighty-eight adult herons."

I held up a clipboard with a drawing of the map of the island's nests.

"I don't want to tell you how much time I've spent on this map," I said. "It's not always easy to figure out which tree a nest is in."

There was a buzz of astonished merriment at the complicated drawing I held up.

"Maybe you need," a voice from the back of the group said, "to get a life."

I suppose the comment was meant lightly. In fact, it plunged deep. At the same time I found myself fascinated by the expression "get a life." There was something in that faddish phrase that seemed to shine a light on some half-formed thoughts.

But just then I didn't have time to be offended or philosophical. I was leading an outing. At that moment, with my back to the shore, I saw a full moon rising over Kent Lake. On the island, I knew, the shadbush was blooming, and the owls were there, and the herons.

"Look," I said, pointing at the moon.

Two and a half weeks later, I stand at the same point, hearing again under my feet the sound of water flowing from Wildwing into Kent Lake. The young owls left the nest a few days after the Sierra Club outing and lingered on the island for another week. But now they are gone—though someone has seen them in the forest north of the lake, with an adult owl nearby.

I am watching great egrets—white, heronlike birds somewhat smaller than great blue herons. They have been coming to the island only for the last few years, arriving late in May. Now I watch an egret fly to the island with a twig in its mouth. I want to know how many there are and what nests they are occupying. Are they building new nests or simply remodeling unused heron nests?

In the period since the outing, I've thought about islands. Contained. Visible. Easily observed. Safe. They can also be separated, static, dying, or dead—the past tense apotheosized. David Quammen's *The Song of the Dodo* suggests that the natural regions of the earth have been carved into islands and are undergoing "ecosystem decay." Lady Bird Johnson Park, wedged in as it is between a Target store and the freeway, represents the condition of the natural world in this view: a place where native plants and animals, cut off from the larger world, dwindle to extinction, a place penetrated easily by the sounds and introduced organisms of the human world.

Of course, neither great blue herons nor great horned owls are threatened with extinction. And the island in front of me hardly seems to exhibit any other symptom of "ecosystem decay" that Quammen talks about. But I believe there is another type of dwindling that takes place in the human mind that Wildwing Island exemplifies: the way it becomes marginal, less important than the human world. The natural world, carved into islands, no longer seems central or essential to human life. Those who develop an obsessive interest or concern with the natural world—unless they are earning money or practicing a profession—might be thought to be exhibiting a symptom of trouble, an indication that what they are living is not quite life. That person might be advised to "get a life."

An impatient critic of popular culture might point to the phrase as an example of how stupid and shallow we have become, to believe that a life is something one can "get." But I think the phrase is intended ironically. What it suggests is that for those who are weirdly, incoherently obsessed, anything, even something artificial, would be preferable. In other words, someone who is too interested in islands needs to "get a life." And an image of the life that that person needs to get might be a river.

A river is open, complicated, never completely available to the eye; it is a flowing away, a carrying on, a joining with others. It gets wider—and dirtier. It is the present tense in all its unraveling impermanence.

Wildwing Island attracted me first because it was isolated and neat. I could see it all at once, could stand on the shore on the busiest of days and look at something free of humanity. In the middle of the nineteenth century, Walt Whitman wrote that from the deck of a ship his eyes "settle the land." A hundred and fifty years later, as I stand on the shore of a small lake in a region aflame with human development, my eyes "unsettle the land" as best they can. And so I turn to this island.

But I have come to realize that Wildwing Island's isolation is an illusion. It is a part of the river—figuratively, in the sense that everything is part of "the river." Since the night of the full moon, the flow of spring has passed over the island: the shadbush blooming has finished, and the oaks are in leaf, so that most of the heron nests are hidden, except to an inquiring eye armed with spotting scope and map. Actually, the herons' habit of defecating generously gives the nests, and many branches, a frosted look. But I can also hear the nests in the synchronized clack-clack hunger call of the heron chicks, hoping in a chorus for the return of their parents with food. In another six weeks, these young herons—about 150 of them—will fly away from the island to find their own food—another type of flow. Finally, the heronry itself is mortal. It has been growing in the eight or nine years it has been here, starting, according to my records, from a scant sixteen nests in 1993 (the first year I kept records) to the forty-five nests this year, 1999. But for some reason, bearing the nests of great blue herons seems to shorten the lives of trees. In a few years, perhaps, the big oaks will all be gone from Wild-wing Island.

But I have realized too that Wildwing Island is also part of the literal river. The water passing through the overflow basin is a part of the Huron River. It comes from the springs that feed Wildwing Lake, and it flows, very slowly, around Wildwing Island.

In a sudden shift of scale, I see the Huron River in the image of an oak tree, with the tips of the outer branches being the springs and small streams that seep into larger branches, eventually joining the trunk. From this per-spective, Wildwing Island is part of the top of the river. It is protected in three ways—first, by being a part of Kensington Metropark; second, by being an island in a lake on which boats are not permitted; and third, by being downstream of nothing but a few springs and short streams, all but one of which originate in the park itself.

But my sense of security about the island doesn't produce much serenity in me. A few miles downstream, the water from this fresh beginning enters a lake where Jet Skis roar and trash floats in the shallows. Ten years from now, urban sprawl will probably increase the number of loud boats and the amount of trash—and decrease the number of species of animals and plants in the Huron River watershed.

Thinking about what is likely to happen, I tend to look at Wildwing Island as if I were looking at a photo of a laughing child who later developed a painful and debilitating disease. The river of loss flows upstream and invites despair.

But here is what I have further come to realize—or remember, for it is not a new idea: this sense of despair and loss is optional. The world produced by future urban sprawl may not in fact come to exist in exactly the way I dread. In any case, it will not last forever. Even the lake of Jet Skis and human feces, though real enough now, might change eventually. One can hope. One can work to make the hope real. Meanwhile, one can look steadily at the island in the river.

After peering through the spotting scope and staring at my map of nests, I finally see that the great egret *is* building a new nest. I look around for someone who might be interested in this news; but for the moment there is no one else, no one hiking the path around Wildwing Lake, no one skating by on the bike path, no car in sight.

CARL R SAMS II

Images by
Carl R Sams II

Huron River rapids

Deer eating lilies

Heron in fog

Huron River in fall color

Canada goose landing in fog

Swan and cygnets

Wood duck

Showy lady's slippers

Waterlily

Tree frog in grasses

Geese in winter

KEITH TAYLOR

Between Freeways

IT WAS YEARS AGO, long before I ever dreamed I would spend a fair amount of time canoeing on the Huron. I was interested in the rough and wild area north of Lake Superior where it's easy to play out voyageur fantasies. This river was simply the one flowing by the places where I lived and worked.

But my friend Dan thought I needed to learn the different calls of the confusing *Empidonax* flycatchers, and he said he knew a good place to study those.

"We'll just float down the Huron, from I-96 to U.S. 23," he said early one May. "This time of year there's a good chance you'll hear them all."

I wasn't overly excited about the idea of canoeing between freeways, but even then I knew enough not to pass up an afternoon with Dan.

He started pointing out the calls to me almost as soon as we put in. I couldn't keep them straight (in fact, I *still* can't keep them straight), but I

was immediately captivated by the river. We were in the Island Lake State Recreation Area. After we escaped from the sound of the first freeway, there were no roads and no houses. I felt as if I were hundreds of miles away, surrounded by woods and marshes, all the spring birds, and even several species of mammal.

When we came to a small creek flowing in from the south, I wanted to follow it. Dan humored me. We wound up the creek for a couple of hundred yards until we came to several houses with manicured lawns running down to the water.

"It's weird," I said. "You feel like you're in the bush, then—bam—you're in someone's backyard."

Dan laughed. "Don't forget where you are," he said. "You're in southeastern Michigan. You're *always* in someone's backyard."

Keith Taylor

Carryover

I WANT TO BREAK IN my brand-new bright-red Kevlar canoe. And I want to do it in a place I've never seen before.

Pete and I start way out on the western edge of the watershed, in the village of Unadilla at the southwest corner of Livingston County. Portage Creek. The connecting point between the Huron River flowing east to Lake Erie and the Grand River flowing west to Lake Michigan. The native people traveled this way to avoid the long trip around the Lower Peninsula of Michigan and the political turmoil that always preoccupied visitors to the Straits of Mackinac. LaSalle may have followed this route when he came east trying to get back to Montreal. We've read about some of this. Other parts of the story are just guesses, our own inventions.

West of Unadilla, past Stockbridge over in Ingham County, Portage Creek disappears into dredged ditches that drain the cornfields. Somewhere close to one of those ditches, separated at most by a couple of hundred yards, is another ditch where the water flows to another creek that connects to the upper reaches of a different river. If we knew which ditches went where, we could put the canoe on our shoulders and make a short carryover to the next place.

But we don't know the way, so Pete and I head back with the flow, toward the Huron and the waterways we do know. The creek is not clean. Cement blocks and bricks clog the streambed. Pipes leak something unidentified into the water. The stream is muddy and shallow. We scrape several long scratches in the unblemished bottom of my new boat during the first five minutes. I know because I look behind and see the red scabs we've left on rocks or the edges of bricks.

Soon, however, the creek enters a series of small lakes, some natural, some formed behind dams. A couple of the lakes are lined with summer cottages, and a few others are in the Pinckney State Recreation Area. They're almost wild, and we actually see an immature bald eagle soaring over one of them. It's one of several times along the Huron watershed where I feel I've simply paddled back in time, away from my urban life and its endless busyness.

At Hell we have to carry my new canoe around the dam. I'm pleased by how light it feels, how easily I can carry it over a portage. We stop for burgers and coffee. It feels like a luxurious canoe trip.

Once we're back on the water, we follow the creek as it loops to the north for a mile or so. It is clean, flowing rapidly over an alternating sandy and gravel bottom, and easy to paddle, the banks lined with wildflowers. Patches of bright red cardinal flowers glow from the late August woods a few feet back from the edge. I wonder why more day-tripping canoeists don't know about this quiet creek, why they all crowd certain small stretches of the river.

When the creek turns south for the last few miles toward Portage Lake, I get my answer. Suddenly and for no apparent reason, every few feet there is an enormous tree blown down over and into the creek. Pete and I can't go a minute without climbing out of the canoe and sliding or lifting it over another tree. The dings and scratches in the unmarked skin of my new canoe are getting obvious. The first few times we have to climb out of the canoe, I try to be gentle with it. But I get tired very quickly and resign myself to a scratched hull, the sign of a canoe that has been genuinely broken in.

At some point Pete and I don't even bother climbing back in the boat. We just slog along in the middle of the creek, avoiding the deep holes and pulling the canoe to the next fallen tree. We are wet and tired and might even be getting grumpy. I'm definitely feeling all of my forty-five years, and I'm impressed with Pete's stamina. He's sixty-five but doesn't seem in any worse shape than me.

"God, Pete," I ask, "did the native people have to do this many lift overs, or have we changed the environment so much that the trees are all falling into the river?"

"No," he answers, "it's just that by the time they were our age, they got to stay at home and let the twenty year olds do this."

Right at the end of the creek, just before it opens up into the marshes above Little Portage Lake, some scrub willow grows out over most of the water. We're too tired to worry about it, so we dig our paddles deeper to build up speed and try to push past it. We're too tired, too weak, or the willow is too strong. It knocks us over, the first time Pete and I have ever been upended.

When I bob back to the surface, I first check to make sure my glasses are still on. Then I check to make sure Pete has resurfaced. He has. I feel for my wallet and am relieved that it's still there, although I already can imagine all my cards and soggy papers sticking together. We pull my new canoe up on the muddy bank and pour the water out of the once spotless interior. We climb in, our shoes and pants covered in swamp mud, and make our chastened way to the Portage Lake public access site.

This charming lake studded valley, hedged about with ranges of rugged hills, has an elevation of 1000 feet above sea level. Geologists tell us that the glacial epoch left it an inland sea on the crest of the Michigan peninsula. But the persistent Huron, in ages past, eroded a defile through the hills that buttress the southern end of the Base and Portage lakes, and the waters of that ancient sea poured forth in riotous abandon to mingle with the flood of Erie, leaving, in the deeper pools of that inland sea, the innumerable lakes and lakelets that lend charm to the present day landscape. . . . This region, now a favorite resting place of the tired dweller of the city, was less than a hundred years ago the summer playground and source of food supply of the Pottowattomie Indians. It is rich in Indian tradition. It was here that the red men came during the warm months to hunt and fish and gather the bountiful harvest of wild berries and fruits. Their lodges were pitched each year on the high and broad plateau that reaches back from the southern shore of Strawberry Lake.

—Charles A. Ward, The Valley of a Thousand Lakes, *1922*

PAMELA REED TONER

The River along
the Lakes

I FIRST EXPERIENCED an American summer in a state of culture shock. I came to the United States as a young child, having been born in Japan at the tail end of the 1950s. During my first summer here, I remember standing in a country grocery store somewhere near Portage Lake, which rubs elbows with the Huron River as it wanders by on its way from Base Line Lake toward Hudson Mills Metropark. A jar of beef jerky sticks sat on the counter next to another jar filled with pink pickled eggs floating in cloudy liquid. On the wall behind them, a calendar, bordered at the top with an eagle, pictured a motorboat pulling a muscled man on water skis. Fireworks flashed in the sky behind him.

A pale man's face with large round American eyes appeared over the counter. I was terrified of Americans I did not know, who routinely lowered their faces so close to mine, staring straight at me and asking questions in their big voices. Japanese people did not stare so, nor speak so loudly.

"Hii-ee," said the face. "What's your name?"

I stared at the floor, examining a knothole in one of the wood planks.

"Pam," said my mother.

"Pay-um," said the man. "Hii-ee, Payum."

The wide vowels and the high volume stunned me. So did the beach. A mosaic of towels lay quilted across the sand. Float toys bobbed, and beach balls flew above a continuous cackle of chatter and squeals. Large people screamed and splashed with little clothing and even less decorum. They ate casseroles with chunks of meat and vegetables sauced together and salads with gelatin, marshmallows, and fruit all intermingled. I watched a boy wipe a swatch of a hot dog bun through a puddle of pork and beans and stuff it in his mouth. In Japan each kind of food was kept properly on its part of the plate, not mixed around with such sloppy abandon.

Although the beach was noisy, I found comfort in the quiet pulse of the water against the shore. I collected tiny stones and shells that shook gently in my bucket as I walked and examined the bits of seaweed that lined the water's edge. My brother and sister and I traced out wet canals with our shovels, scooping uphill through the sand. Eventually a scrawl of waterways was written all over the beach. We finished by shoveling out a final starting point and then made trip after trip with our buckets, refilling our rivers with lake water and watching it trickle back to the shoreline.

This beach is on Portage Lake and is bordered by a long dock. The boats of Huron Portage Yacht Club are moored on one side of it, where dozens of sailboat masts stick up out of the water. The other side is for swimmers, with a tall metal slide whose handles still wobble when my kids climb it as they did when I climbed up twenty-five years ago. Farther out in the water floats a dock with a diving board on each end, one of them a high dive. I remember the days being more cold and rainy back then than in recent summers, but we didn't mind them in elementary school. Despite our lack of body fat, we swam oblivious to the icy water, staying there for entire afternoons, emerging only to scramble up the slide or high dive and splash back in.

On a cool, partly cloudy day after fifth grade, I stepped back on the high dive long enough to look around. The waves swayed the dock, tilting it right, then left, and I had to hold on to the bars atop the diving board to keep my line of sight steady. Back on shore, our mothers lined the grass just beyond the beach in lawn chairs, trancelike expressions on their sunglassed faces, trading comments with each other while staring continuously out across the water. The dark lake shimmered on the other side of me, shaped like a large pear with its stem pointing northward. Three motorboats pulling skiers circled the bottom half of it counterclockwise, round and round, spraying white trails behind them.

These days ski boats still circle, their paths now slashed by zigzagging Jet Skis and bigger boats with earsplitting engines that tear straight across the lake in angry streaks. These speedboats yield grudgingly for sailing races, when a large white flotilla settles on the lake, forcing them to snake their way carefully around and between its folds.

My father sailed in races two or three times a week, often with me as crew. Races were either wild and quick when it was windy or tedious and interminable when it was not. Like a baseball game, a sailing race is theoretically timeless. The course is predetermined, but depending on the wind, our races could take anywhere from less than an hour to several hours. Although sailors make a show of rushing from mark to mark, I think they secretly revel in coming and going mainly at the wind's mercy, whenever that should turn out to be.

Most races begin with a windward leg. The term *beating* is perfect for sailing to windward in gusty weather. Beating involves pointing the nose of the boat close to the direction of the wind, drawing your lines in tight, and leaning out to keep the boat as flat as possible as it heels over, tipping in the direction of its sails. Such legs of races in heavy wind are accompanied by much shouting and cursing as masts strain and pull, punctuated by flurries of flapping sails and snapping lines as booms swing across boats and sailors scramble to tighten the sails again on the other side.

On quieter days, the race was more subtle. My father knew the nuances of the lake, and whispered them surreptitiously to me when the wind was light and other boats were nearby, so they wouldn't hear that the wind would always dwindle off the point near that line of trees but a puff would probably brush our sails if we were patient with the tack we were on. On we would float, on the same tack, waiting for the puff, which sometimes came and sometimes didn't, the wind being the fickle thing it was, and the other boats would bob along too, until eventually, late in the hot afternoon, we all inched across the finish line. Then sailors would share beers, tossing them from one boat to another. One day a friend lofted a can in the air and just missed our boat. Like a good crew, I lunged over the side for the can, but I missed it and watched it swirl downward, shining and flashing up sunlight on its way to the bottom. Sometimes I think about it now, still settled there in the mud, thirty years later.

On another hot, windless day the summer after seventh grade, I swam the length of Portage from bottom to stem. As a defense against motorboat traffic, a friend chaperoned me in a Sunfish sailboat, which she paddled as the sail hung limp above her. When we reached the sandbar that cuts across the lake halfway up the neck of the pear, we pulled up her centerboard, and I walked, the water only up to my waist. Over fifty years ago, this sandbar divided Portage into two lakes. Later, sometime in the 1940s or 1950s, a dam was built, backing up the Huron River just past the lake outlet, and now the lake level is deeper.

Occasional bird's-eye glimpses of Portage Lake came to me from Peach Mountain. More a hill than a mountain, Peach Mountain overlooks the lake from the south. Spread around the base of Peach Mountain lies Stinchfield Woods, owned by the University of Michigan and inscribed with a system of trails. Our hikes in the woods were cool and dark with the scent of pine, but as we ascended the trees thinned out into open sunny meadows, hot and buzzing with flies and bees. From one clearing, I could see the lake in the distance, framed by trees that obscured parts of the shore, and I redrew the lines in my mind. From there it was easy to wonder what lay beyond those imagined shores.

Not far from the clearing, a narrow, bumpy trail led to an old sawmill that we were certain was haunted by the ghost of an ancient lumberjack. The sawmill was composed of a cluster of worn wooden buildings. Next to a large window in one of them ran a sloping series of metal rollers used for conveying logs to the ground. We slid down it ourselves on short lengths of board, and I imagined myself launching off the end and over the treetops to land in the lake below. We shared tales of how rattling could be heard from the mountain at night as the ghost himself rode down the rollers in the dark.

Later my father summarily erased the mystery of the lumberjack ghost when he told me that the saw mill was never a real working mill, just a site constructed to teach students from the University of Michigan about logging. But even with the ghost dismissed, Peach Mountain still held my imagination with its view of the lake that gestured beyond its borders. I still had not connected Portage Lake to the Huron River. For a long time I knew the river strictly as a fall phenomenon, involving annual canoe trips from Hudson Mills southward to Dexter.

At Dexter, we would pull our canoes up on the shore by the Dexter Cider Mill for cider and doughnuts. The doughnuts were the same as now, warm, crispy and greasy on the outside, and sweet and doughy on the inside. The cider press was the same, too, but they used to have a dispenser where you could buy paper cups for a penny and fill them up, as many times as you wanted, straight out of a barrel wedged through a hole in the side of the building. We kids would guzzle the cider furiously until we were bloated, but the taste itself was mellow and slow.

I finally linked the lake of the summer with the river of autumn one summer before high school. My friends and I liked to hang out at a clubhouse next to the beach on Portage Lake. This clubhouse was leveled and rebuilt in the 1980s and is now a fancier place for catered events, but in the 1960s and 1970s it was a sagging firetrap with graffiti on the changing room walls dating back over a decade. It was a friendly place for a kid, with a glass-topped wooden candy counter to peer into and a worn brown piano on which we played endless rounds of chopsticks.

A couple of old aerial maps of the chain of lakes hung on the wall above the piano. That summer I looked closely enough at the maps to realize that we could enter the Huron River from Portage and travel northward from lake to lake, Base Line to the Whitewoods to Gallagher to Strawberry. Another friend and I intended to trace that route when we paddled our canoe up the river from Portage to Base Line. Remembering the book *Paddle to the Sea*, we thought excitedly about navigating the river backward to its origin in a trip punctuated with our own private adventures. We paddled across the bottom half of Portage to a short canal that runs under the road to the Huron River. After ducking low under the metal bridge, we could sit up again in our boat to see the dam on the right and, to the left, the river greeting us on its way from Base Line.

The river between Portage and Base Line, which lakers call the "canal," is a busy place on weekends, with constant boat traffic between the lakes and to and from two party stores with docks for mooring boats during stops for beer and chips. We paddled along, breathing gasoline fumes and rocking from the clashing waves of various wakes. Along the sides of the river, turtles sat on the sunny logs, their color barely distinguishable from their perches, staring silently at the parade of boats.

Once the river widened into Base Line, a brisk wind blew in our faces, and we paddled hard into it. Base Line is a smooth circle of a lake, smaller and more manicured than Portage. A lush collar of large green trees enfolds the shore around its entire circumference, shading expansive lawns and well-kept homes. While Portage hosts a restless and varied mix of social classes and water sports, Base Line has a quieter and more uniformly upscale population.

We pulled hard on our paddles, nudging past the University of Michigan Sailing Club on the south end of the lake. While I knew of people who sailed with this club, it always remained a faint mystery to me as I was growing up. Only a few masts marked its location, and they were tucked back in a little cove, in contrast to the fleet of boats on Portage that so distinctly marked its south shore. I heard that the University of Michigan Sailing Club was used mainly for sailing instruction but that there was also a sailing team there that was once ranked in the top ten in the country. To me, however, Base Line's yacht club symbolized understatement—nothing like the flurry that accompanied sailing at Portage.

As kids we loved the end of sailing races at Portage. We would watch the flock of boats landing at the dock after the race, the sailors squawking as they hauled down flapping sails and tamed them with ropes. They would march down the dock, gesticulating and arguing over who violated whose right-of-way at the mark or why the wind changed so suddenly at one place or another, shaking their heads and lamenting the inscrutability of their sport. And if there were ever a formal protest of a race's outcome, we delighted in watching grownups gathered around a picnic table, fighting over their own games. We came to know each sailor's particular persona in these spectacles and to enjoy the predictability of their scripts. If such drama ever happened at Base Line, it was too colored by my image of the lake's subtlety for me to have noticed or remembered it.

We paddled northeastward across Base Line and continued up what we supposed was the river to what we thought was the first of the Whitewood Lakes. After not finding the outlet that we knew should be there on the northeast side, we turned back, tired, and retraced our route to the beach at Portage. We consulted the aerial maps and realized we had mistakenly paddled toward Tamarack Lake, a short jaunt that dead-ends almost due north of Base Line. And that this journey up the chain of lakes was going to take much more time than we had first calculated.

It wasn't until I was home for a summer from college that I tried the trip again, this time with a boyfriend, beer, and a motorboat, enjoying a lazy parenthesis between the end of final exams and the start of a summer job. Remembering my mistake several years before, we hung right out of Base Line and puttered our way easily and dreamily up to the two Whitewood Lakes and on to Gallagher Lake. Gallagher is now outlined with a thick ring of new homes, but back then we wound through all three lakes, passing just a small half circle of cottages on one side of the first Whitewood, all the rest open and marshy with cattails and grasses and only an occasional house. Next came Strawberry, a civilized lake with pontoon boats moored neatly next to evenly spaced little cottages which I remember painted red, white, and green. The river enters Strawberry Lake from the north, sneaking almost imperceptibly under M-36 on its way south from Ore Lake, but we didn't trace the river beyond the road. Instead, we veered northwestward up a canal connecting Strawberry Lake to Zukey Lake, where we stopped for pizza at the Zukey Lake Tavern.

The tavern side of Zukey was cluttered with run-down cabins facing every which way, as if someone accidentally spilled them there along a narrow stretch of land between the dirt road and the shore. The tavern was dark and wood paneled, with no windows, like an underground burrow. A narrow hallway led back to a main room that had a bar and tables, and another room sat to the side with booths. Televisions were mounted in the corners on both sides of each room so that patrons could watch sports events from any seat in the place. On summer nights the place grew gradually louder and smokier as a series of softball teams finished their games and dropped in for dinner.

Now I make the trip to Zukey Lake by car to pick up pizza for the kids, driving over from my parents' house, which they built on Portage Lake a few years ago. Their house has many windows, and nearly all of its rooms face the water. On the far side of the first floor sits my father's study; on the other end, a breakfast nook rests next to the kitchen, which, slightly elevated, overlooks the dining room. The side of the dining room opens onto a hexagon-shaped great room with tall windows and high white walls. The great room forms the fulcrum of the first floor, jutting slightly lakeward. The nook, the dining room, the great room, and the study all open directly to the lake with sliding doors that slide and click, slide and click with the comings and goings of grandkids on the weekends. The internal flow of the house, however, directs the entire first floor downward and forward toward the great room, which my mother and I supervise from the kitchen, peering over the counter while we work.

On one morning, I stand washing breakfast dishes, looking out past the great room and on to the beach. The kids run circles by me, through the dining room, past the great room, down the long hallway that runs along the back of the house behind the kitchen, and through the kitchen again. The boys, seven and five, are singing the Pokémon theme song. Their two-year-old sister trails along, elated, yelling, "Peekachoo! Peekachoo!"

Outside the window a flock of geese takes off, squawking upward. These days most people detest them because they're loud and messy, but in the 1970s Canada geese were a novelty on the lake. I remember watching a flock in awe one night with our family as they descended to the water in the orange evening sky.

Once the flutter of the geese is gone, I notice a silent heron down by the dock. People on the lake know him as Frank, who comes to fish every morning. By many accounts he has been around for years. Whether he is the same heron or a succession of different birds is unclear. He stands still, staring at the water. Usually I call the kids to come and see, but today I decide to leave him alone. He struts down the dock in slow, studied angles. Frame by frame, he lifts a leg, stops, places a foot, stops, lifts the other leg, stops. He turns, suddenly serious, at the shore by a large rock. He freezes. His beak is poised, pencil-like, above the silvery surface of the water.

The kids charge through again. One of them hurls an imaginary Poké Ball toward the great room and yells, "Gyarados—Go!" My toddler follows with a pink bottle in her hand, trailing a white line of sunblock down the hallway toward the kitchen. I clean it up, grab towels from the dryer, deal out club crackers, and put on my sunglasses. I glance out the window.

Frank still stands by the rock, framed by the branches of a willow tree. Soon the four of us will pour out the door, loud and clumsy, and he will spread his wings and rise, just in time but in no particular hurry, slowly folding his legs as he goes. For just this second, though, he stays, suspended there, beak pointed at the same single spot, the water lapping gently, barely erasing the tips of his claws.

CHARLES BAXTER

A Late Sunday Afternoon by the Huron

A MODEST PLACE, Delhi Metropark stands 850 feet above sea level and is located six miles west of Ann Arbor, Michigan, along the Huron River. This river originates in Pontiac Lake to the north and flows into Lake Erie, eighty miles downstream. The latitude of this spot is 42 degrees, 52 minutes, 30 seconds, the longitude 83 degrees, 52 minutes, 30 seconds. On this particular day, Sunday morning in mid-June, the families begin to arrive at 10:25, stumbling out of their rusty station wagons crammed with bags of charcoal, food coolers, kids, dogs, and pieces of recreational plastic. The lovers, and those coming alone, will arrive later in the day; right now they are still lying in bed, sipping coffee from no-spill mugs, and staring toward the white muslin curtains. What sort of day is it? What's going to happen with the weather?

At 10:40 the temperature is 71 degrees Fahrenheit, the humidity 56 percent, the barometer 29.54 and falling slowly. The midmorning sky is flecked with cirrus clouds, fleecy lines of ice crystals twenty thousand feet overhead, often the vanguard of a low-pressure front. It might rain.

Among these early-arriving families a couple, holding hands at the fingertips, stands next to the water. They appear to be unmarried and in their early twenties. Now he is taking off his blue cotton jacket and dropping it on the grass; then he takes off his shoes and socks and rolls up his cotton trouser cuffs. She removes a light-pink sweater and puts her hand in the small of his back for balance when she unlaces her running shoes and rolls down her white ankle socks. He wades out into the water, stepping gingerly as if on coals, yelping softly, reaching for her hand. They bump hips. She giggles.

His name is Lincoln, and hers is Evie. Upstream from them, sitting on the edge of a bridge over the river, is a thirteen-year-old boy (called Junior by his friends) who gazes at them, annoyed by their exuberance. He grasps a bamboo pole, attached to a red-and-white bobber and drop line. He has a coffee can full of dirt and worms for bait close to his right knee. So far he's caught nothing. Behind him, cars drive over the narrow bridge on their way to the park, rattling the oak planks.

The O'Hara family arrived here thirty minutes ago. The mother has already set up a red checkered plastic tablecloth, while her husband, at the grill, squirts fluid over a heap of coals. Their two children, Barbara, who is three and is watched over by the dog, and Keith, six, have strayed toward the playground. They've been instructed to stay safely within sight. Mrs. O'Hara counts out the tuna-salad sandwiches and the deviled eggs under her breath. The movement of wind traced through an elm stops her, and she sniffs the air. She is lost for two seconds and keeps her eyes tightly closed. No one sees her do this. Then she opens her eyes and begins to count the cookies, separating them into three groups.

For many of these people, the only image of heaven they have ever had, that has ever made any sense, is this: a park, summer, a picnic on wooden tables. Good weather. 11:23. Barbara O'Hara has wandered down to the river. The dog, a female German shepherd named Taffy, watches her. The dog acts, has always acted, as a nanny. She pads along on the child's left and nudges her away from the Huron. From birth, this child has been protected (from stairs, strangers, and rushing water) by this dog.

Lincoln has rolled up his sleeves and is picking up stones from the riverbed and skipping them on the water's surface. Granite, gneiss, a small flat piece of feldspar: the feldspar skips three times before it sinks with a sideways fluttering motion into the water.

This place would not be what it is unless it had a carload of noisy eighteen-year-olds. They are here: Carl, Carl's baby-faced cousin Bob, Bob's next-door neighbor Boone, who wears a pair of glasses with white tape over one lens, and D.F. The four of them have just stumbled their way out of Boone's gray pickup truck. They've left the portable stereo box locked in the cab and are carrying their beers and inner tubes toward the river. Bob and D.F. graduated from high school just last month; the other two have been working for a year now. All four are barefoot and sport T-shirts and cut-off jeans. Barbara O'Hara hears them and scrambles out of their way, followed by Taffy, who starts to growl. As soon as they reach the water they begin splashing each other; unprovoked, D.F. hits Bob in the arm just below the shoulder, and there is a moment of water wrestling before Bob drops his six-pack of Miller Lite and the fight is halted. Carl and Boone take off their shirts; they both have thin, pale chests. Now they drop their inner tubes into the water and sit down, their legs dangling out. Floating downstream, past Lincoln and Evie, who have just kissed, Carl says, All riiiight! and Bob offers Lincoln a beer as he goes by. Lincoln smiles and says no thanks as he shakes his head.

This river is no wider than a residential city street. At this point its rate of flow is approximately fifty feet per minute. Named by the French, it refers to a confederation of four tribes of Indians who lived east of here, all of whom spoke an Iroquoian language.

Another family, the Sinclairs, sets up a complicated lunch. This group includes three children, their parents, the paternal grandmother, and two maternal aunts who are not on speaking terms this particular day. The oldest child, Matt, has brought a football and plays catch with his father, while the two aunts silently take lunch out of the hamper. Mrs. Sinclair, having seen Taffy, the German shepherd, ties their mongrel terrier, Jesse, to the leg of the picnic table. The grandmother sits in a folding chair, touching her gray hair and mumbling commentary. Sometimes people listen to her; at other times they just don't. At the moment she is reminiscing about her life as a child, and a park she once visited in Alabama with her Uncle Tyrone, a park that looked like this, where she ate an orange.

Measured from the horizon line, the sun is at an angle of 84 degrees. The wind speed has decreased to five miles an hour. The cirrus clouds, overhead an hour ago, are now near the east horizon.

Just past noon, Junior can smell hamburgers frying on the O'Hara's grill, and hot dogs cooking over a fire that Mr. Sinclair has started. The river itself smells faintly of iron and clay. From another family's grill, thirty feet away, comes the smell of barbecue sauce. This family, the Bakers, have two children. One of them, a very noisy girl, Cynthia, is begging her mother for a piece of Hubba Bubba gum. Cynthia has a catalog model's face, with two registers, for begging and smug contentment. The other child, Donald, is retarded, with short hair, a sloping Down's-syndrome forehead, slanted eyes, and elongated jaw structure. He sits calmly on the picnic bench staring toward the river while his father spreads his homemade barbecue sauce over the chicken with a little brush. As he stares at the water, Donald opens his mouth, showing crooked teeth. His eyes are a brilliant blue.

Over on the baseball diamond a team from the Dexter A-1 Appliance Store has arrived and is warming up for the game that they are scheduled to play against a team from Groh's Chevrolet. Only one member of the Groh's Chevy team has arrived. This person suspects that the others are getting loaded at Shelley Davidson's house, in Dexter.

> *A prayer, a pledge of grace or gratitude*
> *A devout offering to the god of summer, Sunday, and plenitude.*
> *The Sunday people are looking at hope itself.*
>
> —Delmore Schwartz, "Seurat's Sunday Afternoon Along the Seine"

Junior grabs his bamboo pole and lifts it, yanking the bobber out of the water. The line drips and twitches. Hauling in the fish with a motion of a man pulling at a garden hose, Junior examines his catch, a shiny half-pound sunfish, the size of a man's hand, wiggling in midair and glittering in the sunlight. He reaches out and feels the fish's life flapping between his fingers. After loosening the hook, Junior stuns the fish against the boards of the bridge, then puts it on a green nylon stringer. He attaches his end of the stringer to a corroded nail in the bridge and drops the other end, looped around the gills of the sunfish, into the water.

Lincoln and Evie have waded out of the river, getting their trouser cuffs wet, and are walking back to Lincoln's orange CJ-7. 1:00. They remove a blue cotton blanket and a brown wicker picnic basket from the Jeep's rear cargo area and then stroll away from everyone else, down a narrow path through the cottonwoods, Scotch pine, star thistle, and bur oak.

Now along the river there appears a bearded man, dressed in an absent-minded and haphazard way, without food or blanket, who sits by himself. His name is Rolfe. He strokes his mustache and beard, as a little girl accompanied by a German shepherd walks past him. In his right hand he holds a book, a new translation of the poetry of Rilke. He unlaces his shoes. Something about the day keeps him from opening the book immediately, perhaps the noise of the children behind him, or the sight of two lovers retreating into the woods, holding a blanket and a picnic basket with their outer hands, holding each other with the inner ones. Rolfe tugs morosely at his beard. He exhales quickly, twice. He looks like a man who has spent most of his life by himself. Behind his glasses the wells under his eyes have darkened from sleeplessness. Feeling dampness seeping through his trousers, he opens his book and begins to read, moving his lips as he always does when he reads poetry, following the words in an inaudible murmur.

Grandmother Sinclair comes waddling down toward the water, keeping up a private monologue about her childhood in Alabama. She almost stumbles against Rolfe but at the last moment changes course and heads east. Her grandson, Matt, is sent down to fetch her.

Cynthia Baker is at the playground, climbing up the steps of the slide, blowing pink bubbles with the Hubba Bubba gum that she cadged from her mother. She has to wait halfway up for Keith O'Hara, who stands at the top making wide-angle gestures he has learned from Saturday-morning superhero shows. Now he slides down, facing the wrong way. Cynthia sits down at the top, checks to see who's watching her, blows an aromatic bubble, and pushes herself down. As she slides, the bubble pops against her face, sticking to her cheeks.

1:30. Stratocumulus clouds appear in the west, moving visibly across the sky in a straight-edged line. For the first time today, a cloud covers the sun. But the cloud continues to move eastward, and the sun reappears. The temperature is 81. The barometer has dropped to 29.32. The wind speed has increased to seven miles an hour, blowing from the northwest.

The four guys—Carl, Bob, Boone, and D.F.—can be heard in the distance, returning to Boone's truck, their voices heavy and excited. Boone and Carl have gone through five beers apiece and are bragging about their encounters with women. Carl is saying, You don't know her, man, not like *I* know her, and the way she talks, man, you know, like real low, shit, I could listen to that *all day*. All night, I mean. She ever whisper to you, man? You know, with her mouth right up there in your ear? Carl laughs once, a conqueror's laugh, and Boone looks suddenly angry, but then he spits and says, She never put none of her mouth in *your* ear, she'd be afraid to, with all them bugs flying out. Carl grins, hooks his finger to his ear, and all four of them laugh. Carl and D.F. have latent pink sunburns on their chests from today's exposure; during the week they work on the line in the Ford factory in Saline. Bob and Boone work outdoors for the highway department. Their bodies have a kind of sallow tan, pocked with blisters.

Mrs. O'Hara, Eugenia, has her family seated, and her husband, Roger, says grace: Bless O Lord these thy gifts which we are about to receive from Christ our Lord, Amen. When the prayer is over, Barbara and Keith look up and begin eating their sandwiches. Taffy, the gray-eyed German shepherd, is lying underneath the picnic table, waiting for Barbara to start throwing down pieces of the tuna sandwich to her. Already the dog's tail is wagging in anticipation, and as she pants, she begins, slightly, to slobber.

The softball team from Groh's Chevrolet has arrived in Bart's van, and although they do not look sober, the four women and five men are determined to play ball. They whoop, pat each other on the back, and whistle as they warm up. They give off a powerful smell of hops. The team from Dexter A-1 Appliance cannot believe their good luck, that they're facing nine people who are seriously in the bag.

Measured from the horizon, the sun now stands at an angle of 75 degrees. More broken clouds appear in the sky from the west, greater in thickness, some with dark centers. With these clouds passing in front of the sun, the effect is that of someone hitting an outdoor light switch.

Lincoln and Evie have placed their blue blanket, which Evie received free from a bank for opening a passbook savings account, at the south edge of the park, a section overgrown with wild cucumber, cow parsnip, Norway spruce, and red oak. They are protected from observers on all four sides. Lincoln has taken off his shirt, and Evie is applying the 6–12 mosquito repellant to his back. His skin smells of paint; all week he works at Bill Lee's AMC auto body shop, pounding, painting, sanding, and stripping. Evie is a clerk in the office. No matter how much Lincoln washes himself off, he still smells of the job. When he kisses Evie, she inhales his work, seeded into his skin. She doesn't know yet if she minds it.

Junior, with adult patience, is still sitting on the bridge, having by now caught three fish, including a smallmouth bass. The sun, two hours ago shining on his cap, is now heating up his neck. He looks at the park, yawns, picks up his stringer of fish, and decides to bicycle home.

A huge piece of tuna sandwich falls under the table; Taffy lunges at it.

Look! There's a man, middle-aged, clearing his throat, short-sleeved cotton shirt and white cotton pants, yellow straw hat, walking along the river, accompanied by a raccoon! Not on a leash! Just walking there! People come up to him, look at the raccoon, ask him questions. He shrugs, smiles, keeps walking.

The four guys have brought their portable stereo blaster, a box of cold mushroom-and-pepperoni pizza, and Frisbee down close to the water. They've turned on the radio, loud, to WRIF, self-proclaimed "home of rock 'n' roll," and they are opening more beers, smoking weed, laughing, and stumbling around. Carl makes a comic noise designed to sound like a pig at the trough. D.F. and Bob go off to toss the Frisbee, and Carl sneaks down the river to talk to a girl he's spotted. Boone looks as though he's about to fall asleep. He removes his glasses, separates a slice of cold pizza from the others in the box, and has a bite.

Grandma Sinclair is quiet, eating. Matt and LaVerna glance up at her and wonder how long it'll take for her to doze off. Jesse, the dog, is asleep on his leash in the shade of an elm. His legs pump fiercely: in his dream he follows the scent of a furry rodent into a meadow, and there he pounces on it, picking it up by the neck. Mrs. Sinclair begins to cut a watermelon for dessert, and Matt looks around to see if anyone is going to notice him, out here, eating a watermelon. He hates eating watermelon in public, in a setting like this.

Mrs. Baker has cut up Donald's barbecued chicken for him into little pieces on his white paper plate. Donald, his mouth open, holds his fork in his left hand and spears the pieces; he makes faint vocal sounds whenever he misses. When he is finished, his mother tells him to wipe off his face with his napkin. He smiles, picks up the napkin, and removes the barbecue sauce from his chin. A tiny piece of bubble gum is still stuck to his sister's cheek. Donald asks why Cynthia doesn't have to wipe that off, and his mother says that she does. Cynthia says, Oh, Mom, and begins with violent exaggeration to pull at her face with a paper towel.

Now, at 2:30, I am here, too, with my wife and son. They've walked down to the water pump, to work the handle, listen to it creak, and put their hands in the cold water as it comes, at last, gushing out. Perhaps they will drink the water, taste its heavy mineral content. I'm lying here on the grass in the shade, some distance downstream from everyone else, dozing off for a moment.

In the second inning, Groh's Chevrolet is at bat, Dexter A-1 Appliance in the field. A small woman, a showroom salesperson, is at bat. As in a game of opposites, a huge man who delivers refrigerators and other such items for Dexter A-1 is playing first base. The woman swings, hits the ball toward left field, and begins running toward the huge first baseman.

Rolfe looks up from his book, his eyes slightly wet. He has been distracted by the radio, by its blare, the noise of music he hates, Ted Nugent, Van Halen, and now the Romantics. Hey, he says, turn that down. The music makes him think of shouting, accidents, cultural anarchy. More loudly, he says, Hey, it's too loud. Boone, who is next to the radio, finishing the slice of pizza, doesn't hear him. Rolfe starts to get up. The goddamn radio is spoiling everything.

The Bakers, the Sinclairs, and the O'Haras have all noticed the noise of the radio. They've been looking at each other with irritated glances and shrugs.

Clouds have masked the sun, and the wind seems to have died away. Grandma Sinclair looks at the sky, sniffs, and says, I do think it will rain. She shakes her head. What a pity. Spoiling a beautiful Sunday.

Closing his book and lighting up a Pall Mall he has drawn from his shirt pocket, Rolfe feels his hands tremble with anger and anxiety. He places the book he has been reading inside the sleeve of his jacket, which is lying next to him on the grass, and he stands up, brushing pebbles and twigs off the seat of his pants. He stares righteously at the boy eating pizza and listening to the radio. A ruined life, ruining other lives! After taking a long drag from his cigarette, Rolfe walks over to the boy, who gives off a plaguey smell of body odor, marijuana, and beer. Excuse me, Rolfe says, the cigarette in his tremulous left hand, his right hand tugging at his beard. Excuse me, he says, in his classroom voice, more loudly. Boone, who has been lying on his back with his mouth wide open, blinks his eyes and looks blearily at Rolfe. Boone is blind in one eye; its stationary iris is a milky brown. The noise bothers me, Rolfe says, it's bothering all of us. Could you please lower the volume? Boone closes his mouth, stares at Rolfe, then in an efficient gesture reaches over and flips a switch, turning the radio off. Sure, man, Boone says. No problem. It was keepin' me awake anyhow. Thank you, Rolfe says, amazed at the ease of what has just happened, as he returns to his spot by the river. In the sudden quiet he sits down and stares into the water. There is some noise from the softball diamond, but it is distant, muted.

Tanya, the saleswoman from Groh's Chevrolet, has collided with the first baseman, and she is lying on the ground, her eyes shut tight, holding on to her leg. Everyone is crowded around her. Jesus Mary and Joseph, the first baseman says over and over again. Jesus Mary and Joseph. One man with muttonchop sideburns rushes off to the park headquarters to get them to notify the emergency paramedics. A woman who knows some first aid covers Tanya's leg. It might be a break, she says. Don't move. Tanya opens her eyes and says, I don't think it broke. I got the wind knocked out of me. And my ankle, I twisted it.

As I doze off, I think about all the people here, the beautiful random motion of everyone taking the day off, and for an instant I think of fitting them into some kind of story. But it's impossible. There is no story here.

Lincoln and Evie have been holding and fondling each other for almost an hour now. With some of their clothes still on, they begin to make love. Lincoln's thrusts are slow and gentle. He intends this as a demonstration: that lovemaking can be recreational, and that, despite his occupation, he has enough tenderness to last lifetimes. At first Evie is afraid of being observed, but gradually she loses herself. She loves it, and she loves him. Oh, she says, looking up at the clouds blocking the sun. Oh my God.

> *The sunlight, the soaring trees and the Seine*
> *Are as a great net in which Seurat seeks to seize and hold*
> *All living being in a parade and promenade of mild, calm happiness:*
> *The river, quivering, silver blue under the light's variety*
> *Is almost motionless.*
>
> —Delmore Schwartz, "Seurat's Sunday Afternoon Along the Seine"

Now, at this late midpoint of the afternoon, when almost everyone has eaten, walked, and played, the people here seem to slow down, almost to freeze in time. Barbara O'Hara has fed Taffy her last cookie and is lying with her head against the dog's chest, under the picnic table. Keith O'Hara is playing catch with his father, and Eugenia is cleaning up, wondering if she might be able to take a quick nap. Grandma Sinclair is asleep and snoring softly in her aluminum-tubing-and-plastic folding chair, and another one of the Sinclairs, Matt's other sister, Carmen, is leaning against the trunk of an ash tree, awake but not moving. Mr. Baker, Donald's father, still sits at the picnic table, but his eyes are closed, and his head jerks backward every time he starts to fall asleep. Boone is asleep in the sudden quiet of his radio. I myself have dozed off. Rolfe is not asleep—he has both daytime and nighttime insomnia—but, still by himself, he is staring off into the distance, looking at nothing in particular. He throws his cigarette butt into the river. It hisses, then begins to float downstream at a rate of approximately fifty feet per minute.

D.F. and Bob return from playing Frisbee, Carl comes back with a phone number tucked in his pocket, and the three of them wake up Boone. Come on, Ogre, they say, let's move. Feeling the onset of hangover, the four of them pick up their things, load them into the back of Boone's truck, and leave to buy more beer, before settling down at Bob's place, where they will watch tonight's Detroit Tigers game on Bob's father's twenty-four-inch Sony color set. Jack Morris is slated to be on the mound, against Texas.

Lincoln lifts his hips, as a warmth spreads from his thighs up through his buttocks, and comes into Evie. Straddling him, she has both hands at the side of his head, and now she kisses him hard, feeling herself joining an orgasm. It does not matter to her or to Lincoln that she might become pregnant. She has no fear of this man whose skin smells of paint.

First a siren, and then the clatter of oak planks as an Emergency Medical Service ambulance crosses the bridge, enters the park, and stops at the softball diamond. The paramedics remove a stretcher and load Tanya into the back of the vehicle, while everyone who is down by the river and still awake stands up and squints to see what is going on over there. The back doors of the ambulance are closed, and the two attendants get in at the front. The light atop the vehicle's cab flashes on, and the ambulance rushes out of the park to the hospital, where X-rays will be taken, and it will be discovered that she has sustained no fractures but has bruised her muscles and tendons. Behind her, the two teams call off their game and sit in small groups on the grass and the hoods of their cars, talking about other calamities: falls on icy sidewalks, traffic accidents, drownings in four feet of water, heart attacks, strokes, cancers.

Evie lifts herself up to see over the top of the staghorn sumac blocking the view from where she and Lincoln have just finished their lovemaking to the playing field. No, Lincoln says, putting his hands on her shoulders. Don't look. It's nothing. It's not important. Somebody probably just got a little hurt.

As the ambulance heads out of the park, the Sinclair's terrier, Jesse, wakes up and begins to bark, but in a sleepy, absentminded way.

Hooray! Cynthia Baker says loudly. Look! The sun's out again! Her brother, mother, and father look up in the direction where she is pointing a dirty index finger. The cumulus clouds, now at 4:14, have parted, and the sun's reappearance, as if commanded by Cynthia's grating voice, has scattered the mosquitoes, gnats, and sand flies that have started to swarm around those who have not kept moving. Rolfe adjusts his glasses and watches a swarm of gnats move collectively down the river, two feet above the surface of the water, a small spherical cloud of flying dots. He rolls up his pants and steps into the river, bending down to examine the sedimentary rocks near his feet. Shale, slate, limestone, lignite, gypsum. One stone in particular catches his attention. He rolls up his sleeve and picks it out. It looks like an arrowhead, but only by accident.

The Potawatomi Indians, who once lived here, part of the larger Algonquian group, were pushed during the late-eighteenth-century migrations into this area from the south and west by the more warlike Sioux. The Potawatomis were a largely agrarian people; for the most part, they grew corn, fished, and hunted. Among their tribal rituals was a festival of the sun. They were the last group of any race whatever living in this area to worship the earth.

There's that man again, walking the other way with that raccoon. The animal has been walking a long time and is panting.

Measured from the horizon, the sun is now at an angle of 30 degrees. The barometer is steady at 29.27. The humidity is 54 percent. The temperature is 81 degrees Fahrenheit.

Here are some people arriving: an enormous ruddy fat man wearing bib overalls but no shirt, followed by his gray-haired wife, who has two watches on her left wrist and a thick copper bracelet for arthritis on her right. She clutches a two-week-old issue of *People* magazine. Two women, Cheryl and Lee Anne, have spread out a blanket in the area recently vacated by the four guys. They open a thermos and drink hot Darjeeling tea from ceramic cups. Another couple, quite young, with modified punk hairstyles, come wading down the river from the west and continue until they are out of sight to the east. They are speaking Dutch. An old man wearing purple suspenders shambles toward the river with a pipe in his mouth, the aroma of the smoke unmistakably that of Cherry Blend. His woolly eyebrows are enormous and extend half an inch on either side of his face. The Bakers, however, are packing up and leaving, as are the Sinclairs. The O'Haras, first to arrive here this morning, will stay for another twenty minutes.

My wife and son and I are about to leave. For an instant I glance at all the other people here and try to fix them into a scene of stationary, luminous repose, as if under glass, in which they would be given an instant of formal visual precision, without reference to who they are as people. Even now, with the light changing, the sun moving more rapidly toward the horizon and the light gradually acquiring that slightly unnatural peach tint it has before twilight when the shadows are grotesquely elongated, I cannot do it. These people keep moving out and away from the neat visual pattern I am hoping for. I breathe out, stand up, and walk with my wife and son to the car.

Taffy, the dog, smelling something under the dirt, begins to dig with her front claws. Soon she has a small hole as deep as Barbara's thumb. If she keeps digging, Mr. O'Hara says, she'll get to China. Beneath her in fact is twenty-five miles of the earth's crust, and beneath that a layer of dense rock five to six hundred miles deep, lying on top of an oxide-sulfide zone that in turn rests on the earth's nickle-iron core. Meanwhile, one mile away from Taffy, Evie, lying on the blue passbook blanket next to Lincoln, holds her finger up toward the sky. Sometimes, she says, when I was a little girl, and I was mad at my mom, I'd lie on my back and think of a ladder that would take me up and away from where I was. I couldn't quite figure out where that ladder went, but I didn't care a whole lot. With her eyes still on the sky, she feels Lincoln's face lowering toward hers, and he kisses her. When he lies back again, he says, I remember something from high school science. Mr. Glenn's class. He touches the fingers of his left hand with the index finger of his right. The atmospheric levels. If you climbed that ladder, he says, you'd go up through the troposphere, the stratosphere, the chemosphere, and the ionosphere. But then you wouldn't be able to breathe. He puts his hand over her left breast. So you might as well stay. He feels her nipple tighten under his hand.

Rolfe has mosquito bites on his wrists, neck, and ankles. A horsefly has also bitten him on the back, where he can't reach around to scratch. His pants are damp from the ground. He has read and reread the translation of the tenth elegy. As he holds the book open with his right hand, he scratches his ankles with his left. Feeling hungry, he stops clawing at himself long enough to light up another Pall Mall.

One of the women, Lee Anne, finishes her tea and now takes out a recorder from her bag and begins to play. The piece is a jig, pre-Baroque, English. Cheryl, whose face is hard to see now, in the diminishing light, holds her cup between her hands and looks toward the Huron as her friend plays.

The O'Haras are leaving. Taffy, perceiving this, runs off to the east boundary of the parking lot, squats down, and pees. Keith O'Hara, wearing a Detroit Tigers baseball cap on his head, saunters over to the slide, climbs up, and slides down backward one last time.

The fat man in the bib overalls sits in repose, staring like the Buddha toward the water. In his hand he holds a little transistor radio. He listens to the baseball game, the Tigers against Texas. The game has just started. His wife fans her face with her copy of *People*. Now, at 8:30, with the sun barely visible through the trees to the west—no, now gone—a few more families arrive for some after-dinner recreation. But once they arrive they seem eager to leave, and they check the sky and complain about how difficult it is to catch softballs and Frisbees at this time of day.

At dusk, a woman wearing a tank top and running shorts jogs through the parking lot on her way to the bridge over the river. Around her waist is a small belt on which hangs a Walkman. Through the earphones she is listening to Mendelssohn's *Italian* Symphony, the first movement.

What a relief it is, sometimes, not to have to tell a story about these people.

The O'Haras have left. Rolfe is putting on his shoes and socks. He is waiting for the evening star. When he sees it, he will put his book under his arm and walk to his Renault. In the meantime, he smokes another cigarette and watches the smoke rise and disperse into the sky. It is as if words are bombarding him inside his mind, tugging at him, pulling his thoughts ferociously into terrible shapes. Feeling a wave of word-nausea, he bends down, picks up the book of Rilke's poetry, and throws it under a bush.

With Evie's blanket under his right arm, Lincoln holds his lover's hand as they walk to his Jeep. They throw their things into the back and get in. After starting the engine, Lincoln turns on the radio, and then Evie takes the fingers of his right hand, as he reaches down to shift into reverse. He backs up out of the parking place, and with Evie's fingers still resting on his, he shifts from reverse into first gear, lets out the clutch pedal, and steers with one hand through the parking lot out past the gates.

And now, with the sun below the horizon, the woman who wears a copper bracelet suddenly grabs her husband on the arm. His great double chin shakes as he turns to her, expecting a stricken look, but she has only lost her balance for a moment, and is smiling.

There: the evening star: Venus. Still pulling at his beard, Rolfe trudges to his automobile. Cheryl, sipping her tea, nods to him as he walks past.

The temperature is down to 74 degrees. A breeze seems to be coming from the north. The man in suspenders, smoking his pipe, stands next to the glowing ashes of the Sinclairs' charcoal fire and says to himself, I don't know why his feet was draggin' that way, I really don't.

At this time, when the loudest noise is that of the crickets and the wash of the river's water over the rocks upstream, the last light silhouettes the birds overhead, those that cluster near picnic grounds and water: redwing black-birds, grackles, mourning warblers, waterthrush. But now is the time also for the characteristic irregular swoop and flutter of bats, searching for mosqui-toes above those areas where the water has pooled and is still.

In these pools, away from the river's current, where vegetation can thrive, the carp come to rest in the dark, swimming through the water ferns, blad-derwort, stonewort, and lilies.

The wingbeat, and the pause—half a second, at most—and then the repeated wingbeat, of the bats.

One family, down at the south end of the park, has started a fire to cook a late dinner. From this fire sparks rise into the night sky, bright-red exclama-tion points, commas, and periods thrown up out of the coals and glowing in the air before disappearing.

The park closes at 11:00. In one hour and thirty minutes it will be Monday, the day of coffee, air hammers, and binding contracts. But now, in the dark, with the ruddy fat man and his wife still sitting there in the bug-infested grass next to the Huron River, with Ernie Harwell doing the play-by-play at the top of the fifth inning, Texas leading the Tigers three to two, it is still Sunday, the day of forgiveness.

One day I said to Dr. Curtis, we are talking about the rivers and lakes of Washtenaw County. Why not extend the same concept to the whole length of the Huron River from Big Lake N.W. of Pontiac to Lake Erie and from [the] source near Big Lake of the Clinton River down through the Oakland lake district, Pontiac to Mt. Clemens and Lake St. Clair, and then for a ways along St. Clair and [the] lower Detroit river, the whole to create an outer ring of parkways and parks along the 2 river[s]. . . . So we arranged that I would study the area and draw up the plan, he would take photos, prepare illustrated talks and promote the idea.

    —Harlow Whittemore, on the origins of the Huron-Clinton Metroparks
       (Harlow Whittemore Papers, Bentley Historical Library,
       University of Michigan)

CRAIG HOLDEN

On the Huron
River Drive

THE SECTION OF THE Huron River that winds from North
Main Street in Ann Arbor westward and northward until it crosses Territo-
rial Road, northwest of the town of Dexter, is accompanied by a road with
the obvious name of Huron River Drive. It holds hard alongside the river in
some places, crosses it and crosses back again, goes away and returns. I
remember hearing about it before we lived here. "You have to ride it,"
people would tell me. By bike, they meant. It is a fine road for that, winding
and hilly and largely shaded. I have biked it a couple of times, though mostly
I add to the motor traffic. I find in driving it nearly every day greater peace
than I could have imagined in a car. On this morning our daily commute
along the river is preceded by remarkable creatures. We are sitting at the
table before the wide glass doors that look out over our backyard to the
rolling still-undeveloped farm fields beyond us. (We live just off the Huron
River Drive, probably a half mile from the river itself.) We have views into
two fields that are divided by a tree line running directly back from our
house. In the west field, through a screen of branches, my wife sees move-
ment: a large tawny breast and then another. "Deer," she says. They are
common here. I spot them, too. But something is wrong. They move not
with the smooth gait of a deer but an odd jerkiness, a kind of horizontal bob-
bing. Limping? I see the legs of one animal now beneath the branches and
count: two. The impossible image I conjure, in trying to rationalize this
strangeness, is of a deer with two legs shot off. Then an entire body comes
into view, and it is all wrong, too, as if this deer has had the entire back half
of its torso removed.

When they pass from behind the still-leafless trees into full view, we see
that they are not deer at all but birds. Huge birds. "Emus," I say. It's possi-
ble. There are game preserves nearby, and animals escape from them now

and then. A man encountered a wild boar one night not far from here. "I'm scared," says my daughter, who is four.

They have thick broad bodies with heavily feathered tail sections that droop toward the earth, and long slender necks, and large bird feet that they carefully lift and plant. They're about four feet tall, I estimate, not really as big as emus. The tops of their heads are painted bright orange-red. They stop on the crest of the hill, in full and perfect view, as one of them goes into what is obviously a mating dance. He flaps his wings and turns in circles and bobs up and down, lowering and raising the long neck as he spins. The other merely watches, then wanders off toward the tree line. It is not, apparently, now in early March, time for romance. They wander through the tree line into the east hayfield, and then soon, when one of the neighbors walks her dog, they fly. I rush out front to watch them come over, headed back toward the river, and hear their strange whirring cry. I call my mother, who pays attention to birds. She opens one of her reference books and after a moment says, "Sandhill cranes. Wow."

So on this morning of the cranes, my son, Al, and I leave, as we do every weekday morning, for the Steiner school, where he is in the first grade.

At Mast Road, the real beauty of the Huron River Drive begins. We pass first a couple of small manufacturing plants on our left and then immediately, on the opposite side, the Dexter-Huron Park. This short introduction to the Drive contains, as does any good introduction, a synopsis of the entire thing. That is to say, along with the heavy foliage and sharp hillsides and the curving meandering river, the Drive contains, too, the stuff of humans: businesses and isolated houses and entire subdivisions and high-tension lines and railroad tracks. The Drive is a mixture of the pristine and the utilitarian, of the natural and the manufactured, of stasis and of development.

Just after these plants and the park, we enter a dense canopy of old trees, a long arboreous tunnel. A steep incline plunges down on our left and continues on the right to an overgrown floodplain and then to the river itself. It is all trees here, so closely grown in some sections that when they are leafed out the brightest sunlight will barely penetrate. Now, the trees are bare, but even so the light grows dim, and with the dimness, a silence seems to always come as well. Al and I grow quiet, listening either to a song on the radio or to the sound of the road.

I have driven some great roads.

A lip cut along the edge of a sheer rock face somewhere north of Boulder, Colorado, for instance. This on the way to a local ski hill. Patches of ice caused my old Chevy to wander enough that my heart would seize, for at that time there was no guardrail and there were only a few feet between my lane and the precipice. Occasionally I spotted the remains of a car or truck that had gone over. I am sure it was beautiful up there, the vistas breathtaking. But I could not look. I was worried about dying.

I once rode along the entire length of Loch Ness. I think it was pretty. The problem, though, is that what you do when you drive Loch Ness is to look for that stupid monster. You know you'll never see it, but you can't help watching. And you know that if you look away for two seconds, long enough to take in the hills and valleys and the old stone cottages, that's when it will rear its mythical head and you'll miss it. Your finger sweats on the button of your camera, and you don't see anything but the flat black unbroken surface of water.

These were remarkable roads, through places I was glad to see, but I wouldn't necessarily want to see them again. The Huron River Drive, though, is a different thing. It calms me in a way I couldn't have imagined a road doing. I am not a relaxed driver. I'm no road rager, either, but I admit that I get tense, sometimes. I don't, though, on the Drive. I can actually feel my shoulders relax. Sometimes, when I'm south and it would be faster to take another route home, I don't. I go up to the Drive, and I get behind someone going really slowly, and, inside myself, I smile.

Near the end of the tunnel of trees we pass into a satisfying series of tight curves, a slithering symmetrical back-and-forth dodging that I feel, sometimes, compelled to speed through to enjoy the sense of lateral gravity. More often, however, it is nicer to meander, one curve leading directly into the next and emerging in a satisfying upsurge into full daylight. And houses again, and another factory, and the rails on our right. Sometimes, when our timing is on, we pass the morning Amtrack run headed the opposite direction and wave.

Soon after this, things narrow once more as we approach the old iron Delhi bridge that crosses the river over a section of pretty rapids, really a series of riffles just steep enough to whiten the water. At their head, a flock of Canada geese often congregates, and on these cool mornings of earliest spring, when the water holds more warmth than the air, threads of steam, backlighted by the new sunlight, rise from the surface. My son and I remark upon this every day, and I say the same things about having to bring my camera sometime and find a good place to stop. But not on this day. On this day, as usual, we will just look and admire and continue on our way.

After the Delhi Park, a hard left-winding climb ends this section and lifts us up again and out of the trees. The rise peaks in a vista of broad and distant fields that, in the morning light, look as golden as wheat, though all they really hold now is brown meadow grass. Beyond them, great banks of high deciduous trees rise in graduated layers, like waves following one after another.

As we drive, March passes into April, and the floodplains fill and empty, and April segues into the warmth of May. The trees have filled out now, and the Drive is colored by long strings of bikers, and the river has come alive in a new way with kayakers and canoers and the geese leading lines of new goslings.

Past Delhi and the fields, we spot a particularly pleasing view of the river as it bends south and away from the road in a series of soft bends banked by low overhanging branches. We cross the tracks and then a concrete bridge, after which the river reappears on the opposite side of the road, on our left. The road here takes a broad left-handed curve that will last for maybe half a mile. Only a single row of thin trees separates us from the water's surface now, and the drop-off between it and us is steep and immediate. The river begins to change, to widen, until it becomes a lake nestled in this curve of the shoreline. This is the beginning of Barton Pond, and it is perhaps the most dramatic section of the Drive. The railroad crosses a narrow neck in the pond on a bridge that clears the water by only a few feet. I fantasize sometimes about rowing here, in a skiff, and how, when I passed beneath that bridge, I would have to lie back in the boat so as not to hit my head. Soon, the mansions of Barton Hills will come into view across the water, to the north, but here, in the beginning, all we can see on the far side are beds of rushes and cattails.

As we come out of the curve, past the narrows, and the water widens again, one of us, my son or I, will invariably say something about the swans.

This past winter we read *The Trumpet of the Swan* by E. B. White and learned many things about these graceful porcelain creatures. And then one day on the Drive we discovered the pair that lives in this spot on the river. They were always together, paired for life in their daily routine of diving after greens, until the day in April one of them went missing. It was several days before we spotted, in the rushes across the water, the white form curled upon a bed of sticks and grass.

"She's sitting," I said.

"Like the book," he replied.

And so now, each day, coming and going, we check. One of them is always out feeding, and the other is always curled on the nest. The time will come soon, of course, when the nest will be abandoned, and we will see more than just a pair of mute swans on the river.

But we will see the two of them again this afternoon, on our drive home. And tomorrow and for the next several weeks. And I think we will probably come down here during the summer, once in a while, just to check on them.

For now, though, we continue on, toward our day.

I once hitchhiked out from Anchorage, Alaska, clear along the Turnagain arm and around its end and on down the Kenai Peninsula to Homer. Beautiful? The everyday throwaway mountains up there are bigger than anything you can see in the continental forty-eight, and they are blue and snowy and ragged, and it can make you cry to look up at them. Moose jump out from the weeds like rabbits do here. The air is cold and clean, even in June, and the people friendly enough that hitchhiking is a legitimate way to travel, and you come across salmon rivers that you ache to fish. But it is the Wilderness, the big wide empty. Despite the occasional towns, it is a hard, hard place, and in June it doesn't get dark until after midnight, and a loaf of bread might cost you five dollars. It was good to see it, but I wouldn't live there, I don't think. Not now.

Then there's the road in upstate New York between the west bank of the Hudson River and the base of the Storm King Mountain north of West Point. This, with its heavy foliage and the lighted water winking through and the tight curves and the conflicting desires to accelerate through them and to slow down to watch, probably comes closest, in my experience, to the Huron River Drive. But the road through Storm King is less populated and not developed at all. It exists purely as a beautiful drive. It has no utility in the world other than simply being beautiful. It eventually gets you someplace, but more slowly than other routes.

The Huron River Drive has its pristine sections, but it is also used, lived and worked and relied upon. From our perspective, it is simply the most direct route from our house to school and work. This very fact of its utility, its necessity, makes it more special to me.

As we ride in our morning silence, Al as deeply in thought as I, I sometimes think to myself, "Imagine this: you are commuting." Commuting! I watch the sunlight dappled ripples or the geese or the deer, or I lean into a banked climbing curve, or I look up through the dense trees or at the old iron trestle bridge at Delhi. Commuting. Ha.

It is, I think, better than revenge.

LINDA GREGERSON

Water-borne

1.

The river is largely implicit here, but part
           of what
                 becomes it runs from east to west beside

our acre of buckthorn and elm.
           (And part
                 of that, which rather weighs on Steven's mind,

appears to have found its way to the basement. Water
           will outwit
                 a wall.) It spawns real toads, our little

creek, and widens to a wetland just
           across
                 the road, where shelter the newborn

fawns in May. So west among the trafficked fields,
           then south, then
                 east, to join the ample Huron on its

curve beneath a one-lane bridge. This bridge
           lacks every
                 grace but one, and that a sort of throwback

space for courteous digression:
           your turn,
                 mine, no matter how late we are, even

the county engineers were forced to take their road
           off plumb. It's heartening
                 to think a river makes some difference.

2.

Apart from all the difference in the world,
           that is,
                 We found my uncle Gordon on the marsh

One day, surveying his new ditch and raining
                innovative
            curses on the DNR. That's Damn Near

Russia, since you ask. Apparently
                my uncle
            and the state had had a mild dispute, his

drainage scheme offending some considered
                larger
            view. His view was that the state could come

and plant the corn itself if it so loved
                spring mud. The river
            takes its own back, we can barely

reckon fast and slow. When Gordon was a boy
                they used to load
            the frozen river on a sledge here and

in August eat the heavenly reward—sweet
                cream—
            of winter's work. A piece of moonlight saved

against the day, he thought. And this is where
                the Muir boy
            drowned. And this is where I didn't.

                        3.
Turning of the season, and the counter-
                turn
            from the ever-longer darkness into light,

and look: the river lifts to its lover the sun
                in eddying
            layers of mist as though

we hadn't irreparably fouled the planet
                after all.
            My neighbor's favorite spot for bass is just

below the sign that makes his fishing
                rod illegal,
            you might almost say the sign is half

the point. The vapors draft their languorous ex-
                curses on
            a liquid page. Better than the moment is

the one it has in mind.

A few days after our arrival there, I went back north from where my father was building his house, to the Huron river, which was about a half mile distant. It appeared much larger than it is now, and I think that it was, for it was marked on the maps as a navigable stream. I was surprised at the beauty of the river and the scenery upon its banks. The water was clear as crystal, was well stocked with fine fish and was a great resort for deer at evening. . . . At the point where I reached the river there was quite a large Indian planting ground. . . . At the upper end of this planting ground and upon the immediate bank of the river was an Indian cemetery where many braves and at least one chief had been buried. On my way to the river and about one hundred rods before I reached it, I crossed the Detroit Indian trail—it was the first trail I had ever seen. It was not more than twenty inches wide, but in many places it was as deep as the pony's knees and it more resembled a long, shallow ditch than the great thoroughfare which it was. This trail continued upon the south side of the river until it reached a ford about two miles east of Ann Arbor, where it crossed over to the north bank and from there it took a very direct course to Detroit.

—*J. Warner Wing, recalling his arrival in 1832,*
Michigan Pioneer and Historical Collections 27

KEITH TAYLOR, WITH RICHARD TILLINGHAST

The Local Mysteries: Drifting Home with the Birds and the Fish

A FEW YEARS AGO on New Year's Day, I saw a yellow-rumped warbler flash through a snowstorm beneath the bridge that carries North Territorial Road across the Huron River. The river here, above Hudson Mills Metropark, forms a small rapids over the remains of an old mill run. The stone foundation of the nineteenth-century mill is visible from across the river. Ever since that warbler, a bird usually seen when spring is well under way, I've thought of this as a good place to spot birds: woodpeckers, kingfishers, winter ducks, even the occasional osprey in the fall.

I come out here five or six times a year—to have a picnic with my family, to fly kites in the field just up the road, or to look for birds—mostly just to have a moment away from the usual busyness. And when I want to get in a canoe and float back down to Ann Arbor, this is the place I put in.

This time it is the first Monday in June, about ten in the morning. A few mosquitoes are out, but they don't bother us. The day looks as if it will be clear, warm but not muggy—the best kind of day to spend on the river. My friend Richard and I are beginning our second float down the river together. We did it the previous fall, on the first of October, when the leaves were drifting down around us like big red and yellow snowflakes. The water was much lower then and flowed fairly gently. Today it rushes down.

Richard, who fly-fishes for trout and salmon, often gets away to rivers much wilder than the Huron. And on long canoe trips in northern Ontario, I've seen rapids and waterfalls that are epic in canoeing literature. Those comparisons sometimes make us forget the very real beauty of the Huron. As development creeps or gallops across the five counties that border our river, cutting farther and farther into our sense of untrammeled space, the Huron, at least at its edges, becomes increasingly more important. It feels wild here.

On the banks of the river, late in spring, surrounded by bird call and fresh leaves, it's not difficult to imagine Native Americans paddling downstream toward the big lakes or French explorers coming upriver in their search for beaver.

However gentle the Huron looks as it flows through our collective backyard, it has its own life, its own power. Richard and I remind ourselves that the river can be dangerous; we've heard stories of experienced canoeists who have had accidents, even drowned here. But that, too, is part of the Huron's undomesticated allure. We know that for a few hours, just a few miles from home, we can experience a bit of its wildness.

The friends who have loaned us their canoe and driven us out from town wave good-bye as we push off into the stream. Richard and I are a little self-conscious at first. The water is moving rapidly, and newly launched, we're still uncertain of our balance. We don't want to do anything that will make us look foolish or inept in front of our friends.

Although I'm too busy steering the canoe to put my binoculars up, I notice red-winged blackbirds, jays, a couple of spotted sandpipers working along the bank of the river, and a pair of cedar waxwings hawking insects above the water. Cedar waxwings are not particularly exotic around here—nothing to precipitate a flurry on the local birders' E-mail chat group I subscribe to—but their delicate browns, black mask, and small splashes of red and yellow are still a lovely sight.

As soon as we're around the first bend and out of sight of our friends, we slow down. With nobody to impress, we can be as lazy as we like—two middle-aged and overeducated Huck Finns floating downstream on a summer day. As we drift, we try to reconstruct some favorite lines from Yeats:

> While on the shop and street I gazed
> My body of a sudden blazed;
> And twenty minutes more or less
> It seemed, so great my happiness,
> That I was blessed and could bless.

The river's not the shop or the street, but it's in the here and now, and we feel elated to be out on it.

Richard starts casting his flies upon the water while we are still well within the boundaries of Hudson Mills Metropark, a mile or two above Dexter. The Huron's not a trout stream, but it does have a good population of feisty smallmouth bass. Although we see fish scurrying across the rocks below us, none takes Richard's bait. Much like finding the balance in a canoe, he has to make a few casts to get his rhythm.

Fishermen aren't finicky about fly selection when angling for small-mouths. Bass—the linebackers of the piscatorial world—are aggressive predators that attack whatever darts through their territory. Smallmouths are attracted by anything big and black, fished "wet," underwater. Richard casts something called a Wooly Bugger and lets the current drag it downstream against the pressure of the line. The graceful looping of his casting accompanies us as we drift downstream. I'm content to float, using my paddle more as a rudder than as a means of power. My canoeing friends would be ashamed of me. But who cares? I'll watch some birds.

A red-tailed hawk floats over, then several turkey vultures. I catch a glimpse of a small hawk, probably a Cooper's, disappearing off toward the new golf course north of Dexter. I hear, but don't see, several warblers—one or two black-throated greens, a common yellowthroat, a yellow, and a black-throated blue—and a couple of vireos. Some of those are probably late migrants, still heading north for their short breeding season. Catbirds are doing their odd imitations from the bushes at the edge of the river. At one point a noisy kingfisher flies over us, lands on a dead limb above the river to study the water briefly, then dives in. I don't get a chance to see whether he has any luck, more luck than Richard has had so far.

On our fall trip we smelled the doughnuts and cider from the Dexter Cider Mill long before we rounded the corner and saw the houses of the village. We were tempted to stop, and several other canoeists had already yielded to the temptation. Today, however, we're the only people on the river, the cider mill is boarded up, and the water is carrying us too fast under the bridge. We barely notice the town as we try to avoid the rocks and bridge abutments.

Below Dexter we come around a small island and drift right up to a great blue heron. Astonishingly large up close, it stands motionless in the water, with its spearlike bill poised to stab at anything that swims below it. We startle it, and it startles us in turn, opening its five- or six-foot wingspan and lifting into the air right beside our canoe.

Richard and I stop at Dexter-Huron Metropark to eat our lunch. The park is empty, and we stretch out on the grass. Just glancing at a couple of the oak trees, I spot four species of woodpecker: two little downies engaged in something that resembles the mating squabbles I've read about; a hairy, easily distinguished by its size compared to its smaller cousins; a red-bellied, with its call like something from a jungle-movie soundtrack; and a yellow-shafted flicker, noisily pounding away on a dead branch.

When we're out on the river again, the sun slips behind a cloud. "A good sign for fishing," my companion says and continues his rhythmic casting, dropping the fly behind submerged rocks and into the lines of foam that trail slow ripples in the stream. Suddenly the rod jerks sharply down. Richard strikes back, the reel clicking wildly as the hooked fish darts downstream, taking out line. Richard grins and starts to stand up until I remind him to stay put. He holds the rod tip high, playing a give-and-take game with the bass: letting the fish run with the line, then reeling it in again, back and forth until the foot-long fish is netted, held up to be admired, then unhooked and released. While the Department of Natural Resources places no warning on fish taken from the Huron, many fishermen, concerned about the runoff of agricultural chemicals into the stream, shy away from eating them. And like most fly-fishermen, Richard prefers the catch-and-release approach anyway.

Farther downstream we begin discussing the rapids at Delhi, one of two places between Hudson Mills and Barton Pond where canoeists can experience an adrenaline rush. After the short paddle there, we get out to study the rapids. On our last trip, in October, the water was very low, and the passage through the rocks was exceptionally narrow, barely the width of a boat. We had studied it carefully and navigated through the rapids and under the bridge without a problem. Today there is much more water, and even though it is moving quickly and making a fair-sized rumble, we think we can do it easily.

We are overconfident. About halfway through the rapids we slip out of our narrow channel and smash headlong into a trough between the rocks. In the stern, I'm knocked off my seat and onto my knees. I notice that Richard, a tall thin guy who usually sits as straight as a great blue heron in the bow, is lurching perilously close to the edge of the boat. A lot of water comes over the side, and we both get wet, but the river is strong enough to push us off the rocks and back into the channel. By the time we're under the bridge at Delhi Road, we're laughing.

After Delhi comes a long oxbow bend that turns the river quite a distance to the south, away from the cars on Huron River Drive. It's a quiet place that has not been completely spoiled by the construction of a few expensive-looking homes on the high south bank. There is a path along the river here. It's a good place for warblers in early May: my daughter and I counted eleven migrating species of warbler in an hour's saunter around the oxbow a month ago.

It's a bit harder to see the birds from the canoe, but their calls are all around us. We catch a glimpse of a couple of white-tailed deer on the north bank, before our presence spooks them and they bound away over the bushes. At the end of the oxbow, just before the river cuts under the railroad bridge and the Huron River Drive bridge, is the second place for some canoeing excitement.

This little stretch of rapids is the last of the fast water before the river widens and slows from the effect of Barton Dam. People often approach it casually, a bit tired as they near the end of their trip. On our fall trip we went into it without studying it first and smacked into a hidden stone. Although we weren't upset, we were jarred, and we knocked a hole in the outer layer of our friend's fancy Kevlar canoe. She had taken that canoe, perhaps her most prized possession, on some of the roughest rivers in northern Ontario and never got anything more than some interesting scratches. We took it out on the Huron and punched a hole in it. I felt terrible about it, but she patched it and said she forgave us. Nonetheless, I think she looked relieved when we asked to borrow her aluminum canoe this time.

Because of our mishap last time, we get out to study the rapids, looking for the safest passage. This time we run it easily and with style, then settle in for the slow water that will last all the way to Barton Park.

There are often good ducks during the migrations along this section of the river. If the ponds don't freeze in winter, hundreds of Canada geese can

Canoe outing, c. 1910

collect. One of my favorites, the common loon, stops through almost every spring. Several birding friends have told me that in early April they've heard the call of the loon in the evenings from Barton Pond. Although I keep hoping to hear its haunting call from the very edge of Ann Arbor, I haven't heard it yet. But I'm still waiting.

Richard and I continue to paddle until we get to Barton Pond. We see several more great blue herons and what seems like thousands of red-winged blackbirds. As we make our way down the pond, Richard catches and releases the last of our trip's half dozen bass, all about the same size as the first.

I've heard that during some canoe races, teams get from Hudson Mills to the pond in two hours or less. Today it has taken Richard and me six and a half. Last time it took us seven and a half hours, and we didn't arrive until after dark. Then we sat out in the middle of the pond for a half hour or so, watching the moon come up, not saying much, a little reluctant to get out on dry land and begin our usual round of duties and responsibilities.

When we finally land at the portage point beside Barton Dam, I hoist the canoe on my shoulders and set off down the trail to our car, parked earlier in the morning near Huron River Drive. Richard carries all our gear. Back at home my wife asks how the trip went. "It was fine," I say. "Fun and relaxing."

What else could I say? It's hard to find words to explain a day on the river. It's a day when nothing happens but a day when we can relearn the easily forgotten lessons of the local mysteries—and a chance to catch a few glimpses of those beautiful creatures in our own watershed, our own backyard, creatures that often live their quiet lives just outside the window frames that usually circumscribe our sight.

PAUL SEELBACH

Huron Hex Hatch

IT'S A WARM, QUIET August evening and I'm wading slowly upstream, fly-fishing in the Huron River near Dexter. I've caught and released a few modest-sized smallmouth and rock bass, but mostly I'm just enjoying the scenery: clear water, an interesting riffle, a pool, and here and there a crayfish or a freshwater mussel. The moving surface waters dance, sparkle, and laugh. I keep watch for a great blue heron, a green heron, or perhaps a mink along the bank. Good numbers of the white mayfly Ephoron have been performing their serial mating dance—this is a fairly large concentration of flies and is quite a sight to behold!

But then the cedar waxwings appear, sentinels in the treetops that line the river's edges—how do they know? It's getting towards dusk and, sure enough, now the first hex mayflies are in the air; dancing up and down above the river. As each of the first flies appears, a waxwing swoops and takes it. The hex hatch—my favorite time on the river—is beginning.

The hex hatch is a major happening each August on the Huron. The intense concentrations of these large food items trigger a late evening feeding frenzy, something akin to the Manchester chicken broil. The knowledge that large trout are out slurping bugs likewise triggers certain instincts within fly anglers, who go to great lengths to outwit each other (unlike the flies, anglers do not prefer swarms). I used to stand in the Little Manistee River for several hours before the hatch, reading a book, laying claim to my favorite river bend.

"Hex" are mayflies of the genus *Hexagenia,* one of several genera known as burrowing mayflies. Juvenile mayflies live under water and are called nymphs. Hex nymphs create burrows in soft spots in the river bottom (silts) and filter-feed on particulate matter and debris. They require clean waters with a fairly high oxygen content and are indicators of a healthy river ecosystem. After several years, the nymphs come to the water surface where they transform into winged adults and emerge. Predators, like the cedar waxwings, make emergence a dangerous business for them. In fact, just about every larger organism likes to eat hex nymphs (sold as "wigglers" in bait shops).

An adult mayfly is about two inches long and has delicate, many-veined, transparent wings which are held together vertically when the fly is at rest. It has large eyes and vestigial (non-functioning) mouth parts—adults do not feed. From its abdomen protrude three tail filaments. The swarms that form above the river are comprised mostly of males, who each fly rapidly upward within the swarm and then float gently downward. Single females enter the swarms, find a mate, and lay their eggs beneath the water's surface. Adults typically die within about twenty-four hours. Piles of dead hex flies can be found the next morning, especially near lights. Huge piles of these "fishflies" used to occur near Saginaw Bay and Lake Erie, requiring shoveling of sidewalks and streets, but water pollution eliminated these populations during the mid-1900s. Fishflies have rebounded in Lake Erie in recent years, often stimulating headlines about the "nuisance" they cause, despite the fact that they are an important sign of the lake's returning health. A river hatch continues each night for about three weeks.

But hex fishing or hex watching is mostly an excuse to get out on our backyard river.

A change in my business prospects induced me to remove to Ann Arbor. Accordingly in the autumn of 1825 I hired a small row boat into which I loaded my goods and chattels and getting my family aboard we started. I knew the journey would be long and tedious, but at that time I thought it preferable to journeying by land with no other road than an Indian trail. The first day of our journey we glided down the Detroit river as far as the mouth of the river Ecorse, where we went ashore and spent the night. The next day we reached the mouth of Huron river about thirty miles from Detroit. Here a family by the name of Truax permitted us to remain with them over night. On the morning of the third day, we left the Detroit river and entered the Huron. Thus far our journey had been performed with ease, but now we must row against the current when the stream would admit of rowing, and when it would not, the boat was propelled by means of poles. The third night we reached Smooth Rock and stayed in the house of a Mr. Vreeland. The next morning I heard the boatmen talking about a bend in the river which we must pass that day. On making inquiries I learned that the land route to the house of the brother of our host, Mr. Vreeland, was but two miles, while the route by water would consume most of the day. I then proposed to my wife that I would carry the babe if she would walk across and wait there for the boat. Our journey was soon accomplished, but we waited till the stars shone that night before the boat arrived.

The Huron from Smooth Rock to Ypsilanti is very crooked, and this day's experience induced me to procure some other mode of conveyance for my family. I purchased a yoke of oxen and obtained the services of a man named Johnson with another yoke of oxen and a wagon, and taking from the boat such articles as we should need, on the morning of the fifth day we again set forward, leaving the boat to make the best of its devious course. The country through which we passed was rolling; there was no road, so we dodged here and there through the openings, over hills so steep that it required all the strength of both yokes of oxen to make the ascent, and to descend safely we would take one yoke of oxen and fasten them with a chain to the back end of the wagon and they would pull back while the other yoke went forward.

We reached Ann Arbor on the seventh day after leaving Detroit, but the boat containing our goods did not arrive at Snow's landing, four miles below Ypsilanti, which was as far as it could come, till the fifteenth day. It cost me forty dollars to come from Detroit to Ann Arbor.

Bethuel Farrand, 1852, Michigan Pioneer and Historical Collections *6*

RICHARD TILLINGHAST

What We Bring to the River, What the River Brings to Us

Open-throated chuckle of a wood dove,
flow over flatrock   spruce branches sough,
   the regressive *jug-jug* of a bullfrog.
Then fish fins   evolved to the shape of the current,
      divide the ripples as a carp roots
   face-down in the muck
            downriver from the Ford plant.
And something obscure splashes
      where you can't see to assign meaning.

Canoeists (the good kind) appear,
paddles imprinting the stream with C's and J's,
      voices pitched at water temperature,
not rising above the birds' unceasing ostinato.

The river has breathed up to me
      old mustiness like air trapped in an antique drawer
and chilled me with its coolness
            at the close of the hottest day.
I've walked by these waters in despair and abstraction,
I have brought my dailiness here,
I've made it my church.

May our chain-link demarcations never
         intimidate the river.
May our culverts never contain its waters for long.
May our chemicals cause no more than a blip
      in the life-graph of the smallmouth bass,

Huron River scene

and the shells of endangered birds regain
        their power to nurture generations.
Let the river assimilate our broken-up pavement
        into its pebbles
and wash away   with its gravity-drawn continuum
        every disturbance we bring to its banks.

KEITH TAYLOR

Black Ice

SOME THINGS shouldn't frighten me. I should know better. If given half a chance at a party or over drinks, I will bore my friends with stories of ice-skating across prairie sloughs forty years ago, learning how to turn quickly and handle a puck. Yet when my seven-year-old daughter and I drive down by the Huron after a two-week cold snap and find the large pond behind Barton Dam completely frozen and carrying several families of skaters, I feel the flutter of my new and overeducated fear. Of course I let her go out on the ice. I go with her. We stare down through several inches of black ice at the plants drifting in the slight current. We hope to see a cold fish swim by. She kicks a stone across the ice, squealing with pleasure at its speed and distance. She wants to kick it all the way across, over to the marina below the rich people's homes.

That's when I get scared. I call her back and climb out on the dike above the water. She keeps kicking her stone across the ice, and I notice pressure cracks. I begin to imagine the groans and cracks of ice.

"Come on, Faith. We have to go," I call out, and she ignores me as she has done for most of her life, at least when she's having fun.

I keep calling, and still she ignores me, kicking her rock across the frozen river, sliding on her feet, her knees, even her butt, laughing and laughing. I call again, more urgently, and then again. I try to sound tough and threaten loss of privileges. She kicks the rock out farther and keeps going.

BOB HICOK

Borrowed Soul

-at Barton Dam

I'll think what the river thinks.

All its mouths gather at the falls
to taste the air.

In the prisming spray below, the bundled
minds of light are loosed in halos.

I'm seduced by my watching
because I squandered my soul.

For years I complained about the cost
of nails and lectured the posture
of friends so it left.

I can't dream or smell tar or discourage
my loneliness without it.

Can't ask the sky for a date
with a voice that sounds
like the white keys of the piano alone.

They say each molecule of water
licks the earth for years
before slumming into us.

So this rush and bedlam is home.

Even the green slime, the shouts of water
that fall and curl into whispers,
know well how to be what they are.

I see that everyone wants to lug
a piece of this certainty away.

That's why the fish are removed
and eaten for the peace
locked in their flesh.

I'm learning to come here
when I'm supposed to be anywhere else.

To break the sign's commandment
and wade into the water.

It doesn't know I'm there and still
embraces my knees, reminds me
I'm mostly made of a noise
that doesn't belong to me.

"Take Me to the Water"

Autumn 1961

A FRESHMAN AT THE university, Blinx has been in Ann Arbor for a couple of months. The small town with its two gas stations and single stoplight where she grew up, marking time all through high school until she could get out, lies a comfortable 160 miles to the northwest. Though Blinx is wildly excited that her real life is at last getting under way, the Blessed Virgin still hangs on a fine silver chain from Blinx's neck, and each night Blinx winds her hair in pink rollers whose bristles poke her scalp, disturbing her dreams. Though her perfume is a little tigerish, Blinx's pale lipstick and pale nail polish still match nicely, and Blinx still curls her eyelashes, powders her shiny nose. Her closet is crammed with pastel shirtwaists with straw belts, madras bermudas, Pendleton skirts with matching crewneck cardigans and kneesocks. There's a gold circle pin glowing on Blinx's dresser.

Long-legged and skinny, not needing one at all, Blinx still tugs on her Playtex Living Girdle when she goes to Mass on Sunday. The girdle has about as much give to it as an inner tube. It holds Blinx's stockings up and makes absolutely certain nothing moves. Blinx wonders what the girdle thinks about at night lying in its drawer.

For some time Blinx has had her eye on a boy from her English class. Perpetually rumpled, a first-generation Italian roughneck from Rochester, New York, Dom is a former quarterback, a former altar boy whose moody eyes and unruly heart overbrim with angst and "Who am I?" Not having been washed since his arrival in Ann Arbor, Dom's Levi's and sweatshirts are grubby; at night his roommates park his smelly sneakers out in the hallway. Dom showers, but days go by when he doesn't shave; dark stubble sprouts on his cheeks. By mid-October, Dom's ROTC instructors are getting on his case: "Cut that hair, soldier, and where's your goddamned cap? That uniform's a mess." Dom's piling up demerits, threats to his scholarship, but he doesn't care. Sometimes he just shoots pool instead.

Like Blinx, Dom knows incense and his catechism and some Latin, recognizes a sacramental when he sees one. But also like Blinx, Dom is letting his attendance at Mass slip—he lies to his parents when they phone up on Sunday afternoon—and doubt is muddling his head, scalding his soul, making him miserable late at night. If there is a God, they wonder, and He's truly all good and all powerful, how can He allow babies to suffer, innocent people to starve or be carried off by hideous diseases? Where did He go during the Holocaust? How can He give Evil such free rein in the world?

Already by the third grade, Blinx had been sent over one wintry morning to the empty church to pray for faith, a concept that even then had struck Blinx as somewhat odd. All Blinx had wanted to know was why, if He already knew everything, God would make certain people, knowing full well ahead of time that their souls would end up frying in Hell for all eternity. It seemed like a mean trick. The priest's angry reply that God can do whatever He pleases failed to set Blinx's heart at ease. "Yes, but . . ."

The boiler having been shut down during the week to save on heating costs, when Blinx dipped her hand into the holy water font in the vestibule to bless herself, her fingers hit ice. Pulling her mitten back on, she genuflected, slipped into her family's pew, and with only poor punctured Christ on the Cross for company and the saints glaring down at her from the side altars, Blinx whispered several Hail Marys and Our Fathers. Quickly running out of things to say to silent God sitting up there in the ciborium behind the locked door of the tabernacle, Blinx shivered, gnawed her mitten, and wondered if she was doomed. The small red flame of the sanctuary lamp flickered in the gloom. Blinx watched the long hand of the clock above the confessional taking forever to tick away the hour until she could rejoin her classmates.

"In nomine patris, et filii, et spiritu sancti. Amen," Dom intones, describing an elaborate sign of the cross over cherry Cokes, french fries and fresh packs of Marlboros. Though they're full of bravado and irreverence, feeling their faith slipping away terrifies them, leaves their hearts deeply fearful, timid, scrambling for safe hiding places like newly molted crustaceans. What if they're wrong? Suppose God does have this fantastic plan that's just too big for their minds to take in? And suppose it's true that the fires of Hell give off no light, just an ever-intensifying heat? But if there's no God, what difference does it make what you do—you could kill somebody and it wouldn't matter. But, most of all, what're you supposed to do with all that love, all that reverence?

"Things aren't always what they appear," the priest at the student chapel assures them. "Cool," says Dom. "Then what are they?" The priest shakes his head sadly, writes himself a note on the pad on his desk, and warns them about the necking and heavy petting that are rampant in the bushes outside the dorms at night. He also reminds them to drop their envelopes in the collection basket on Sundays. Pray too, he tells them. Make a novena. In free fall, they read Donne and Cardinal Newman, but the universe feels drafty and spooky, an empty house to abandoned children.

Meanwhile, mercifully, also like Blinx, Dom is discovering that he loves language, that words thrill him; that somehow they seem to know him, to seek out corners of his heart obscure even to himself. Lines of poetry, beautiful passages of prose astonish, anatomizing the soul's desolation but holding out as well the promise of a wide, wide, greenly spinning world with plenty of oxygen for breathing, for an altogether different kind of burning. Avid learners, the two of them revel in words and images the way Scrooge McDuck glories in his pool of gold doubloons, diving into them, preening, rubbing the gleam all over their feathers.

Following their ten o'clock Intro. to Poetry, Dom and Blinx make a beeline for a booth in the basement of the Michigan Union. Dom's green book bag hits the table with a solid clunk; these days he carries everywhere the *Merriam-Webster* the nuns gave him after his valedictory address. Blinx delivered a valedictory speech too; it was patriotic and heartfelt and rousing—something about Jack Kennedy and the price of liberty being eternal vigilance. Behind the podium in her cap and gown, Blinx went on and on about Kennedy and the New Frontier, what a great and generous world it was going to be soon. She rubbed it in good. The town being Protestant and Republican, Blinx's name had been withdrawn from a list for a DAR scholarship when someone reminded the committee that she was Catholic. They couldn't do a thing about her grade point, however, and graduation night the gym was full of people who loathed Kennedy, who gnashed their teeth, anticipating the Pope's imminent arrival at Dulles. From his folding chair down in the front row, Blinx's dad grinned up at her.

Shoulders touching, smoking cigarettes and gulping down far too much awful black coffee, Blinx and Dom huddle over their *Norton Anthology*. "Anthology," Dom has shown Blinx in his dictionary, derives from the Greek, and it means "a collection of flowers." Hearts thumping from caffeine and nicotine and the proximity of their shoulders, their hands on the page, they take turns stoking each other's ears with Dylan Thomas and Whitman, Eliot and Yeats and Auden, whose voices whirl around their heads in a fearful, jangling, and joyful chorus, exhorting the two straying lambs to risk all for love, to plunge ahead, to sign on to be lonely and scared, uncertain of Heaven, but to dance, to sing in their chains, to celebrate this mortal world at the tops of their mortal lungs.

While they're enrapt, caught up in rhythm and song and not even look-
ing, along comes that troublemaker Beauty. All gussied up in her red-rose-
bordered gown, she sidles up to the Naugahyde booth there in the Michigan
Union whose air is inauspicious with the grease of cheeseburgers and the
clatter of commercial china. Unbeknownst to the pair, Beauty leans down,
herself a little disheveled for all her dangly earrings and rosy breath, mur-
murs a tricky benediction in their sizzling ears, eggs them on. "Tra-la. The
first one's free." Smiling like some goofy, know-it-all old aunt, she vanishes
into the elevator.

"I am a man of constant sorrow," sing Peter, Paul, and Mary from a
speaker off in a corner. Growly Bob Dylan's warming up in the wings. Some
evenings at parties in dim apartments where Blinx's not supposed to be,
Blinx and Dom lean together, drink Chianti, and listen to koto and flute
music, to Nina Simone and Joan Baez and Judy Collins. "I've seen trouble
all my days," Dom sings along in a sad voice from deep in his chest even
though his dad works for Eastman Kodak and wears Perry Como cardigans
and his mother stays home and cooks great sauce. Before long, on an over-
cast afternoon after her French class, bypassing the Village Store where they
peddle the spiffy shirtwaists, Blinx heads farther down Liberty to Sam's
Store, lays down her money, and walks back out again with a black turtle-
neck tucked in her book bag.

But on this particular early October morning, though it rained during the
night, the clouds are gone. The light spilling down over the newly washed
town with its changing maples and tall elms is brilliant, and Blinx is dazzling
in her white tennis shoes. Her blouse with its sprinkling of tiny flowers and
Peter Pan collar is freshly ironed. Her shorts match the blouse. Her hair
band matches both of them. It's a football Saturday. Across campus over by
the stadium, the Michigan marching band is practicing "Hail to the Vic-
tors." Fairy-tale handsome, blond, athletic, and pre-med Warren has invited
Blinx canoeing.

Warren and Blinx met at a dorm mixer. Halfway through the evening,
Warren detached himself from a clump of boys, crossed the lounge to where
Blinx was standing with her roommates, and asked her to dance. Later, when
the housemother called it a night and shut down the music, Warren asked
Blinx out for a Coke. He's from a suburb of Detroit, and he plans to be a
psychiatrist, Warren informed Blinx across the wobbly soda-shop table.
"The human mind," Warren declared firmly, nipping in the bud any possi-
ble objections Blinx might raise, "is interesting."

"You bet," nodded Blinx, who knows perfectly well that someday she's supposed to marry someone like Warren—intelligent, polite, a good provider, etc. "Clean and decent and respectable," Blinx's mother adds.

Though the morning's plenty warm, Blinx brings along a cardigan—just in case. Warren's serious, intent, very handsome like somebody from a storybook. A flannel shirt tied around his waist, he's wearing sneakers, a tucked-in white tee shirt, neatly pressed khaki shorts. Patting her forearm, Warren greets Blinx, then checks his wallet and their lunches before they pedal off across town on their bicycles for Wirth's Canoe Livery. Blinx has to admire Warren's take-charge attitude, his determined jaw, the pretty fuzz on his muscular legs. Warren doesn't look like somebody who spends a lot of time fretting about what God is up to.

Along with scores of canoes, the ramshackle livery on Argo Pond houses a humming Coke machine and a big collection of old nickelodeons. Blinx is curious about the nickelodeons and the tinkly player pianos, but Warren's all business. He negotiates with the man behind the counter, thanks him for the pair of varnished wooden paddles, then lifts down a red canoe from a rack, settles it on one broad shoulder, and carries it down to the rickety dock, where he slides it deftly onto the river. Blinx trots along behind with the paddles and their sandwiches and pop and the bag of New Era potato chips.

Warren climbs in first. "Careful," he warns Blinx, steadying the canoe and reaching for her hand. Blinx knows about canoes, how tippy they are. She was a Girl Scout, after all, Curved Bar and the whole shebang, lots of patches on her sash for which she'd fed the dog for a week, bathed a doll, or learned ten trees or ten birds, ten embroidery stitches, ten things to do if you come upon somebody knocked out cold in the woods. But Blinx gives Warren her hand and steps in gingerly as if she were Cinderella and had never laid eyes on the inside of a canoe. Warren takes the stern. Her back to him, Blinx sits in the bow. The lunch sack rides on the middle seat.

Even in the shade of the giant old willows and cottonwoods that line the Huron's bank, Blinx feels the day heating up. She leans back to set her cardigan beside the lunch sacks. Warren folds his plaid shirt, lays it on the other side, and prepares to cast off. He'll steer, he informs Blinx, which he does, expertly guiding the canoe out into the middle. This stretch of the river is broad, quiet, the current scarcely discernible. Warren's J-strokes are smooth, efficient, all but silent. "You can paddle if you really want," he tells Blinx, "but don't worry about it."

Blinx does paddle some at first, but before long she lifts the dripping paddle out, lays it across her knees, and just watches. Growing up, she played whole summers and long afternoons after school with a creek that ran through the woods below her parents' garden. Night after night, her mother would scold her for coming home soaked and muddy after splashing in it, heaving rocks in it to watch it fly up sparkling, floating rafts of twigs in it, damming it up and then letting it loose, chasing after it as it flowed around boulders and ducked under fallen limbs. Now as the river ripples around the bow of the red canoe, Blinx sits quietly watching the water glitter in the sunlight out ahead or shimmering on the undersides of turning leaves along the bank. Trailing a hand over the side, she feels it cool on her fingers. Lines from Yeats drift up from the floor of her mind.

> Come away, O human child!
> To the waters and the wild
> With a faery, hand and hand,
> For the world's more full of weeping than you can understand.

Blinx wonders where Dom is, what he's doing, if he's all right. Catching a glimpse of a silvery fish over in the shallows leaping after an insect, Blinx turns in her seat. The blade of her paddle dips, sloshing a bit of river into the canoe. The fish leaps again, splashes, disappears. "Watch out," Warren says. The water's not cold, but Blinx tells him she's sorry.

"So, do you know what you want to major in?"

"Well, when I first got here," Blinx begins, realizing it's time to get a conversation going, "I was thinking I'd major in political science. Last fall I worked in Kennedy's campaign—my friend Dolores and I hopped his train and traveled around the state with him in October when he whistle-stopped out here. It was amazing listening to his speeches. He really makes you believe things can be fixed; that the world's got problems, that people are poor and hungry, but we can do something, help them, take care of them. The man's got so much energy," she tells Warren, remembering Kennedy's thick eyelashes, his gorgeous Irish-setter hair. The river widens briefly, going around a bend. There are geese in the water and ducks dabbling, tails in the air, or resting on logs. Blinx unties her shoes, drops them with a thunk into the bottom of the canoe. She slips her paddle back into the water and takes a few strokes, careful not to splash.

"Kennedy asked me and Doe all sorts of questions about our town and our parents—he got a big kick out of it when I told him my mother and father were from County Kerry. His grandparents were from Wexford, he said." Blinx glances back over her shoulder. Warren's frowning and still brushing droplets of the Huron from his shorts between strokes. "Sorry," she says again. He shrugs, shifts in his seat.

"Anyway, Kennedy made sure we got some lunch, and he had us ride into Saginaw with him on the back of the train and wave at the crowds and everything. And he promised us we'd get invited to his inauguration if he got elected, and, sure enough, by God, one Saturday in November the Democratic chairman showed up in the middle of a snowstorm at my house with these great big engraved invitations. My dad couldn't believe it. Doe and I took a train to Washington to watch him get sworn in—it was freezing, but it was great. I was so excited, I was shaking. We saw Robert Frost and Jackie and when the lectern started smoking and caught fire and everything. It was fantastic."

"Must have been," allows Warren. "My father's a Nixon fan." It's Warren's turn to tell Blinx about camping and canoeing up in the Boundary Waters. Black flies were terrible, but his troop saw moose. They got pretty close. He took some pictures. He had his camera.

"Neat," Blinx says, then tells him she's just read *The Sound and the Fury*. She was so blown away that the minute she finished it, she flipped right back to the beginning and read the whole novel all over again. Now she's reading *Absalom, Absalom*. She thinks she'll maybe major in English instead.

"That's nice. It's important to read books."

Not watching where they're going, Blinx is startled when the nose of the canoe bumps the bank. There's a dam, and they have to portage. Blinx scrambles to gather the lunches and their belongings. Warren grunts as he hauls the canoe out. No, he doesn't need her help. He can do it. Blinx grabs both paddles. After last night's rain, the path up the bank is muddy and cool under her bare feet. The air smells good. Blinx wiggles her toes. Mud squishes over pale opalescent polish.

Back out on the river, Blinx raises her paddle to wave back to an old man in a green jacket who's fishing from the bank with a bamboo pole and a striped bobber. "Any luck?" Blinx calls out to the man. Reaching down into a bucket half-hidden by the tall grass, the man smiles. On the tip of his index finger, he holds up four or five wriggling fish tied together with line looped through their gills.

Warren resumes his steady paddling, and soon they've left behind most signs of civilization. Arcing high into the blue sky above the river, the buzzy voices of cicadas drown out the murmur of traffic. Willows and dense thickets of alder crowd the banks. Painted turtles bask on downed logs, slip into the water as the canoe glides toward them. Half-mesmerized by the cicadas and dancing sunlight, Blinx is getting drowsy. A smallish, funny-looking, big-headed bird with a big bill takes off from an overhanging branch and flies rattling away up the river. A belted kingfisher. Blinx doesn't yet know the bird's name, but she'll find out.

Blinx and Warren make an easy progress up the easygoing river. The current's mostly mild, and Warren's Eagle Scout paddling is even, methodical. Blinx lets her paddle trail in the water. In the shadows beneath the trees, she watches synchronized schools of shiny minnows darting this way and that like giddy impulses. Bigger fish leap, slapping the water with their sides. Out ahead of the canoe, a great blue heron takes flight from a shallow reedy patch along the shore. A small greenish heron hunches motionless on a low branch over the water, watching for a frog or a crayfish. "Would you like a sandwich?" Blinx asks Warren. He shakes his head. He's not hungry.

Gaps in the foliage reveal farmers' fields lying quiet. The corn has been harvested by now and stored in cribs. Winter wheat is springing up in neat bright green rows. Blinx hears crows cawing, the whistle and churrr of grackles and blackbirds. They pass a field of pumpkins, big ones, lying on their sides. The river narrows. Out ahead, wary of the nosy canoe, frogs plop from grassy banks into the river. Shapes shifting, overhanging leaves are reflected in the water. The canoe glides noiselessly through shimmering color. Blinx watches a muskrat slip below the surface, smiles as he swims away, his small sleek head leaving a glimmering wake. Dom read somewhere that, toward the end of it, Thomas Hardy had confessed to a friend his life was a failure, that the one thing he'd wanted to do was to make the world safer for hedgehogs and he'd failed.

Mindful that she mustn't splash Warren, Blinx paddles a few desultory strokes whenever the spirit moves her. She's been aware for the last weeks of a new warmth around her heart, a dreamy eager softness stirring somewhere in her belly. She's feeling restless, impatient for it all. Warren's not that bad, she starts in on herself. A little boring, but he is handsome, and he says he plays the violin. Oh, come on. He has no use for her. He doesn't need her for a thing. Any one or two or fifty of the thousands of freshman girls could be sitting in the bow of Warren's canoe right now, and, as long as they were halfway pretty and didn't think out loud too much, he'd just paddle away, happy as Larry, as Blinx's dad would say. But it doesn't matter. None of it. Auden's got it right, Blinx realizes. "The desires of the heart are as crooked as corkscrews."

Sighing, Blinx plucks the guy in the stern out of her mind, drops him gently over the side. He barely makes a splash. Half closing her eyes on the shining river, Blinx listens to the cries of birds, and she thinks about Dom. She thinks about the ache of melancholy and the long struggle to find out who in the world you are and what matters, the right way to spend your life—how some days it feels wide open and thrilling, a splendid adventure, and other days all you know for certain is loneliness and a blistering confusion. Blinx wishes she could hold him, comfort him when bleakness settles over him.

Sighing again, Blinx hunches forward on her seat, banging her knee. The canoe rocks gently in the current. Gazing down into the weeds, she trails her fingers and the paddle in the river languidly like Ophelia or whoever that was in the picture of the painting of the woman in the embroidered gown lying on her back in the boat full of flowers that Blinx saw in her roommate's art history book. Actually the woman's arms were folded across her heart. Her eyes were open, Blinx thinks, but she might have been dead. Blinx couldn't tell from the picture. If she wasn't dead, she was just lying there staring up at the trees and the sky as the boat drifted along. But how did she wind up there anyway? Where was she going, half dead or half asleep, all dressed up and alone in a boat?

Suddenly, with a jolt, the paddle's nearly ripped from Blinx's hand. What! She jerks it back. The canoe lurches. "Hey, watch out," Warren yells. "What're you doing? Look out or we'll tip."

"My paddle's snagged," Blinx tells him, struggling to free it. The canoe is rocking wildly with her exertions. River comes in over the sides. "Something's got hold of it." Turning in her seat, out of the corner of her eye, she sees her immaculate sneakers and Warren's nice ones and their lunches sloshing around in the bottom of the canoe. Blinx tries to stand. Again from the stern, louder: "Hey! Hey!" Warren sounds a lot like Blinx's high school principal at basketball games when kids leaned over the railings up in the balcony.

Right foot propped on the bow and bracing the handle across her thigh, Blinx heaves her paddle up out of the river. Jaws clamped around the blade, beady eyes glaring, the horny beak and thick warty neck of a huge turtle break the surface. Webbed forefeet with long claws rake the air. The animal's shell is covered with muck and algae. "Watch out," Warren yells. "That's a snapper. He'll take your hand off. Let go."

Heart thumping, Blinx won't let go. Neither apparently will the turtle. Staggering with the weight of him, Blinx is half standing now, and the canoe's going nuts. More glittery river sloshes over the sides, washing over Blinx's bare feet. Peanut butter and jelly float in waxed-paper boats. The bottles of pop clank against each other, clunking against the bottom, as the canoe rocks crazily and Warren hollers at Blinx some more. His face is red. He's sunburned or furious. But she's got this wild, mucky turtle all the way out now, suspended from the blade of the paddle nearly a foot above the splashy riled-up river. Blinx's arms are going to break, or the paddle will snap—this thing must weigh forty or fifty pounds. So heavy, and he's thrashing about, clawing the blue air, lashing his long, saw-toothed tail, but he's not about to let go.

"Gimme my damned paddle." Glimpsing something incandescent gleaming in the turtle's ancient reptile eyes, something she suddenly knows she has to have, Blinx tightens her grip on the handle. Lurching around in the bow, trying to keep her balance, Blinx is laughing out loud. Turtle mud spatters the sprigs of violets on her shorts, on her blouse.

"Sit down," Warren barks. He lunges for her elbow. Blinx jerks her arm away. There ensue more wild rocking, much arcing and splashing of glittering river water, a shriek, several whoops, additional barking—entirely too much commotion, clamor, hullabaloo. The red canoe won't stand for it. They're going over.

Still clutching her paddle and hauling the clamped-on snapper nearly into the canoe with her, Blinx clambers up onto the narrow, slippery seat, steadies herself a moment, glances over her shoulder. Hearing an irate yelp, she grips with her toes and dives off.

The consequences are predictable. The canoe flips. Waxed paper floats, but pop and soggy white-bread sandwiches drift down through the kicked-up silt to settle into the riverbed. While she's under, eyes open to the swaying weeds and the rocks on the bottom, Blinx swallows a few good gulps of muddy water. When she comes up, her hair's streaming, a god-awful stringy

Canoe dating c. 1910

weedy mess. The current carries off her head band. Where they go over, scaring away the birds, sending them flying with their racket, the river isn't deep or dangerous, just weedy. Warren loses a sneaker. He curses once, sinking past his ankles into the muck. She's still laughing. In all the commotion, the turtle slips away with the paddle, drags it up the bank and off across the grass.

Warren has grabbed the rope. He tows the canoe to shore. Groaning, he manages to right it and mostly drain it. He is very strong.

"Just get in and sit down," Warren orders Blinx when they're ready. "You just sit down." Now he sounds like Blinx's exasperated bus driver from elementary school.

Paddling and paddling, Warren is silent all the way back down the river. The sun slides lower in the sky, and the air cools. Blinx shivers. Back at the livery, Warren pays for the lost paddle with a couple of damp bills from his damp wallet. Blinx offers to pay him back. "Forget it."

That night Blinx is falling off to sleep in her bed in the dorm. Drifting off, smiling, Blinx thinks about it all. Though maybe it was just a trick of the light, the sun glancing up off the water, tomorrow she'll tell Dom about the amazing snapping turtle with the blazing red lamp in his eyes, how beautiful he was and how tight he hung on. She'll make him laugh when she describes her dive off the bow into the Huron. "While I was down there, I drank muddy river water that's got minnows in it," she'll tell Dom. "Muskrats and frogs and turtles. Man, I drank holy water."

The old pond above the Delhi Dam often has about as many people in it as it will hold on a warm summer day. There is a bath house. The water is only about four feet deep. . . . There is considerable swimming from the bridge at the upper end of the Barton Pond and a number of private bathing places on the pond itself. The sand bar at Fosters is well used with a life saver from the Washington Cabin of the Boy Scouts just above. The City bathing beach showed an attendance of 14,800 last summer.

> —*Henry S. Curtis, from an unpublished article, "Recreation on the Huron," c. 1940, Harlow Whittemore Papers, Bentley Historical Library, University of Michigan*

JULIE ELLISON

Looking Backward

In the rowers' peripheral vision the oar ticks.
With a caw, a flex to throw open its wings
the heron strokes the haze above the oar.
The horn sounds from the dam,
and water lets down on the other side,
overflown by cedar waxwings. The boat
spins in place, starboards to back, ports to row.
Backfacing torsos rock and recoil.
Each rower looks straight at the next,
at her rotating hand, her tattoo, the eyes of the man
on the back of her T-shirt, her compressing knee.
Later in the day, each will stare ahead out of habit
into the space where that rower should be.

Before the leaves come out,
the rowers mark encampments from the water:
a blue tarpaulin hooked by scrub willow,
tabloids woven through vines.
Last year, a white sailboat immigrated.
It housed the ghost of Andy Warhol,
a bleached thin man in a cracked keel.
He played *The Blue Danube Waltz* on a harmonica
as the rowers filed past. In August he floated
the white hull across to a one-man isthmus.
Then he may have wintered over, blond
and boatless, narrow as the monitoring birds.

The rowers see sideways: Men are stationed
along the river until they are not.

Women's crew, 1878

Today lime-yellow willows curtain
no one's belongings. Still without turning
their heads, the rowers try to look into the shore,
beyond gray blades, beyond gray heron Ichabods.

Ken Mikolowski

View

The view of the river
from the eighth floor
University Hospital
room is not the same
as from the Arboretum
I guess it's the perspective.

Little or Nothing

there are these trees
and beyond these trees
trees, and beyond that
little or nothing. Little
fields and nothing but sky.

Nichols Arboretum, Ann Arbor

DAVID STRINGER

Balancing

My son sends me whirlpools, his back
too broad for the short paddle. We probe
the Huron River west of our dock:
wind abrasion in open water, heavy
plants just under the surface where
bass swirl and disappear, a stagnant
channel which almost defines an island,
a film of dust and insects, fields of
waterlilies rasping the canoe. He shifts
sides, I shift against him. A blue heron
lifts from a high nest. A stream emerges
in a small cascade. We pass downed trees
where rough winged swallows wait
to skim the river. We lurch the canoe
over sunken logs jammed between piles
of a railroad bridge. Two thwarts apart,
we slide west between steep banks,
past stumps and fence posts. A hawk
cries from a speck in the evening sky.

"Dance-Modern," 1929

Nicholas Delbanco

Witness

Time now to take him his coffee: second duty of the day. I'm the appointed cupbearer, his personal assistant and bright boy with a tray. At this hour every morning coffee's ready in the kitchen, and it's my job to hunt and fetch and haul breakfast up the stairs. Eleven o'clock and he wants his first cup, and as with every other thing in the great man's household this procedure is a ritual: he wants it with warmed-up skim milk. He expects it with two cubes of sugar, and although the night nurse tells me that I ought to halve a single cube I cheat on her cheating and give him the two that he wants. Why not; what difference does it make if he's at risk for diabetes or his teeth will rot?

Blue Mountain; it's his chosen brand; he talks about Jamaica and the time he spent there in the mountains and what it felt like when the world was young to go to a cockfight and drink their strong rum. When we're alone he shuts his eyes and talks of sugarcane and palm trees and machetes and then about the octoroon he stayed with near Negril. The great man describes her dancing and lifts his hand and beats the air as if he still can *see* her, as if we both were watching and I am young along with him and a houseguest sixty years ago at her plantation in the hills. And then he starts to cry. "Don't cry," I say, "she's laughing," and then he starts to laugh. Blue Mountain Coffee, one spoonful per cup, and sugar cubes and warm skim milk; it all comes rushing back. . . .

That's what the Frenchman meant, he tells me, by sensory recall and involuntary recapitulation, a cookie dipped in tea so after the first taste or two you can remember everything. I ask him, "Who?" and he says, "The Frenchman," and then I ask, "Do you mean Proust?" and he says, yes, that faggot, that little Albertine. "It was a Madeleine," I say, a particular variety of tea cake that Marcel's mother gave him, and he says what a piece of ass she was, that octoroon. You would have loved her, kid, he says, you wouldn't believe that smooth rum. Or the way she moved when dancing, which is what she liked to call it, or what she did with sugarcane: you would have loved it, kid. . . .

His cup is big and blue. It is the Master's cup, of course, with double handles in the shape of an inverted **E** and a white strip at the rim, and chipped, and with a matching saucer, and he wants it on a tray. By eleven o'clock every morning our Edward has been washed and shaved and brushed and changed, and he's sitting in the easy chair behind the double-hung window and staring at the river and the trees in Gallup Park. I knock and enter and bring him his coffee, and sometimes I too take a cup, and then we go through the mail. The junk mail I've already chucked, and bills that go directly to the accountant or the requests from charity functions there's no point pretending he'll attend, and then I sort the rest of it into three categories: **O**ffers, **A**lms, and **F**riends.

This had been his idea, I'm told: the first letters add up to **OAF.** We proceed this way always, up there in his room: first "**O**" then "**A**" then "**F.**" The categories overlap and it's not always easy to tell them apart, but I do try. My first job every morning is to spend ten minutes sorting mail, deciding which is which. The great man corrects me, of course. This system of his is a system he likes and he himself invented; he says it's gotten him through an amazing quantity of horseshit and if I have a better idea he hasn't heard it yet. Not from me or from my predecessor or from the one before that. And not, he likes to threaten me, from the one who'll come to work for him when I decide to leave, when I like everybody else just put my tail between my legs and run and say I quit. You pissant college boys, he says, you ones who pretend to be writers once they give you a degree. . . .

That's not my way, I tell him, I'm not a quitter; no? he asks, you're certain? and I say I'm certain, yes. We do this all the time. We have this conversation every time I bring the tray. Hannah the Housekeeper taught me the drill; she's been working here for thirty years, and very little has changed. He lived in this house when there wasn't a park, when all you saw was fields and ponds and not rows of starter castles down along the Huron, the wetlands filled in for a golf course and farms with lawn tractors not sheep. This city has grown up around us, Hannah says, but we pay no attention, we don't let it bother us now do we, Mr. Ed? He nods at the window and pays no attention and she wipes the drool off his cheek. Why what a commotion they're making, she says, the geese on the river this morning, they're honking loud enough to wake the dead.

The Master shakes his head. "Not quite," he says, "not yet."

His letters arrive by ten-thirty, sometimes sooner, rarely later, and I chuck the junk and do the arranging and slit open the sealed envelopes for easy reading access. Next I pile the mail in three piles and knock three times and whisper low and enter what he likes to call Edouardo's Hideway, his little arbor harbor and inner sanctimonious, to bring him the news of the world. We talk about who's in, who's out, who's bombing what and where the fires and the earthquakes and the oil slicks and the mud slides and starvation look the worst. Eleven o'clock in the morning, and he wants to hear about weather and where the catastrophes are. Some days he's peaceful and happy or, if not happy, reconciled; you can tell it by the way he swivels and raises his right arm and the welcome-expression he wears on his face. It's like he's had a good night's rest and wants to make amends for things: Enter to grow in wisdom, kid; come on in, the water's fine. But other days—and it takes about a second to decide which one is which—the door should have a sign on it: *Abandon hope, all ye who enter here.* . .

In "Offers" there's only good news; I've been warned to make certain of that. There are articles, if favorable, that the clipping service provides, and reviews that still refer to him or to his influence. There are royalty statements he studies at length. There are translations of his books into Italian and Korean and Urdu and Japanese. Every month or two a contract comes, or the inquiries his agent sends and the proposals forwarded from Hollywood or Paris or New York. But it's important that the news be good, because the message and the messenger are, to the great man, indistinguishable: you bring bad news, you're dead. His last assistant failed to screen a reference that called him "more than any other author of the period pernicious in his use of sexual stereotype and the sado-masochistic strategies of machismo from the onanistic yet invaginated I/eye . . ." And that was the end of his job. That was *his* last day of work. . . .

In the second category, "Alms," we get the things E. doesn't do: speak, read, respond in writing, send photographs or autographs, consider manuscripts with an eye to prepublication blurbs, sign books, offer opinions, judge contests, consent to meet with strangers or would-be biographers. "Alms" is the largest of the letter-piles—often as many as twenty a day—but the one that takes least time. He's got a rubber stamp ready to answer, and the answer's always No. In the third category, "Friends," there's not much mail to deal with; his friends are dead. And he never had very many of these in any case, he says proudly, what he had were hangers-on. He was a whale, he likes to say, and some of them were pilot fish and some of them were sucker fish, but all of them were parasites and now they're dead and gone.

A postcard comes, from time to time, from the son of some old hunting buddy or the daughter or granddaughter of some long-extinguished flame. When this happens it excites him; he stares at the picture and rocks in his chair while I read the message loudly and repeat it once or twice. Sometimes I have trouble with the signature or, because of the handwriting, the message itself, but this never seems to matter and he doesn't seem to care. What matters is the postcard, and the place it comes from and the stamps; all this excites the great man palpably and he shifts in his seat and pulls at his cheeks and rubs his nose and tells me, Wolfie—he likes to call me Wolfie, since I went to school here and on football Saturdays I like to watch the Wolverines—let's get some writing done, let's go to work. Then I position my own chair where he can see me as well as the trees and the geese and canoes; *Hup two,* he says, get crackin', rise and shine.

We are writing his memoirs. Third duty of the day. And so we proceed from the coffee and mail to the next stage of the pilgrimage, the one that takes till lunchtime and the sandwich tray or until he falls asleep. He's had a long important life, he's written all those books and known a lot of people and been a lot of places, and he's rich and famous and believes the world wants his opinion and requires his memoirs. What this means is he talks to himself and sometimes it's intelligible and I write it down. Also, he wants a recording, and there's this big brown vintage ancient tape recorder on the table by the window that he likes to think still works. I've tried to explain it; I've told him it doesn't, it belongs in Greenfield Village or the Henry Ford Museum or maybe the Smithsonian but doesn't qualify as a recording apparatus, sir; there are better and smaller machines. Why don't you let me purchase one or we'll order a Sony or a Blaupunkt or a Panasonic on approval and run a comparison test?

He refuses to do this, of course. He won't or can't believe that there's been real improvement; the advance of electronics and the age of the computer make about as much impression on the great man as a flea does on an elephant; he barely notices. He doesn't care at all. What makes you think that newer is better, kid, he likes to ask; show me anything that's better now than how it used to be. Just because you went to college doesn't mean that things improve. It's not an argument I'll win and so I don't bother to argue, and the house has nothing in it that could make my point in any case: old rotary phones, old long-fluked fans, a black-and-white seventeen-inch Philco that he thinks of as TV. He's a relic and an archive and a man who likes his coffee just the way it used to be; his concession to modernity and the terms of his present condition is he used to drink cream with his coffee but has been reduced to skim milk. He tells me I should order Blue Mountain only, a *doppio,* because any other brand will wreck your heart and your kidneys and liver and gut. It will wreck everything, he says, it isn't a question of whether but when, and what you therefore want to do is postpone the business of wreckage as long as you possibly can. Blue Mountain coffee, and grappa, and skim milk and Château d'Yquem; it's all the great man drinks.

So what we have is a reel to reel recorder made in 1951 he likes to watch revolving, the still point of the turning world, and I maintain the tapes. I rewind and splice them and make a great show of reversing the spools. Except it's gibberish, of course, and he never asks to listen, and I just press the Record button over and over again. It erases what he said before, but what he said before erases what he'd said still earlier, and so there are layers of static and silence and the tape squeaks out cacophony if you bother to press Play. There is, as he says, no real reel. Every time a postcard comes he cranks up what he likes to call the memory-machine and I get set to listen and take notes.

This morning there's a picture of the Alps. It's a snow-covered mountain range and a blue sky up above the rocks and on the flip side it says *Jungfrau* and he asks if I know what that means. "Young woman," I say, though my German's not good, and he says, correct, but it really means virgin, it's what they used to mean by an unconquered mountain peak. When there were such things in the world. Hey Wolfie, he inquires, winking, do you know the definition of a virgin forest? and when I tell him that I don't he says it's someplace on this earth the hand of man has not set foot. Get it? he asks me, wheezing, coughing, and I tell him yes I do. Well there's the Matterhorn and then the Jungfraujoch, he says, and I have a story to tell you, and therefore I pull out my notebook and set up the tapes.

Two days ago it was Versailles: a postcard depicting the Hall of Mirrors and sent to him by someone whose name is Janine. I can't tell if they ever met or if she's somebody's daughter or granddaughter, but she wrote she thought about him in this place: that scene where the Colonel confronts himself and his reflection in the ornate gilt mirrors at the signing of the Treaty of Versailles. It's a fine scene, I have to admit it, full of bitterness and vanity and bitterness *at* vanity and of a kind of foreknowledge that the peace will fail to last. It's cross-cut, you'll remember, with memories of his wife dying and the way she gripped his hand above the blanket she was covered by, and how the Colonel kept fighting back crying and finally failed and the other members of the deputation believed it was laughter and asked him what was so funny and he turned his back on the mirrors and said, nothing, nothing at all. In the Hall of Mirrors, when the novel ends, there's this endless allée of motorcars and sentries standing at attention and carriages reflected beneath the dripping trees. . . .

The day before it was Egypt, and a picture of the pyramids with a camel and a Bedouin, though I doubt in fact that Bedouins encamp in front of pyramids. The message had been written in capital letters and so it was easy to read. DEAR EDWARD I THINK OF YOU OFTEN AND ALWAYS WITH PLEASURE. WISH YOU COULD BE HERE. But the signature itself was scrawled, illegible, and I had no way of knowing or guessing who might have sent it from Cairo five weeks previous, since it took that long to arrive. Also, the ink had been smudged. Not by water or teardrops or anything instructive: the signature just trailed away in dots. When I asked him if he knew anybody who had lived in Egypt, or had been planning a trip, he waggled his head in the way that he does and answered yes, of course. Then he reminded me about that scene in "Nile"—the final story in his third collection, the one that won the Pulitzer—where the girl gets off a steamer that is going up the Nile and a tour guide steals her suitcase or maybe just collects it because of a misunderstanding and she follows him and ends up that night in a Bedouin camp on a trade route in the middle of the desert, staring at the stars. It's a fine scene too, you have to give him credit, there was a time the man could really write. There's a camel and a vista of wind and sand and stars. There's this enormous nothingness—he called it *nada,* you remember, *le Néant de nada y pues y despues*—and the girl gives up her travel gear and her planned-for destination and renounces her companions since it's all a part of nothingness, and then the moon appears.

Picture postcards arrive from America also, of course; he wrote most of his books in this house. He's been living here for decades, and most of his readership still is American; he's our great white not-quite-yet-dead male writer, and if he were an athlete he'd be in the Hall of Fame. But Ann Arbor isn't Cooperstown, it isn't a place where you purchase a ticket and camp out on the property for a look-see after lunch; he isn't selling T-shirts or giving autographs to fans; the driveway gates are locked. So there's no one now who visits and what he gets instead are postcards from Yosemite and the Golden Gate Bridge and the Grand Canyon and the Mississippi Delta and the Black Hills and Charleston and Truro and Ketchum and Key West. . . .

These cards don't seem to signify; he studies them less eagerly and makes me read them only once; we haven't returned to America yet in the story of his life. I've been working here since April and he's only twenty-three or -four and hasn't finished with his period of expatriation, his cutting-of-the-eyeteeth in Italy and Switzerland and France. And therefore the particular glazed I'm-writing-my-memoirs expression on the Master's face requires that we go way back and cross a body of water; he's remembering the nineteen twenties or the thirties, the time when he was happiest before it all went bad.

"When Mr. Hitler came to town," he likes to say, "the town went to hell in a handcar, and the name of that town is the world."

"Handcart," I tell him, "I think it's called handcart," while he peers at the photo and turns it over and over and sometimes licks the stamps.

"All gone," he says, and claps his hands. "All gone."

Most everything has gone by now; he only half listens and only half tastes what he eats. I could bring him a cupful of Taster's Choice Freeze Dried instant coffee, for all the difference it would make and if Hannah would allow me to; he lost his sense of taste, he says, when they made him swear off shellfish and after he had his first stroke. In 1961. He used to watch the setting sun with a cigar and pitcher of martinis or bottle of Mount Gay and, for the guests, since those were the years when there *were* guests, smoked venison he'd bagged himself with his famous bow and arrow, or maybe trout and whitefish from the lake. Underneath the red and blue and yellow striped umbrellas they'd speak, he says, about careers: much irony and pity then, many suits and countersuits and accusations. Those were the years when there were actresses, often, and the models and photographers would flock to the house and come upstairs to look at what he liked to call his itchings, his scribble scribble scribble, Mr. Gibbon. The society beauties, the long-legged swiftly tilting and not always upright girls. Come to visit from the newspaper or Diag or the Law School, come to interview the great man where he wrote. Not Canada geese or herring gulls but storklike in their two-piece suits and afterwards on towels or rubber inflatable mattresses or deck chairs offering themselves up to him like spread extracted entrails to the sun. . . .

His nose is no good either and I expect he'd burn himself if given half a chance. He doesn't seem to care how hot or cold the coffee is and doesn't seem to notice if the room is hot or cold. Outside it can be pushing ninety, with that hot steamy windless waiting-for-tornado weather that makes everyone else in this godforsaken part of the Midwest sweat buckets and go crazy and huddle by the vents for the A.C. But all the Master has are long-fluked fans, and he doesn't even notice if the fan in the bedroom is working or not; he sits there with that dry papery old-man skin of his that doesn't even sweat.

I come in and turn on the fan. I open the windows and wish I could go swimming in the forbidden pool downstairs, or take a canoe on the river, and dream of ice and air conditioning but all he says is "Mornin', kid, get crackin', rise and shine . . ." I say, good morning sir, did you sleep well? and he says, where's the mail today and I produce the tray. Then he lifts his cup of coffee and we work through "**O**" and "**A**" until it's time to look at the pictures again.

This he does attentively and for minutes at a time. He's got no taste or sense of sound or smell or touch worth mentioning, but what he *looks* at counts. The body on Mary the day nurse engages his attention—popping out of that green uniform—as though it were a Goya or the man he calls Pablito who I'm pretty sure was Picasso: that bald buttfucking Spaniard, he calls him, that nasty little man. Were you a friend of Picasso's, I ask? and he says, no, Cézanne. When was that, I inquire, and he tells me, I forget. *Where* was that, I prompt him, and he says the town of Aix. In Paris also briefly but mostly in Aix-en-Provence. And then he's off again and telling me about the oranges in Cavaillon, the flower sellers in the covered markets and how he used to go at dawn to watch them wheel in their carts full of flowers and hose them down and set them up in stalls, the way the flower water dyed the paving stones beneath the trestle tables and the colors of the high-heaped roses and anemones and how one day he took a gypsy standing up behind a flower cart because she pointed admiringly to the piping on his coat. And that wasn't all she admired, he likes to inform me, not the only thing she wanted, kid, I'm telling you, no sir. Oh you would have enjoyed it, he says, the sweet tart taste of the olives from Nyon and the harsh local rosé and the way they prepare their birds and rabbits in blood sauce after a good day's shooting and the *lavandin* and sunflowers and the sheep beneath the olive trees and jasmine-fragrant air. It was before it all got spoiled, before I wrote about it and the world came in truckloads to visit, which is what always happens, kid, when you describe it truly enough you wreck what you try to preserve. Before Mr. Cézanne started painting them those mountains were something to see. When he told you to look at the mountains you *saw* them, Wolfie, he says. When he said, hey, have an apple you could *taste* it on the plate.

The problem with all this—I've looked it up—is Cézanne died in 1906. And even if he knew Picasso and is old as the Apennines hills, even if you stretch it back as far as things can stretch the great man was seven when Paul Cézanne died, and a continent away. He was playing baseball at summer camp in Wisconsin, he was doing his multiplication tables maybe, he was learning about bows and arrows but not about Mr. Cézanne. . . .

One day I press him on it; I ask who exactly was that gypsy and where exactly is Cavaillon? He doesn't blink; he doesn't even pause for breath, he's saying, well, he got it wrong, he just remembered how it happened in the town of Blois that dangerous summer by the Loire. There's this family circus, these gypsies, and they've been on the road forever, for three generations anyhow, and they pull their painted wagons up like settlers in a circle, and where they settle for the night is where next day they mount the show. This girl is someone's cousin and she's best at doing backbends, and her uncle is the troupe's leader, the one who does the juggling and the trapeze and high-wire stuff. Also, they have a bear. The great man himself was maybe twenty at the time, and he hangs around them watching, it reminds him of the black bears in the garbage dumps outside of Ironwood, but that afternoon the troupe is acting a bit worried and shorthanded, since the bareback rider's husband is too drunk to work and has been sleeping it off. When he asks if they could use some help with the ropes and ponies, they nod their heads; they let him feed the horses, and also he waters the dogs. Another thing the husband does, he understands, is pass the plate—but this the gypsies don't trust him with, naturally, and so the girl goes around with her tambourine held out instead. When the show is over and they break the tent he helps them haul the ropes and stow the gear and feed the bear, and then she says they've got no cash to spare but everybody's grateful anyhow and she'll pay him back in trade. She says all this in Romany, which is not a language that he speaks, and mostly using sign. He says no problem, that's OK, it was a pleasure helping out, and then she loosens his belt buckle and undoes his tender buttons and then she does a handstand and drops her legs around him in a scissors grip. Wheelbarrow style. That's right, he says, it wasn't Cavaillon, it was where we tethered horses by the Loire. . . .

So one story leads to another and they're tailored, a little, to fit. It's not that he's lying exactly, it's just another version of the truth. He does admire the work of Cézanne and knows a good deal about it and when I try to challenge or correct him he pays no attention, he talks about apples and Mont. St. Victoire as though they were part of his personal history, the way that he talks about Proust. He *does* have that framed drawing by Picasso, after all, the one with a bull and girl and bottle of wine and the inscription, *Pour mon cher Édouard.* He did know Picasso in Paris, and maybe on the Riviera in Antibes or Mougins. And I suppose when you're as old as he is and dreaming by the window it doesn't matter all that much if there was an actual gypsy, or if he just imagined one and then composed the scene. The edges blur, I mean; things bleed into each other and if you're famous for invention why not invent that too? If almost eighty years ago you've been to Cavaillon or Blois or to the flower market on Thursdays in Apt and eaten an apple or looked at his mountain and maybe watched a gypsy dance then why not say you did it because of your good friend Cézanne?

Our boy was born in '99, and part of the reason we're writing memoirs is because he plans to stay alive into his third century. He might just do it too. *Witness,* that's his working title, and when I remind him that Whittaker Chambers also called himself a witness he says what the hell does that have to do with anything and, I have to admit it, not much. There can't be all that many people in the world who were alive in the eighteen hundreds and remain as strong as he is; our Edward's doing fine. The night nurse says, as old birds go, he's a very tough old bird. Once when he couldn't sleep at all and was recovering from the last stroke she asked him what he'd like to have and he said, so loud it startled her, "Strychnine, my dear."

"I'm afraid all we can manage is Valium," she said, and he responded to her, gently, "Then that will have to do."

We aren't alone together, ever; this house is a full house. What he says is, Beats a flush. For breakfast I bring him his coffee; at lunch there's a sandwich and pickle or two to masticate, that's the word he uses, anyhow: come let us chew the fat cud. There's the cook and the day nurse Mary with the romantic entanglements and her green blouse and matching skirt and the night nurse and the gardener and every Monday afternoon the good Doctor Stephens arrives. He registers the patient's temperature and blood pressure and looks in his ears and throat and eyes and nods approvingly and takes out his stethoscope and then I leave the room. They were wartime drinking buddies, the doctor likes to tell me, which is why he makes a house call when he's mostly quit his practice and ought damn well to retire before he kills anybody else, or at least that's what he tells me he likes to tell the Maestro, and I hear them laugh and grumble together, and then the doctor emerges again and slaps me on the back and says, Keep up the excellent work. He's doing fine, he says, he's got real staying power, does our Edward. I say you can say that again. You're doing fine, the doctor assures me, if I still had a practice I'd want you for a junior partner and your name up there right alongside my very own moniker on the shingle. I say thank you and ask myself why. He's very grateful, Doctor Stephens says, he's very happy to have you here, son, to imagine he's still writing things and to tell his lies to and impress. Then he puts on his hat and nods at his reflection in the mirror and pats me on the back again and I open the door and he leaves.

We study the postcard from Switzerland. White mountains and blue sky. The legend announces we're looking at the alpine villages of Zermatt and Zaas-Fe and the Allaline Glacier between. He peers at it, flips it around. He touches the stamp with his tongue. Because his hand is shaking he slops a little coffee in the saucer and nods at the machine until I turn it on. Then the great man reminisces, sighing, saying what a morning, little Mr. Wolverine, what a day it was when she arrived to visit me. I ask him who, and he says, who do you think? I don't think, I want to tell him, I'm not paid to do the thinking here and he says my first goddam beautiful wife. Her wild free way with dismissal, her easy available scorn. The skullcap of her hair, he says, the corona of her hair. When she got off the train and before I even knew it, before she could tell me, he says. Milady of the baggage car before it all went bad, when everything was Jungfraujoch and not as yet corrupt.

My own day's work is done by four but at four o'clock Mary comes to his room, and so I hang around in case she might want company, which hasn't happened yet. I'm fiddling with the tapes and making sure the reels are turning and I don't really know what he's talking about but smile and make encouraging noises and watch the guy beyond the window cranking out a white hose from a service van for the chemical mix in the pool. He's wearing a blue uniform and cap and using the scoop net and mixing and adjusting things, as if anyone ever could swim in the pool, as if we were allowed. The pool guy's weight has settled in the gut, so when you see him from behind he's still a slim-hipped kid but when you see him turn around or from the side he's fat.

Wind rattles the leaves of the trees. There are sparrows feeding by the ornamental pond. There's the pool the great man nearly drowned in when he had his second stroke and although they keep it full no one wallows in the water, Hannah says, not on my watch, not so long as I'm running the show. Down below there's joggers jogging, and a bunch of kids on roller blades and across the river I watch Amtrak heading west. It's a busy imitation of silence, the hum of the fan and the train whistling and on the table the sound of the tapes, his labored exhalation and stertorous intake of breath; it's a lot of noise but nothing worth hearing and I ask once more, what morning, sir, and he says the one she came to see me down in the valley in, where was it, Wengen? Gründelwald? Mary Mary quite contrary plumps the pillows on the daybed, then puts her finger to her lips and nods at me and tiptoes out again.

And now he says it's like this window, isn't it, the way the light falls glancingly and Thermopane can keep at bay what nevertheless it both frames and contains, a screen of second growth and scree of rock, a patch of lawn for men to mow and pool to fill and this city enlarged from a village, a village sprung up near the creek bed it was. Hear how the fen beneath us percolates, the Master says, and cocks his head, and listen where the glacier halts, extruding rock by Allen Creek where once they traded furs and beads so we may watch the time lapse of a photograph and f-stop of remembrance as though it were a semipermeable membrane, kid. For through this lens and glass emerges a solution now, the interlocking cones of memory and hindsight, and therefore I myself incorporate surveyor and the thing surveyed, at one and the same time both subject and object, a helicopter circling down with kidneys for the hospital, or maybe what that rising spiral signifies is how they hunt some donor's heart: let's hope the transplant takes. He crosses his fingers and knocks on the wood of his chair. For all is as once was, he says, and soon or late the Huron will reclaim its proper place—and now he's coughing, hawking phlegm—and swamp the golf course and the cookie-cutter condos and the shopping mall and lap at the bridge pilings where they span the road. Because when I first came to town it wasn't much more than a whistle-stop station, six musicians every year, a serious winter, a wildness if no longer wilderness, with cow barns and old Germans and the smart money in Detroit sending its smart children east and south. But then I built this house, he says, and settled in and settled down before your parents' parents met with only this foolscap and dunce's capped pen, just language inspissated and ephemeral and lifelong, evanescent, just the visible and quasi-palpable damp residue and aftermath of speech. A pair of cracked bellows pump-pumping. And hiring and firing the children from school, the literary aspirants, the ones who believed themselves promising, promising, who dreamed of an imprimatur or connections or advice, who wanted to include in their own professional history the fact they'd been employed here once, and sending them up like a series of mates to this topgallant squall of a room. Those were the years I was writing, he says, still writing every morning and standing upright at the desk no matter how tardy or busy the night, and those were the years when I flattered myself—for others were flattering also, of course—that language still could matter, that a place and time and people would require attestation and it somehow might fall on these shoulders of mine to act as scribe and mantled witness, the green mantle of the standing pool and so on and so forth. He had been trying very hard, he says, to keep up with the Jonahs and the Jonasses and the Jackasses and Jills, but it took concentration like pulled skeet to shoot, and it isn't all that easy for an old pro any longer, what did you say your name was, Wolfie, well you come here with high marks and positively glowing references. From little Albertine. And so no interval occurs between the first and final line, and what I forget or don't choose to remember is detritus and the chaff of it, the town of Montalcino and the village of Ann Arbor and the gypsy camp along the Loire, the Po and Seine and Huron and that vanished Allen Creek itself still flowing softly where we take our ease: my self-deluding self-appointed mission to impart to others afterwards that *this is how it was.*

An old man maundering about his vanished youth.

Who sits dreaming in the sun.

Who picks at his nose and his nails.

Who enjoys or is not troubled by the whiff of urine that permeates his clothing, and tries to remember the name of the nurse who suggested he warn her whenever he needs, as she puts it, to go.

Potty, go potty? she asks.

Yet all of this but clouds the act of observation, kid, the sustained rapt revery and syntactic rendering that is the writer's trade. And therefore what I'm after now, our Edward says, is the glottal stop and hush of, why not call a spade a spade, devotion to the visible, the radiance inhering here and I mean by that no fuss and ruckus, no TV or traffic or laughter. Except what you must understand—what I need to make you understand—is how everything that happens happens in sequence simultaneously and if I put it in and don't know about it truly then it truly isn't there and if I leave it out it isn't not there still.

What year was this, I want to ask, what season, what are we talking about? And then his voice trails off and his great head drops a little the way that it does, that great white shock of hair of his falling, and he puts his coffee down, which is a good thing. When was that, sir, I ask him, but he's crying now, the tears tracking down the wrinkled and striated rum-wrecked delta of his face, and he says it was the day my first goddam beautiful wife arrived and told me we were finished, *finita la commedia,* the day it all went to hell in a handcar, *passata la festa,* you've understood nothing, I see.

ALICE FULTON

The Permeable Past Tense of Feel

Let the barbaric flowers live, I'm living.
I'm liking the meadow blobbed with birdsfoot trefoil,
      with earth-gall and the creeping
wheatgrass anciently known as felt. I mean nonelites
that live in disturbed soils, nuisance shrubs
      whose fragrance
exceeds exaggeration. Isn't it green.

      These days everyone wants
two acres gated with herbicide. Everyone wants
to eat high on the food chain while—

Contain yourself. We need less
impervious surface per person

      beginning with the mind.
      Oh, the blisters sustained
      while blaming others. The indignation of!
      Only the sky has a right to such
      disdain. Isn't it blue, my companion
      animal said. And doesn't the body extend

      into other endowed stuff. Feeling things,
      with blue irises and pink or brown
      fleshy hairless ears
enrobed in fat and skin,
that chew and breathe and joy themselves
by twisting, aerodynamic, when they jump.
That have soulweight and intestines.
      That like Mozart,

which is played to calm them since calm
things are easier to kill.

Felt comes from "beat" and from "near."
As hooks pass through, the fibers entangle
till our presence is a double-dwelling = =

Why must I say they are like
us whenever I say let them live? Speak eco-speak
like "eat no flesh and save the watershed, like
maybe the whole blue-green."

How have I inconvenienced myself
in service to this feeling?
Felt is ideal for padding and sealing.
How have I left the earth
uncluttered with more me?

The inhabitant cleans and wipes,
eats and spasms. Cruelty exasperates
reason. At the top of its range,
ah is the only sound
the human voice can make. So felt

takes on the shape of the flesh
it covers, and the animal is understood

beyond resemblance
into same, a thou-art-that that oscillates
through pollen-throwing and clasping devices,
ovaries and arms. So lid and lash

close over iris and pupil, dissecting tables drain
into our sweet spot.

The century heaves. Nowever. Who has time?
With primates to raise, important hearts
to hold down.

When the box is full, hammers beat the felt,
which turns to present a new surface
before it's struck again.

Lovers, givers, what minds have we made
that make us hate
slaughterhouse because it tortures a river?

[157]

As the prescribed burn begins, I see the warmth
sculpture rise higher, twisting from the base.
As the body extends into other
infused stuff. And though the world consists of everything

that is the case,
I know there are ways to concentrate
the meanings of felt in one

just place. Just as this flame
assumes the shape of the flesh it covers.
I like to prepare the heart
by stuffing it with the brain.

On the 27th day of February, 1824, a son was born and named Alpha Washtenaw Bryan, the first white child born in the county. Mr. Bryan being a carpenter built the first bridge across the Huron River, at Ypsilanti.

—Michigan Pioneer and Historical Collections *17*

Mill, Ypsilanti, 1892

JANET KAUFFMAN

Buried Water

WATER IS WILD, it's outlaw. It takes topsoil, it channels serious and grand canyons, it collects in wetlands and goes no place. It stinks. It sinks, it springs. Water falls, flows, gathers, floods.

Even so, human beings want to *walk* on it. And not get their feet wet.

A miracle's a passionate, compelling story, not the usual muck and mire. And if it takes the special effects of engineering, dredging, blasting, bridge work, drainage systems, and various metal-clad machineries to work miracles in nature, well, that's good business, too.

We walk on water every day of the week in southern Michigan.

It's a classic American story—domination of the elements—and the action has been most ruthless and visionary and violent when the main players come upon water.

Water starts out simple, very clear. But as soon as it hits the ground we claim, things get murky. And you know how much we claim: every square inch.

Look at some square inches and acres around here. Ypsilanti, for instance. A narrow, funnel-down point in the Huron River watershed, Ypsilanti has been claimed ground since the French Claim of 1809. On early maps—1825, 1874—the Huron River takes a sprawling turn at Ypsi, with marshes on both sides of the wide floodplain. A small stream flows into the river near Forest Avenue. A bit later, in 1907, on the delicate, hand-colored survey maps drawn up by Gardner S. Williams, they're still there, the marshes, the stream.

But look around now. Walk around town, along Forest Avenue to the Eastern Michigan University Campus—you won't get your feet wet. That ground where the stream should be, through the middle of campus? Dry ground, sidewalks. Water, water, is not anywhere.

Except for the Huron River itself, other visible waters—the original swamps and streams—have been disappeared from the city (as from almost every city), and it didn't take long, a few generations. *Miraculous* is the word people like to use when they hold Nature down for the count. The most cinematic miracles in the Bible are water ones—Moses parts the Red Sea; Jesus walks on water. But if God isn't on your side in these matters, if you can't single-handedly part a stream and cross it, well, you can bury it.

The place I work in Ypsilanti, Eastern Michigan University, stands on a slope falling away to the south bank of the Huron River. Around EMU, the river takes that wide, formerly swampy, turn after Leforge Road, swings around to the Forest Avenue bridge and then runs more or less straight into Depot Town and through Riverside Park. The Huron River isn't buried, it isn't completely barriered, but most students at EMU don't notice the Huron River and don't think of it as part of campus. They know the river as part of the scenery in Depot Town, east of school, where Frog Island and Riverside Parks open up the water to view.

In Depot Town, you can walk on a scaffolded wooden walkway that connects the parks and crosses over the river, under the Cross Street bridge. It's the one place in town you can meander, get close to the churn of the water, hear it wash around the rocks there, and check out whatever debris has snagged in the brush and slung off to one side—a couple of tree stumps, clutches of cans in branches, a tire, some fishing lines.

On campus, though, you don't think about water flowing nearby. Everybody drives on Huron River Drive; but at Eastern, close as the river is, Huron River Drive is a *drive.* The name becomes the road, cut off from view of the water by the Riverrain apartment complex and the Eastern Plaza mini-mall.

Most students could draw you a decent map of the campus with the streets intersecting at exact angles, but the river wouldn't be there. If you said, "Draw in the river," they'd probably have to think about it. "The Huron River," you'd say. And then they might be able to backtrack the river in their minds, coming upstream from Frog Island and guessing about the turn and about what happens behind the railroad tracks, the old Peninsula Paper Company building, behind the mini-mall.

But where the river comes from—back toward Ann Arbor and Gallup Park—and where it goes—someplace after Ford Lake—that would be distant territory, unmappable.

We're explorers now in watersheds, with no signposts and few maps or with blank territories on our maps, those drop-offs at the edges where cartographers used to draw dragons in threatening seas.

We believe we know where we are. And it's true, we have some very good maps. But, it is also true—we have no idea where we are.

We know road maps, not watershed maps. Not vegetation patterns. Not soil maps. Not buried water maps.

An address? Most of us know the street number, the ZIP code. But who knows the watershed or its number?—the digits tracking back from outlet to large rivers to streams. The Huron River Watershed: #04090005.

For many of us living and thriving in watersheds, ecosystems, and climates, those elemental systems have become deep background, lost to our thoughts and experience. The more a place is settled and built up, the more uncharted its natural features. The lay of the land, the landscape, the fall and flow of water—they all disappear.

And if you decide not to bury water, you can blur it away, set it aside pretty completely. Just about every river, for our safety, is bridged and barriered—there's no drive-by viewing. Most old-style see-through pipe railings have been replaced with reinforced concrete sections, shoulder to shoulder. We drive over rivers without knowing it, without seeing their course, their width, their particular ripple. Since they are out of sight, most highway departments don't label the rivers with signs anymore. You're on a bridge, you know that, but what you're crossing—who knows? You can drive across the Midwest on interstates and not know you've crossed any river, any watershed.

Not long ago, the Cuyahoga River near Cleveland was labeled with a big sign, a presence on the Ohio Turnpike. From a car, you could look through pipe railings, dizzily, at the river below and know its strange name, maybe hum a few bars of the R.E.M. tune. The river was a clear water stripe, a twist coming out of trees, with high banks and a visible floodplain, some rocks spitting white streaks in the water. The turnpike—any driver could see—was a road built from high ground to high ground, landforms the Cuyahoga River had cut. Now, with the concrete barriers, you can't see the river, you don't know you're on a riverbank, there's no sign with the river's name. It's not clear what carved out those cliffs where the condos sit now. And half the time when I drive there, even though I'm determined to hum "Cuyahoga" in tribute to the river, I miss it and drive right through and feel too bad about it later to sing anything, retro-honorifically.

When we cross over water, we're safe. (And sorry.) It's a clear cut, a straight shot. No scenic distractions. No notion of waterways, watersheds, landforms, nature.

Out of sight. Out of mind.

Water is wild. It obeys the invisible and elemental laws of gravity, absorption, evaporation—not human laws of boundary, possession, property.

Until we get our hands and machines on it.

Water's our source, our sustenance. It bore us, it buoys us, it can bear us away.

Still, we believe that we, and by law we do, *own* water. In the past, we've pretty much done what we pleased with it. In the West, with water a rarity, the story's an old-time romance, an ongoing saga—with schemes to conjure up water, claim it, carry it across state lines, and marry it to dry cities, dry farms.

But in the Midwest, in southeast Michigan, where water stood around just about everywhere, such a common thing, the story has always been: ditch it, drain it, bury it, forget it.

DITCHED & BURIED, TO START WITH

When I first farmed in southern Michigan, I farmed dry ground. The fields were sandy loams that drained so fast after rains I could often work the ground the same day. The only water on the farm was a stream in the woods at the back of the property. One year a sinkhole appeared in a low spot in the hayfield, and, when I checked it out, dug down into it, I pulled up a chunk of broken clay tile—terra-cotta, the color of the bricks of houses around here, like a shard of a flower pot.

I had no idea. I'd never seen water collect in those fields, and I'd never thought about it. Or about Michigan soils and glaciated ground. About its watersheds and drainage. Even though I was obsessed with weather and watched for the high cirrus clouds, drawn back like hair, a sign my grand-father taught me meant a low pressure system moving in, with rain maybe, within thirty-six hours. I farmed hay, and I had to think about rain, know when it would come and how long it would last. I watched the sky and I watched the TV.

But I thought rain fell and flowed downhill to the stream or percolated down into groundwater somewhere, the way it did on the farm where I grew up in Pennsylvania. There, everything sank through fine clays into porous limestone or flowed downhill, you could see it, through the network of streams to the Conestoga Creek and on to the Susquehanna River.

But here in Michigan, with the complex and mixed soils, glacial hum-mocks, sands and gravels overlaying marls and clays, water collects. It stands around.

Until somebody digs a ditch, carefully sighted downslope, lays some drainage tiles, and buries the water.

On most of the farmland of Michigan now, the watershed lies under-ground, where water flows at terrific pace during thaws and rains. Buried, water is invisible, silent. You walk right over it.

All eighty acres of my farm were ditched and drained. I had no idea. There was no record of the work, no maps. But in the years I farmed those fields, the old clay-tile drainage system broke down, one tile after another. The tiles filled up with dirt or roots. Or the clay just shattered like stomped-on glass. Low spots got wet and stayed wet. Unplowed places sprouted sedges, loosestrife, and clumps of reeds.

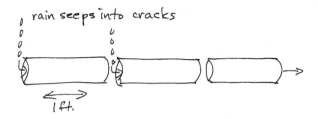

Clay drain tiles

When I plowed the bottomlands, I'd sometimes cut through the tops of strange gray-dirt chimneys that crayfish kicked up in wet ground. I could look straight down the chimney hole to water, six inches below the surface of the field. I was farming a bog. The tractor would push out a kind of waterbed ripple through the dirt.

In the end, it wasn't worth it, working that ground, and I quit farming the low spots. As more tiles broke, small wetlands formed, and the extent of the tiling was clear. This was a huge water network, a watershed underground—coursing, flowing, lying low.

I see any farm field with a different eye now. I can see what's in it, and I can guess what's under it.

In Michigan, if it looks like dry ground, you can bet somebody's buried the water.

I still don't know where all the tiles are on my farm. It's a patchwork system of arteries. A map of the old drainage system, the watershed underground, might look like this:

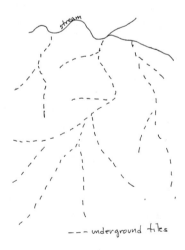

Underground tile system

After walking the stream in rubber boots, I spotted several outlet points of the tile, three places in the banks of the stream. In the fields, I know the main tile lines because I've broken them now, crushed the tile, and let the water collect, as part of the Federal Wetlands Reserve program. Five huge wetlands formed—these would have been woodland swamps, in beech and oak forest, before the white settlement here. All that water restored, resurfaced. Out of sight!

Acres of water on a dry farm.

In the decades that closed out the nineteenth century, almost all of southern Michigan's woodland swamps were cleared of trees and drained with clay tiles for farming. In many towns, along with the sawmill, the brick and tile works was the major industry.

Nobody wrote much about it, but the southern Michigan landscape in those days must have been nightmarish—trees cut, stumps uprooted, brush burning in huge heaps of flame; families in fields with shovels or with animals harnessed to ditching blades; children hauling in and setting those tiles, one at a time, thousands and thousands of tiles in the trenched fields; then the work of shoveling dirt and covering it all up.

Burying the water.

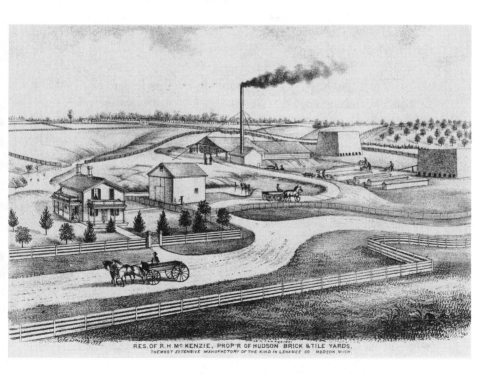

RES. OF R. H. McKENZIE, PROP'R OF HUDSON BRICK & TILE YARDS,
THE MOST EXTENSIVE MANUFACTORY OF THE KIND IN LENAWEE CO. HUDSON, MICH.

Hudson Tile Works

Today, to keep a farm dry, fields are drained and redrained with plastic tiling. The process is fairly quick, surgical, with laser transits, trenching machines, and huge rolls of yellow tiling unwinding into the ditch. But the thinking and consequence are the same: ground is a surface for farming, for human use; and water must go underground.

In towns, too, like Ypsilanti, water was ditched and buried. Water had its use, but it had its limits. To run flour mills and sawmills, the Huron River was cut into in several places, channeling water to the mill wheels and returning it to the river. Frog Island (which is not an island at the moment) was no island to begin with, until a millrace was dredged in the 1840s, cutting a good chunk of ground away from the bank. Frog Island stood apart in the river for over one hundred years, long after the mills were gone, until gradually, through the 1960s and 1970s, the millrace filled in with years of sediment and became a dump for concrete, construction and railroad debris.

Ypsilanti is a small point, one turn, in the Huron River watershed, but it's got it all—the love and desire of water, the loathing, the ditching, the burial.

Every water affair goes on and on. It just won't quit. Settlers drained foul swamps with clay tiles; they dredged stream banks and cut out millraces. A few years later, in a kind of wild digression, a fling in the water story, Ypsi entrepreneurs drilled bedrock wells and pumped up waters from the "Atlantis" well. Then, later, a real dissolution, a *thunk,* a hush of a close, civic leaders drained the city watershed and separated themselves from whole streams.

The *work* it took. To work these miracles. And still takes. The labors of love and of machineries. To bury water, walk on it, and walk away.

DRILLED, BOTTLED, & BOUGHT (THE FLING)

In the hierarchies of waters, surface waters are sluggish, sluttish. We don't like things easy. But, oh, the seductiveness of well water! And the deeper the water lies, the more miraculous. In Ypsi, for a few years, there was a regular crush of men, good businessmen, out to *resurrect* mineral waters from bedrock wells. They bottled and sold the water, a miracle cure—three glasses a day for whatever ills, chills, the nineteenth century gave you, whatever "disordered blood."

In 1884, on sixty-five acres of the property where EMU's central campus now stands, lived the oddly named Tubal Cain Owen. He was a nut ("a bit peculiar," the *Ypsilanti Commercial* called him), a man "of capital and push" in Ypsilanti. Tubal Cain Owen put together a small domain on this property—a wife and three children, a house on the hill in a grove of hickory trees, 6 1/2 acres of tropical plants and lawn, with pretty Owen's Creek running through the grounds.

Tubal Cain Owen, was an entrepreneur and a believer in the Book of Revelation and a great believer in scientific principles. He was a success in most of his endeavors and businesses—shipping, milling, farming—although his belief that the Bible prophesied "flying machines" led him to construct, on scientific principles, years before the Wright brothers, an "aeroplane" in his backyard. The construction never flew, but that one failure didn't diminish T. C. Owen's faith in technology and his visions of a fantastically improved life.

Water was a curse in the lowlands for farmers, but it was also a cure one took at that time in the many popular springs and sanitariums: Saratoga Springs in New York; Hot Springs, Arkansas; Mount Clemens in Michigan. In 1883, a well drilled by the Cornwell Paper Company in Ypsilanti hit "evil smelling" water, and it didn't take many months to find backers with money to build a sanitarium, the Ypsilanti Bath House, which opened for business January 10, 1884.

Six months later, Tubal Cain Owen drilled his own, very deep, 740-foot well and struck salty water on the Forest Avenue property. A flamboyant competitor, Owen called his well "The King of Mineral Waters" and christened his product Atlantis Mineral Water. "We have no myths nor Indian legends to relate to appeal to the public's credulity," Owen pronounced in his brochure. "We sank our well on scientific principles in search of HEALING WATERS." He invited comparison with the Cornwell water, and the *Ypsilanti Commercial* wrote in June 1884 that the Owen well water "very nearly resembles" the Cornwell water but lacks "the stench." The writer, no doubt guided by Tubal Owen in the experiment, goes on to describe "a curiosity." Rub a silver dollar with Cornwell water, and it is blackened at once. "Wash it with this [Owen well water], and it is restored to its original color."

Okay. Not quite parting the Red Sea. But Ypsi applauded.

Stand-around surface water had to be ditched, but *bedrock* water—that was a moneymaker. For a while, Ypsilanti was a watering destination, with its mineral bathhouses and sanitariums known "the world over."

Early photos show a derrick and a smokestack on the Owen property, but Tubal Cain Owen quickly built a brick factory around the derrick and manufactured a slew of deep-well products. He bottled Atlantis water and Ypsilanti Mineral Water and marketed them as "Nature's Greatest Remedy for Disordered Blood," a curative for thirty-two diseases including hay fever, hemorrhoids, pleurisy, diabetes, cuts, burns, venereal disease, bee stings, and cancer. In Owen's 1885 advertising brochure, three wineglasses a day, "no matter how nauseating it may be," were recommended; and "as an enema," he wrote, "this water has no superior."

Owen shipped mineral water in state and out of state to Chicago; he evaporated water into salts and sold that; he manufactured Atlantis Mineral Water Salicura Soap and Paragon Ginger Ale.

The *Detroit Herald of Commerce* claimed that "the natural water has been deodorized and carbonated and makes a palatable drink of great potency in the relief of all persons afflicted with skin or blood diseases. The granulated salts obtained from the waters are highly recommended by the most prominent medical exponents for the cure of catarrh, headaches, and bilious or malarial disorders."

This water was big, flashy business. The Cornwell brothers, backed by investor George Moorman, drilled more wells. Several Ypsilanti doctors had Cornwell-Moorman mineral water pumped to their offices. In a famous quote people still like to haul out of the archives and twist around, the *Ypsilanti Commercial* declaimed in 1884: "Ypsilanti has already come to be the centre of attraction for the halt, the lame, and the blind, the palsied, the paralytics. It is by no means a crippled city, but a city of cripples."

Disordered blood was a boon for Ypsi. The *Commercial* goes on: "The cry is every day, still they come! Let Them Come. The Hawkins House, the Follett and the Barton, and all the other hotels and numerous nice boarding houses are full. Ere another season a mammoth hotel may be in the process of erection." An anonymous "Farmer" wrote a ballad published in the *Commercial*, with a couple of verses that tout the success and the dream of these waters:

> If you are sad, with sickness worn,
> And have the headache every morn,
> Just come and drink a healing horn,
> Of Ypsilanti's water.
> There's forty new baths agoing,
> And all the healing waters flowing,
> Better days and health bestowing,
> On many a weary one.
>
> . . . .
>
> It's true, it has a woeful smell,
> But if your stomache don't rebel
> It's just the thing to make you well
> And praise up Ypsilanti.

Owen and the others had drilled through more than two hundred feet of glacial deposits and drift into bedrock, where aquifers trap Paleozoic marine waters in the sediment. Owen's mineral water was ancient seawater. Those salts were real sea salt.

Atlantis Mineral Water labels

Groundwater geology studies in the 1960s noted that "water obtained from bedrock in the Ypsilanti area is not potable in the ordinary sense, although small quantities are consumed." During the bathhouse boom years, small—and large—quantities of salty bedrock water were bought, bottled, and consumed from Ypsilanti wells.

The fling didn't last long. Around 1902, new owners of the Ypsilanti Sanitarium began admitting "many d.t. victims" whose "yells annoyed other patients and staid Ypsilantians." The social status and respectability of the bathhouses declined, and in 1906, with the passage of the Pure Food and Drug Act, requiring—alas for Atlantis waters—truth in labeling, the business of miracle waters wound down. No more cures for thirty-two diseases, no more fantastical labels. The well water was bottled and marketed as simple mineral water for another decade, but then the wells were capped. There's a pipe in the ground someplace on that hillside at Eastern, probably just about under the President's House.

DITCHED & BURIED, AGAIN

With surface water, *not seeing* things is the trick, the magic, the miracle. Invisibility is better than any one-shot parting of seas. The permanent disappearance of water—so we can walk from any point A to any point B and do whatever we want with the ground between—that's the dream and deepest desire. The American dream doesn't take long to move past the manufactured pastoral and into an engineered territory of full and free enterprise.

Tubal's lawns, with Owen Creek burbling there behind the Atlantis well and manufactory, took shape in the first dream. And all that came next took shape in the next, the ongoing dream.

On an 1874 map of Ypsilanti, Owen Creek winds around and flows more or less parallel to Forest Avenue, down to the Huron River at the railroad bridge. If the creek were there now, it would run behind the I-M sports complex and down the street past Pray-Harrold and on under the Alexander music building.

Of course, there's no stream, and there's no mouth of a creek downslope at the Huron River.

What there *is* at that point (walk down Forest Avenue to the bridge and look north) is a 6 1/2-foot reinforced concrete pipe: The Owen Outlet Drain.

On early Drain Commission maps, it's the Owen *Creek* Outlet. But more recently, the maps say simply Owen Outlet. The file folder in the Washtenaw County Drain Commission office is labeled Owen Outlet. No creek no more. It's ditched, piped, buried. Done for.

Like the wetlands that farmers drained and tiled underground, many streams and some rivers—the Grand River in Jackson, for instance—were buried in Michigan towns, to facilitate city construction, to control the storm water and flooding caused by that construction.

Gulf air might build up in weather systems and dump on EMU, but the rain that falls no longer follows the watershed topography into Owen Creek; it's channeled underground in the Owen Outlet Drain. Grates in parking lots and cuts in sidewalks collect water into a network of buried streams and tributaries. But in spite of the extent of storm drains—or because of their miraculous invisibility—buried water remains somehow mysterious, a hidden knowledge. Who knows where the water goes? A few engineers?

Not many people in Ypsilanti know. The map of the storm drains on file in the Ypsilanti Office of Public Works was drawn in 1960! It's a beautiful yellowed map, frayed all around, with a few penciled additions.

"They told me to guard this with my life," the woman said who set it out on a table. "It's the only map we've got."

"Nothing more recent? How do they know where to fix these things?"

"Well, some of these guys have worked here a long time."

Buried water's a mystery. Cultish. Out of sight. Secret, forgotten, hushed up. Did somebody say *repressed?*

At EMU, drawings of the campus's storm drains, including the Owen Outlet Drain right down the middle, date from 1970, before the Alexander Music Hall was built on top of the drain. If you put your ear to the ground during spring thaws, could you catch a murmur? A hum?

Dan Klenczar, project manager for EMU's physical plant, knew about Owen Creek. He's the only person I found who knew that there had been a creek on campus and that the creek had been put in a drain. He wasn't sure when. The County Drain Commission knew the date of construction, 1929. Seventy years ago. Nobody knew why, although "construction, probably," "expansion" was a good guess.

In some places, seventy years would be recent history. But here, and in the United States generally, landscape memory is short-term memory. And when we bury water, the first thing we want to do is forget it.

Still, sometimes old names carry watershed history.

Check out a map of the Huron River watershed. Ypsilanti's the base of a bottleneck. The watershed narrows there between two hills, and the river starts to pour itself out toward Lake Erie. At this point in the watershed, you can literally see from one side of it to the other. From the hill with the Ypsi water tower, on Summit Street, you can sight across to the other side—the old Highland Cemetery and, beyond that, Prospect Road. The names recall what the settlers and early surveyors knew. What we've forgot.

On the other sides of these hills, water flows away through other watersheds, finds different rivers and different outlets to Lake Erie.

Without a map, who would know? We count on the names, Summit, Highland. But what if the name shifts—Owen Creek Outlet to Owen Outlet? The creek is gone from the maps, gone from the name. Out of sight. Out of mind.

When it comes to water, we've lost our senses. We bury water. We forget we bury it.

Who buried Owen Creek?

It wasn't Tubal Cain Owen. The stream fit into his lavish and sweeping design of the property. And nobody then knew the scientific principles for the construction of pipe big enough to hold the stream. By the time Tubal died in 1913, the state of Michigan was anxious to purchase the land, to allow the Normal School, now EMU, to expand. The buildings of the sanitarium had been sold for residences, although water from the Atlantis well was still pumped by Owen's son and shipped in bulk to Chicago and Boston. EMU's president, Charles McKenny, argued that the Atlantis well and facilities, though in competent hands with Owen's son, could become "a serious menace" if passed on to other interests.

The Owen family resisted sale of the property and battled the state in court, but they lost; and not long after World War I, the Normal School gained title to all the property, including the well, the stream, the homestead, the old factory buildings. The place would be cleared to make way for, one after the other, buildings on the expanding campus: Roosevelt, Jones-Goddard, Pray-Harrold, the IM building, Downing, Quirk, Alexander Hall.

About the time of the Owen buyout, in the spring of 1918, another event may have contributed to the fate of Owen Creek. With heavy snows and a sudden thaw that year, the Huron River flooded through Ypsilanti, breaking both Superior and Peninsular Dams and inundating the low-lying parts of town. No doubt Owen Creek flooded as well. As a consequence, the Washtenaw County Drain Commission began a series of storm drain constructions along Owen Creek, first a short drain near the source, in 1922, and then an extension drain in 1925. The main section of Owen Creek remained intact, though, flowing all the way through the campus and into the Huron River.

In the end, it wasn't fear of flood so much as love of power—the power of light—that buried Owen Creek.

In May 1929, Clayton Deare, the Washtenaw County drain commissioner, wrote a letter to Michigan's governor, Fred W. Green, asking for state funds to cover drain work on the state's property at the Normal School. He wrote, "As you formerly lived in Ypsilanti, you will probably recall the old creek that empties into the Huron River near the Lake Shore Freight Depot [Forest Avenue]. A petition has been filed with me to inclose this drain. It passes in between houses and continues on up through the Normal property. I have talked with President McKenny who stated they would like the drain inclosed on part of the State Property for the reason that they intend to build a new power house on the spot where this creek now lies."

A power plant it would be. And continues to be. On the spot where the creek now lies buried.

The Washtenaw County Drain Commission put out a call for bids on the Owen Creek Outlet Drain, specifying precast reinforced concrete pipe, 6 feet 6 inches in diameter, for a drain that would follow "the general course of a creek, at some places being in the present creek bed and in other places in a new course."

Water and power. Power and light. To have light, we ditch and drain a creek. Or dam a river.

We walk on water. We run on water.

We have the power to do what we want.

On the slopes and streets of Ypsilanti, water falls and it disappears. It goes underground. We forget all about the sprawl and the spray of water, its name, its course through the watershed, its stink or its skid over rocks, the body-roll turns, and then we forget we've forgotten.

Peninsula Dam, Ypsilanti

The maps of water and watersheds are ancient—as rare, as recondite, as maps of the psyche. Memory fails, and fast.

It may be a miracle to walk on water. Make that wishy-washy stream look like ground. Tame it. Shut it up, shut it down. Forget it.

But, Lethe, remember, that river of forgetfulness, we cross over into hell. And then if we bury the river! There it is—we forget we've forgotten. The place may be tillable, arable, a good site for a power plant, but how will we know where we are when the water's buried and there's no map?

What kind of miracle is it, if we don't know we're walking on water?

LAURA KASISCHKE

Our Lady of the River

Something cuts straight through us. It is

the physical world, in which

there's mostly water. *Saint*

Teresa, when she died, they cut the heart from her
and found a fissure, a little river. It is dark, except in winter

when snow undulates on the ice, like
a rug dusty with stars and talcum powder
shaken out in the night. *She*

claimed an angel pierced her with a spear. In summer, the ducks

swim with the styrofoam cups. It's what
we drink from, and it's why

the tribes gathered here
instead of over there
It's why we'll have to leave
or die together when it runs dry.

The angel was golden
He came to her in bed.
The piercing made her moan.

In autumn, the dead leaves fall upon the river
as on the freeway, upon the sinners

as on the saints. *The spear*
was tipped with fire. When he

withdrew it, she sighed. It is

the same river in the bathtub of the mayor, in the garden
hose of the shirtless boy, who
scrubs down his car, becoming
the feverish fantasy of his neighbor's wife. It washes
the make-up from the exotic dancer's face. It baptizes

the innocent child. *Many*

have laughed at Saint Teresa's angel
and his spear tipped with fire, which

penetrated the core of Saint Teresa
and left her praying for more. In

the physical world, there's water. It
comes from a single source. It is

the mystery running
divine and dirty
straight through the center of every town

then through the heart of us.

We started again as early as possible, all who could walk moving on a little in advance of the wagon; the small children were the only ones who thought of riding. Every few rods it would take two or three men to pry the wagon out of the mud, while those who walked were obliged to force their way over fallen timber, brush, etc. Thus passed the day; at night we found ourselves on the plains, three miles from Ypsilanti. My feet were so swollen I could walk no further. We got into the wagon and rode as far as Woodruff's Grove, a little below Ypsilanti. There were some four or five families at this place. The next day we left for Ann Arbor. We were delighted with the country before us; it was beautiful in its natural state, and I have sometimes thought that cultivation has marred its loveliness. Where Ypsilanti now stands, there was but one building—an old trading house on the west side of the river; the situation was fine—there were scattering oaks and no brushwood. Here we met a large number of Indians and one old squaw followed us some distance with her papoose, determined to swap babies. At last she gave it up, and for one I felt relieved.

—*Harriet Noble, in* History of Washtenaw County, *1881*

Fishing under the bridge, Ann Arbor

John Knott

Serious Fishing

CHARLES MORRIS HAS BEEN fishing the Huron River for fifty-five years, since he was six. He can tell you about every good hole and fishing place from Barton Pond to Belleville Lake, with the kind of affectionate detail that suggests long and intimate experience. He can tell you about the ones that have changed or disappeared, too, like the sandbar that's harder to get to now because of a wall along the bank, or the large pond that was filled in when the Ypsilanti Ford plant expanded, or the marshes that used to be where the parking lot for the plant is now. He remembers how the big kids used to club spawning carp in the spring in those marshes. If you wonder about eating carp, he'll tell you that it's as good-tasting a fish as you can get out of the river, that it seasons well, and that when it's smoked it can be mistaken for smoked coho salmon.

Huron River Carp

Fillet the fish and take the mud vein out. Use seasoned pepper and garlic pepper. Squeeze a lemon over the slabs. Slice the peel up and put it around the sides. Bake the same way you would salmon.

Morris doesn't plan fishing trips: "If you've got the time, you take off." He might try a favorite hole at 8:30 some summer evening and come back with an eighteen-inch walleye and a sixteen-inch channel catfish caught in the same spot, using the same lure, as he did on one recent outing. Since he has always lived within walking distance of the river (in Ypsilanti) and keeps a couple of rods "loaded," spur-of-the-moment fishing is no problem. He uses waders, and sometimes a canoe, to get into places he couldn't otherwise and sneak up on a few bass. He fishes a lot in his fourteen-foot wood and canvas rowboat, now sixty years old, and has a bigger boat that he can use to fish the Detroit River with his father-in-law. Morris likes fishing the cuts that go back into the marshes on Walpole Island and will spend several days with friends catching and cleaning fish there, but he finds all the fish he can eat in the Huron: "You can catch everything you want just below Peninsula Dam." Sometimes fishing the Huron is "almost too easy," he says.

Charles Morris

Morris knows the fishing scene up and down the river around Ann Arbor and Ypsilanti and can tell you what you can expect to find at just about any time and place, not only the fish but the people. Fishing for crappie off Barton Dam in the spring, he says, you practically have to make reservations. If you leave your spot for a minute, you lose it. Every fall along the river he sees some of the same regulars who come out from East Detroit or Lincoln Park or Livonia to fish for walleye in Ann Arbor. If there are too many people trying to fish the same ledge, they just cast in rotation. They get along because they know how to fish, according to Morris. He now sees kids fishing the same holes he did when he was their age. Sometimes older "kids," in their twenties and thirties, watch him fish a hole to see if the fish are biting. They call him "the jig man," because he likes to fish with jigs. He will fish in the winter near the dams, where the river doesn't freeze, and has caught walleye on Christmas Eve and given them to friends for Christmas dinner.

Walleye

Cook walleye any way you want. To fry, put fillets in a bowl with Drake's batter mix, add seasoning, and pour in some good Canadian beer. The best way to eat it is to start with the "cheeks and chins." The cheeks are the round pieces behind the eyes; the chin is the triangular piece behind the gill plate (where the fish's chin would be if it had one).

Morris knows what to do with the various kinds of fish he catches in the river, including Northern pike, a notoriously bony fish that he claims to be able to debone. He tells a story about the time a friend suggested a fish fry, and he said, "Give me two hours." He went to his favorite sandbar and caught four carp on dough balls in the first half hour, then spent the next hour and a half cutting them up and cooking them, for four couples. He and his friends and family obviously know how to eat well, and they enjoy some dishes many of us would not recognize as part of the local cuisine, like turtle gumbo, made with snapping turtle meat.

Turtle Gumbo

Always use snapping turtle. Chop up bell pepper, green onion (maybe yellow), and garlic. Add tomato sauce and a couple of bay leaves. Add okra (or corn cut in two-inch rounds), canned tomatoes and a couple of fresh ones. You can season the meat and batter fry it just enough to seal it, then add it to the pot. Cook it until the meat starts falling off the bone.

According to Morris, a friend from Louisiana makes spaghetti sauce with turtle meat, so hot that you can hardly eat it and so good that you can't stop.

Fishing is so natural and habitual for Charles Morris that he talks about it easily, with a ready supply of metaphors. He describes fishing the holes along the Huron as like going shopping. If you don't find what you want at one store, you just go on to the next one. He tells friends that he shows where to fish: "I took you to the market. You do your own shopping." Years of watching people fish have made him a shrewd judge of human nature. He talks about three kinds of fishermen: people who go out and hope something will come by, people who know something ought to come by, and people who don't care whether something comes by or not. They just want to get out of the house. You can usually find Charles Morris at the front desk of the Ann Arbor Public Library, bantering with patrons while he checks out their books. If you ask him about the river, you'll get some stories.

KEITH TAYLOR

Floating over the Lines

As soon as we put our canoe into the river below the Dixboro Dam, my family and I notice the difference. Other than a couple of elderly African American men fishing the rapids, there is no one here. On a warm Sunday in June like this one, it seems as if a canoe passes us at least once a minute on the stretch of river between Portage Lake and the east end of Ann Arbor. A good deal of the riverbank along that stretch is protected, and many of the people who live there think of the river in terms of recreation.

Suddenly things have changed, as if we have followed the river across one of those real but invisible lines that divide our watershed as they divide our country. There are no canoe liveries that help people paddle to and through Ypsilanti, and the access here is more difficult. But there seems to be a different attitude toward this part of the river. Some of this may be aesthetic. The first big landmark after the dam is the Ann Arbor water treatment plant at the point where Fleming Creek comes down from the Botanical Gardens and Radrick Fen. The water treatment plant stinks. Apparently it is a very good one, and Ann Arbor is certainly not the first community on the river to use it this way, but it is hard to think of the water the same way after smelling the plant. All the way to Lake Erie, even past creeks that we know leak industrial toxins into the system, we can't forget the Ann Arbor Waste Water Treatment Plant.

But we paddle on. There are some lovely houses on Superior Pond, and the people who live in them certainly think about the river. We know this, but we don't see any of them on this Sunday. We share the whole stretch of the river with a large flock of turkey vultures and, just a mile east of Ann Arbor, one bald eagle. The river seems surprisingly wild and forgotten, all the way to the old Peninsula Paper dam just below the campus of Eastern Michigan University. There the big sign rising above a burned out power plant is gothic and picturesque, looking haunted above the shimmer of the dam.

After that portage, the river pushes us quickly through downtown Ypsi-

lanti. When we drift past the strollers in the parks, they seem almost surprised to see canoeists on the river.

"Where did you come from?" they call.

"Ann Arbor."

"How will you get back?" And we have gone too far to yell back the explanations.

South of Michigan Avenue in Ypsi, we cross another boundary. The river is quiet. Two fishermen in hip waders pull in their lines to let us past.

"What are you trying for?" I ask, as we try to float carefully over their lines.

"Smallmouth," the older one says.

"Anything that bites," says his friend.

Otherwise there is no one around. We see the backs of buildings and chain-link fences. There are old machines and chunks of concrete in the river.

"It looks abused and forgotten here," my wife says. And for a short distance there is an eerie quietness: no birdsong, no traffic noises, no conversation between fishermen, no children playing.

But just a bit farther to the south, some kids, maybe ten or eleven years old, have found their way over or through the fences and have built their forts just up from the water. They peer out at us, and we pretend not to see them.

Closer to the Ford plant and I-94, more fishermen are out, even though this is one of the most industrial sections of the entire 125-mile riverbank. The river, sluggish and dirty, runs between metal pilings and cement embankments until we pass under the low bridge beneath the interstate—the semis and endless cars moving just above our heads at 75 miles per hour—and out into Ford Lake.

Abruptly, things change again, even though we can still hear the traffic behind us. We hug the shore, heading around the large bays toward the condo developments that line the east shore. We try to face into the wake kicked up by the speed boats and the Jet Skis. Now the river has become a lake, and the people who live here obviously think intensely about their lake. Their windows all face it, and their boats line the docks below the developments. Ford Lake is their pleasure and their recreation.

And some of their boats get perilously close to us before they realize what we are. In our canoe, we make sure our life jackets are tight. We paddle grimly forward.

KEITH TAYLOR

Contradictions

IT WAS A CLEAR DAY in July after the second heat wave of the summer had broken. The humidity was low, and the temperature never went above eighty. The sky was crystalline blue, and what clouds there were stepped away in O'Keefe-like series. We were putting our canoe in just below Interstate 94, in Wayne County. Despite the three large metroparks we were going to float through, the Huron here felt very much like a city river.

In the downriver metroparks—Lower Huron, Willow, and Oakwoods—the river runs deep and fairly straight toward Lake Erie. In the nineteenth century, before the dam was built at Flat Rock, boats came up the Huron from the big lake as far as French Landing, just east of the village of Belleville. Some southern species of tree, butterfly, and bird are found along this lower stretch of the river that are found nowhere else in the state.

The riverbanks are lush and thick with trees, broken occasionally by the few areas of private property or by the metropark golf courses. Just after we started out, a woman with a three-iron yelled down to us, "Can you stop and find my ball? It's somewhere in the middle, about where you are." It was a few seconds before I realized she was kidding.

The river is dirty here, silty and smelly. Pete and I tried to tell ourselves that this part of the river, flowing through the clay of the prehistoric lake bed, would have always been brown. Since so much of the lower Huron is marshy, we argued that it would have always smelled of decaying vegetation. But despite our best efforts, we knew too much about cities, development, and industry upstream to convince ourselves. I felt an odd reluctance to get my hands wet.

For the first two or three hours we had an easy paddle. The river was full and fast, carrying us quickly toward Flat Rock, but it slowed down as it widened in Oakwoods Metropark. The last part was quiet and marshy. But early on, when we still had to pay attention to the rocks and the riffles, we were directly under the approach pattern of the airplanes landing at Detroit Metropolitan Airport.

Every thirty seconds or so, a DC10 or Boeing 737 (once even a gigantic 747 arriving from Europe or Japan) came right over us, certainly not as close as they seemed but nonetheless casting large shadows across the river like the science-fiction image of an invading fleet of alien ships. Their roar drowned out all the sounds of the river and our attempts at conversation. After just a few planes, my ears felt stuffed or covered by earmuffs, as if I had been at a rock concert.

Pete and I stopped to watch a wood duck shepherd seven tiny ducklings, barely two inches long, away from us. The little birds were panicked by the canoe and skittled along the edge, peeping loudly. When a plane came over almost deafening us, the ducklings didn't seem to notice.

"I wonder if they hear the planes," I said, once the roar had died away toward Metro Airport.

"Maybe," Pete said, "but they seem much more worried about us."

It was not until 1925 that the Edison Company built the French Landing Plant creating a lake through Belleville to Rawsonville . . . following 1925, the Edison Company began selling its rights. A purchaser who came into the market was Henry Ford. He bought the rights at Rawsonville and built that dam in 1930. Mr. Ford had novel plans in connection with water powers. His small plants were to be assembly centers for workmen who would devote a part of their time to farming small plots of adjacent land. He bought the rights on Mill Creek at Dexter, [and] the dam at Sharon and rebuilt it; also dams at Manchester, and Saline, and Milan, and at Brooklyn in Jackson County, and Dundee in Monroe County.

—Louis E. Ayres, "Uses of Washtenaw County Streams," 1949

STEPHEN LEGGETT

Starting from a River

Time folds forward on itself. *Mammut.* Three of them.
They cross from a forest of tamarack and spruce and move
slowly down into a meadow, a deep yellow in the distance,
and across it toward the lower woods where the clear pools
wait. The sky is the darkening gray of time building, and the
rightward edge of the meadow is spongy and gives a little
as they cross it. They slip into the trees where the snow
still lingers, melting into clear pools. Here is a watery world,
time layering beneath the cool cathedral of trees, beneath
the gray of time building above it. Two fast flying birds
cross over, fleeing the storm front. Water seeps from the earth.
The clouds darken. Time is a pool that seems never to
diminish. Time folds forward. *Mammut.* Three of them.
The world glistens in the spring melt. The forest is thick
with haze and fog. The old paths to the river are watery.

The Drowning of
the Rhea

I heard it on the radio.
Somebody lost a rhea.

We're used to things being slightly
out of place: nails in the road,
barbed wire around swimming holes,
cars rusting deep in the woods,
milk cartons and toilet paper
hanging like fruit in the trees . . .

Now it seems we have a lost rhea
to ponder, last seen in a cornfield
just south of Willis Road. You can't

miss it: a large flightless bird the size
of a collie. Poor lost soul.

What on God's good earth
is a five foot flightless bird
from the plains of Argentina
doing running loose in Wayne
County some forty minutes drive
from the Windsor Tunnel?

We want the story to end
but we don't want the story
to end. The Great Lost Rhea.

Do rheas like corn? Driving
home I imagined dark shapes
moving along the corn rows,
peering over fences in the moonlight.

I admit it. I want to see
a rhea in the headlights.
I admit it. I kept my eye out.

Imagine the two fishermen
who found it just east of the
Rawsonville Bridge, a rhea washed
ashore, a tangled, fish-eaten mat
of feathers whose bright eye
can't catch the morning light.

Imagine what the river
brings each day . . .

Fishing from the dam

[When one of the local boys, Ed Clarke, saw a sturgeon in shallow water he leaped in] and succeeded in getting astride the big fish and after a good tussel got his hands in the gills. It was for some time a wonder with the spectators on shore to know which would come out best in the rough and tumble fight till finally when both were nearly tired out the fish was landed safely. The sturgeon measured over six feet and the adventure was the principal topic of conversation in the village for several days. A week or two later the New York pictorial papers had fine illustrations of young Clarke astride the fish.

—Freeland Garretson, on the early days of Flat Rock

Under a promise of protection, Cadillac, in 1701, persuaded the Hurons to settle near Fort Ponchatrain in Detroit. From this time on they are called "Wyandots," their name for themselves, which means "islanders.". . . During the 1700's they occupied many small village sites on both sides of the Detroit River. Treaties with the United States in 1789, 1808, and 1818 resulted in the eventual consolidation of the villages onto two reservations, one in Sandusky, Ohio, and a 4,996 acre tract straddling the Huron River in Huron Township, Wayne County, Michigan. . . . By the early 1840's the Wyandot were once again considered to be in the way of "progress." The Treaty of Upper Sandusky was negotiated, resulting in the moving of the Wyandot tribes in Michigan and Ohio to reservation lands west of the Mississippi River. A monument commemorating "the last reservation of the Wyandot tribe of Indians in Michigan" was erected in 1926 by the Wayne County Board of Park Trustees. The tepee shaped marker can be seen today in a small park on the Huron River west of Willow Road.

—Robert Wittersheim, supervising naturalist, Oakwoods Metropark

GERALD P. WYKES

Clamming on
the Huron

BY THE TIME DON WOODRUFF began to ply his trade along
the Huron River in the late 1920s and early 1930s the object of his search was
already on the decline. Don was one of a select few who once gathered fresh-
water mussel shells for the pearl button industry and one of the last surviv-
ing Huron Rivermen known as "clammers."

A stained 1932 "License to Take Mussels" (No. 359) and a few small jars
of rough looking pearls are the only physical evidence of Don's activities as
a clammer. "I didn't do very well that year," he confesses. He once worked
the river from Flat Rock to Rockwood in waders as he handpicked living
clams from the bottom. He would steam out the meat, feel them out for
pearls, and save the cleaned shells for a buyer who would come through each
fall and load up a train car at Flat Rock. Although the buyers came seeking
shells, which were rendered into exquisite buttons, they also had an eye out
for pearls. Don never sold any of his misshapen pearls, but he recalls that
there was plenty of incentive to search for them nonetheless. "One fellow
found a pearl the size of a cherry pit near Flat Rock," said Don. "It sold for
$1,200."

The Huron River was one of a half dozen rivers in southern Michigan
which produced enough freshwater mussels, or clams, to nurture a
significant but brief industry in the early 1900s. The concept of making but-
tons out of the pearly white shells of freshwater clams (marine shells have
long been used by button makers) was spawned by J. F. Boepple, a German
immigrant. Boepple came to Muscatine, Iowa, and set up a button factory
along the Mississippi River in 1891 based upon the abundant shells available
there. The idea soon spread throughout the Midwest and was a full-fledged
industry by the turn of the century.

As the local mussel population was depleted, outlying sources were
sought. The clammers came to western Michigan by 1908 and established

Fox River Clammers—
from an old photo depicting crew
working with Jim Kerr's dad
Coleman, Ill.

detail of "mule"

Clammers

several button factories along the Grand and St. Joseph Rivers and sought further raw material in the Kalamazoo, Maple, Muskegon, River Raisin and the Huron.

The idea was simple enough. The clammer gathered the mussels from the river bottom by hand, rake, tong, or crowfoot bars. The crowfoot bar was the preferred method. The bar itself was 1-inch iron gas pipe, 12 to 20 feet long, from which were suspended dozens of four-pronged crowfoot hooks. The hooks were dragged along the bottom from a flat-bottom "john boat." Upon contact with a living clam, the clam instinctively clamped down fast on the prong. The bar was lifted to the surface, and the tenaciously clinging clams were removed. The cleaned clamshells were brought to the factory and button blanks cut out with a hollow drill. The blanks were finished off, sewn to cards, and marketed in various sizes.

The Huron River never produced a tremendous quantity of clams and consistently ranked sixth among the Michigan streams in numbers. Thick-shelled commercial species with colorful names like Hickory Nut, Pimple-back, Maple-leaf, Pigtoe, Three Ridge, Mucket, Pocketbook, and Black Sand Shell were present in sufficient quantities to support a few part-time clammers. The Mucket was the largest and most prevalent species. According to a 1913 Bureau of Fisheries report, listing the Huron and River Raisin jointly, 16 people were engaged in the activity. They netted 51 tons of shells worth $1,506 (at $19 per ton).

A significant part of that number was harvested from the lower stretches of the river by the Tures and Smith families, who lived across the river from each other. Mr. Jim Kerr, a descendant of the Tures family, still lives in the old homestead and has a set of huge scissor-like tongs, with 6-foot handles, and a few crowfoot hooks left from his grandparents. (The descendants of Owen Smith have a set of identical tongs which sports 12-foot handles!).

"Grandma" Tures wrote a series of letters to her daughter Irlene in July of 1918. "Last week dad had a little time so he and I flew at the claming [*sic*]," she states. "We set out to make over a pile of shell 3 tons and I guess we did all right but we were dead tired every night. We had a buyer here Sunday and he offered us 60 dollars a ton for them. [He] wants us to save all for him . . . if he gives $60 maby [*sic*] someone else will give more." Later on she writes, "Dad and I cleaned all forenoon got about 7 hundrid [*sic*] right along here by the house. I did not think there would be so many left after all it has bin clamed [*sic*]."

Mrs. Tures later commented in a June 1920 letter that "Henry Ford . . . will build a factory and within a year he will employ 3 to 19 hundred men . . . he intends to raise the dam five feet . . ." That dam, completed in 1924, would completely change the face of the lower Huron River as dams upstream did over the ensuing decades. At French Landing the Detroit Reduction Company had been pouring raw, lethal sewage into the river since the early teens. The clams that survived the harvesting could not cope with the habitat change brought about by these actions.

Don Woodruff ended up working for Mr. Ford and appreciated the opportunity to earn a decent living. The descendants of the last clams he gathered are still present in the river, but their role as button material has been supplanted by plastic.

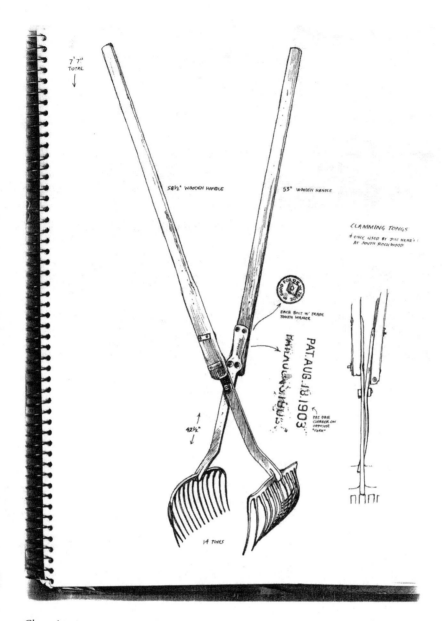

7' 7"
TOTAL

58½" WOODEN HANDLE

53" WOODEN HANDLE

CLAMMING TONGS
+ ONE USED BY JIM KERR'S
AT SOUTH ROCKWOOD

EACH BOLT W/ TRADE
TOKEN WASHER

PAT AUG 18 1903

PAT DATE
CLEARER ON
OPPOSITE
"FORK"

42½"

14 TINES

Clamming tongs

Park and dam at Flat Rock

John Strong built various mills near the Chapman Road crossing (Dixie Highway), starting in 1863. It wasn't long before steam barges loaded with apples, cordwood, lumber, and mixed freight plied the Huron River. Traveling at six miles an hour they sailed from Strong's Landing, at the bridge, to Detroit and Toledo. The Alice Strong, the Cora Strong, the Mayflower, and the Ida Burton sailed their way past the swing-bridge at the railroad in South Rockwood and on through the new swing-bridge at the Military Road. Excursion rides were given on the Alice Strong during the summer months, and there were "moonlights" on the Ida Burton, with a fiddler playing for dancing on the deck.

Patricia Quick, in Histories along the River, *Huron River Watershed Council, 1993*

MACKLIN SMITH

Pointe Mouillée

ONE SUMMER MORNING as I was walking my birding loop out and around Mouillée, having seen impressive numbers of short-billed dowitchers and lesser yellowlegs and many other shorebird species (even a rare avocet), I looked down at the gravel roadbed I was on and realized that I shouldn't be here. It wasn't the humidity, or the biting insects, or my guilt at wasting yet more time birding. It was the sense that but for the grace of man I couldn't be here—except in a flat-bottomed canoe. The shorebirds possibly wouldn't be here either, although they might be, depending on the natural fluctuation of the Lake Erie water level.

It's odd how easy it is to ignore how we have altered what we call Nature. I cross the Huron River in Ann Arbor via the Broadway Bridge to buy supplies for cooking Indian food, and if my mind is focused on a particular recipe or the samosa-to-go that I might order, I don't know that I am crossing the river. Alternatively, when I am at Pointe Mouillée I forget that I'm walking a road system. I think I am in a marsh. Which I sort of am.

A SOFT, WET POINT

Unlike Lake Erie's more conspicuously pointed points—Point Pelee, Long Point, Presque Isle, and Cedar Point—Pointe Mouillée lacks a history either of glacial scouring or of swirling lake currents, although it has been badly storm battered over the last century. Its name in French (still pronounced MOO-YAY) means something like "soft wet point," referring accurately to the vast muddy cattail marsh it once was, interspersed with shallow open ponds, generally called "soft water."

Pointe Mouillée marks the delta of the Huron River. The delta is skewed to the south, its right bank extending an extra four miles, because the Huron enters Lake Erie from the west not far below where the far bigger Detroit River enters from the north. The Huron either enters the Detroit River or it enters Lake Erie. No one has figured out the distinction. In either case, as the Huron carries forth the runoff from its modest watershed, silted now from fertilized farms, forest seepage, and bank erosion, the Detroit brings relatively huge numbers of water molecules—along with other chemicals—from all the northwestern Great Lakes. The Huron River delta, then, is blindsided by the Detroit River at their confluence, leaving a discrepancy between the right and left banks of the Huron.

Although Pointe Mouillée has now been filled and diked, we can still imagine it as a soft wet marsh, washed by both rivers. It used to be called Dead Man's Point by the locals, not because anyone had ever been murdered out there but because drowned bodies occasionally washed up, carried down by either river.

Both the Huron and the Detroit flow into what limnologists call the Western Basin of Lake Erie. The Western Basin is shallow and richly nutrient, unlike the Central Basin, which comprises the great deep part of the lake and is glacially scarred. Ice Age history is more visibly evident in the Portage Escarpment to the immediate south of Lake Erie, from Sandusky to well past Cleveland. The lakeshore there consists of steep bluffs.

Separated from the Central Basin by Point Pelee, Pelee Island, the Bass Islands, and connecting shoals, the Western Basin has little depth and no escarpment. Its shores are flat for miles inland, preserving the contours of "Lake Maumee," the huge prehistoric lake bed left when the last glacier receded. Historically, the entire Western Basin between Detroit and Sandusky was bordered by cattail marshes. These marshes were huge and extended many miles inshore. They teemed with birds, mammals, reptiles, amphibians, insects, and great plant diversity. For the colonists, wild rice was a main attraction. Fish were also extremely plentiful. G. T. Hopkins described catching "upwards of five dozen black bass weighing from four to six pounds" in the Western Basin in 1804. What the early pioneers and missionaries can't have known is that the Western Basin was also the main spawning area and nursery for much of what would become the rich Lake Erie fishery, to include sturgeon, blue pike, lake trout, muskellunge, and lake herring.

From the Huron and its kindred rivers (the Raisin, the Maumee, and the Sandusky) excess silt from agricultural clearing has flowed into the lake as a result of seasonal flooding. The introduction of carp (*Cyprinus carpio*) has destroyed many aquatic plants and contributed as well to the turbidity of the lake. And dredging, diking, and draining most of the marshland for industrial, agricultural, recreational, and even "wildlife" areas have only compounded the problem. It's hard to find clear water in the Western Basin, and the fish know it. More than half of the eighty-eight fish species—including sturgeon, muskellunge, and walleye—have been drastically reduced or extirpated.

For millennia, these rivers contributed their water and soils to the Western Basin. After the retreat of "Lake Maumee," they maintained its shallow, clean-silted character, enabling the profusion of marshes at its edges. Today, almost all of these marshes have been degraded or destroyed, but you can see what it must have looked like, sort of, by driving to Point Pelee and walking on the Marsh Boardwalk Trail. It's a cattail marsh. It's extensive. From the boardwalk, you can hear common yellowthroats and marsh wrens all around you. At Mouillée, these species are less common.

MUSKRATS AND MAYFLIES

Two hundred years ago, the Lake Erie marshes were all but unaltered. The Potawatomi, Wyandot, and Ottawa had hunted the wetlands, spearing muskrat, shooting ducks and geese, and harvesting wild rice. The French did likewise, adding their trapping technology for taking muskrat. Although most later settlers maintained an aversion to this clean-water-loving, vegetarian rodent, some appear to have been persuaded by the dictum of Xavier Francis, an expert French hunter and cook: "You cook it wid onion you shant tole it from duck." Today one can order Rat in Creamed Corn at several restaurants in Monroe, although home-cooked muskrat is usually prepared with onion, catsup, Worcestershire sauce, and salt and pepper to taste. Although I wouldn't recommend it, I've eaten it. The presentation can be startling. The head, traditionally prized for its brain and tongue, is intact. The taste is gamy, with a fish-oil aspect concentrated near the spine, which leads me to wonder if this critter sometimes deviates from its vegetarian diet.

Early in this century, annual muskrat banquets sponsored by the Monroe Yacht Club at Christmas time attracted over eight hundred guests, most served a rat. There were many other feasts, some all male, others mixed. If women were present, an alternate meat would be offered, but all men were expected to eat muskrat—pronounced "mushrat." Legend has it that an archbishop of Detroit sometime in the nineteenth century granted a dispensation allowing the consumption of muskrat on Fridays during Lent. Everyone of French descent in Monroe County believes this or pretends to. Supposedly the rationale was that muskrats, as underwater swimmers, were related to fish. In some homes even today, a mock benediction is offered: "God bless dee mushrat: she's a fish!" Although not all dispensations are documented, the one about eating muskrat on days of abstinence is almost certainly a folktale. It attests both to the persistence of remnant French culture in the Downriver area and the willingness of parish priests to respect local customs. As the *Homiletic and Pastoral Review* (1933) puts it, "even St. Thomas in speaking of the distinction between fish and flesh says that the common estimation of the people and the opinion of medical men should be consulted." Were the archbishop to overrule his mythic predecessor, he would be regarded as an interloper. Still, the archivist at the Detroit Archdiocese assures me that no record of a dispensation for Lenten muskrat exists. Although an archbishop might be more interested in spirituality than science, he would certainly know a mammal from a fish.

Muskrat populations have declined in the Lake Erie marshes, mostly through habitat loss. Ironically, muskrats at Pointe Mouillée currently fare quite well when water levels rise above optimum levels for "waterfowl management"—but then they destroy vegetation needed by ducks. The number of currently licensed trappers is half the fingers on my right hand, and these men, although skilled and willing, are constrained, for example, by the value of the Russian ruble.

Less culturally significant than the muskrat, but still remembered, are the ephemeral mayflies. Their story more graphically illustrates marsh degradation. Mayflies (*Hexagenia bilineata*) depend on clean water, and they constitute a key part of small fish diet. They used to be superabundant in the Lake Erie marshes. They spend almost all their life cycle as larvae, but when nearly mature they come out of the water in subimago form, experience a final metamorphosis, and then breed and die in a day. The mayfly swarms were legendary. In 1953, the population crashed, so that by 1961 the mayflies numbered less than 1 percent of their population in 1930. Subsequent efforts to restore this species have largely failed. It doesn't take much to imagine the consequences.

Why did the mayfly population crash? Why are muskrat populations down overall? Why are many species of fish depleted or extirpated? Because of industrial and agricultural pollution, the increasingly turgid water quality from agricultural runoff, and the loss of marsh habitat. However, degradation of Lake Erie has proven in part reversible. Although the vast cattail marshes will never be restored, and although agricultural silt will continue to cloud the lake, great progress has been made during the past two decades in reducing chemical pollutants. In recent years we have seen modest mayfly swarms. The walleye population is up. Charter boat captains are doing a good business. Colonies of fish-eating double-crested cormorants have increased dramatically, to the chagrin of some fishermen.

WHAT HAPPENED?

Most other habitat destruction in Michigan, especially the almost total deforestation in the nineteenth century, was pursued urgently as a capitalist enterprise. The timber harvest was immediately lucrative and then sometimes yielded up valuable farmland. Comparatively, there's not much money in a marsh—unless it is drained and developed.

Consumers Power Company filled in a significant area of shoreline just north of the Ohio border in order to construct the Erie Power Plant. In the 1940s, the Ford Motor Company cleared the Monroe harbor and adjacent shores of marshland in the interest of its industrial expansion. By 1956, another swath of marshland had been filled to enable the construction of the Fermi II Plant. Finally, the Detroit Metroparks system, favoring beaches over marshes, converted some wetland into parking lots. At present, the only extensive marshes in the Western Basin are former gun clubs: Mouillée and the Erie Preserve.

The marshland at Pointe Mouillée meanwhile deteriorated. By the late 1940s, high water levels and a series of major storms had obliterated the barrier island that had headquartered the Pointe Mouillée Shooting Club, and the marsh to the east had become largely submerged—no good for hunting dabbling ducks. The club disbanded, selling its assets to the state. By the 1960s, the expansion of Great Lakes shipping and enlargement of the freighters necessitated the dredging of the Detroit River. Where to deposit the sludge? Pointe Mouillée.

Rather than wait for lake levels to decline, and rather than accept lake fluctuation—and erratic hunting opportunities—as a norm, the Department of Natural Resources agreed to use the Detroit River fill to rebuild the barrier island (now known as the Banana), to dike the perimeter of the marsh, and to subdivide it into impoundments. By means of pumping stations, the water level in each impoundment could be controlled at optimum level for various uses. For example, water could be drained completely in midsummer—a drawdown—allowing either for natural reseeding or for cultivation of grasses and reeds. The entire area, theoretically, could be maintained as a fifty-fifty marsh: half open water, half cattails and other vegetation. After a drawdown, an impoundment could be refilled with lake water at just the right level for the dabbling ducks, and this could be timed for the start of hunting season. Meanwhile, certain impoundments could be maintained as dry cropland, with corn planted for the geese.

The Michigan Department of Natural Resources has managed Pointe Mouillée as a state game area since 1945, gradually adding to the 2,600+ acres purchased from the Pointe Mouillée Shooting Club an additional 1,200 acres of marsh and upland. In 1963, 365 acres were diked during a period of low water, but by 1972 much of the marsh had again been destroyed due to storms and high water levels. Enter the U.S. Army Corps of Engineers. As they state on their web site,

> The Pointe Mouillée Confined Facility is a 700-acre crescent-shaped dike designed to contain contaminated dredged material from the Detroit and

Rouge Rivers. . . . [Its] primary purpose is to contain 18 million cubic yards of contaminated dredged material that will be removed from the existing navigation channels . . . which carry a large volume of waterborne cargo, requir[ing] periodic dredging to maintain the depths necessary for ship traffic.

By the 1980s, the Army Corps of Engineers had also reclaimed 1,900 acres of marsh by construction of 10,000+ lineal feet of dikes. After that, it was a matter of pumping water, replanting, and drawing down, to be carried out by the Department of Natural Resources.

On paper, "waterfowl management" seems like a great idea, and it may well prove workable. The new, optimistic term is marsh "emulation," not "reclamation." We'll see. Until recently, state funding has declined, making the cost of drawdowns in some years prohibitive (even with generous contributions of local hunting groups, especially the Michigan Duck Hunters' Tournament Committee). More state funding may be in the offing. It should be. If water levels remain too high, the plants cannot reseed themselves, and neither the waterfowl nor the shorebirds will have feeding resources. If water levels remain too low, alien species can take over, as they have. The cattails are gone. In their place we have phragmites, an utterly sterile reed that supports no native species; and we have purple loosestrife, whose beauty belies its capacity for degrading an ecosystem by crowding out native plants.

THE GOLDEN AGE OF HUNTING

Most prior alteration of the marshland, relatively benign, was done by the gun clubs, some as early as the mid–nineteenth century. These clubs were corporations with very restricted membership, and they held the best hunting land on Lake Erie. Hunting also occurred on marsh tracts owned by individual families, but sportsmen who belonged to a gun club had the advantage of punts (flat-bottomed canoes) at the ready, personally assigned punters, a marsh maintenance crew, individually owned cabins, and a clubhouse offering lounging areas and cooked meals. The Pointe Mouillée Shooting Club was located on a barrier island some four miles from the shore. It overlooked both Lake Erie and the vast marshes between the island and mainland. Alteration of the marsh was minimal: annual clearing of wild rice in some areas and the construction of one long channel between the club and the mouth of the Huron River. Most shooting occurred in the fall, but some went on in the spring. When water levels were high, access from shore to club was easy; when low, members sometimes had to resort to the use of "mud-skis." The club focus was on dabbling ducks, not bay ducks. This meant traversing shallow water, poling through the reeds. Some punts were equipped with built-in blinds at the bow, but members would ordinarily be punted out to a favorite blind already set up in the marsh.

The marsh also provided good habitat for shorebirds, rails, bitterns, and songbirds—no matter where the lake level stood—for the terrain was subtly varied in depth and in vegetation zones. Although the club members were duck hunters, they also would shoot, spear, or hook other prey—but they only kept records of ducks. On September 14, 1899, the height of duck season, one of the members, Alex Gunn, made this comment in the *Record Book:*

> Item:—It is to be regretted that only a record of ducks is kept here. The ducks are very well, but silence broods over Sora Rails or Ortolan, and snipe, plover, reed birds, frogs, and fish. Today there came to the larder from the marsh: 85 Sora Rail, 7 yellow leg Plover, 6 mud hens, and 15 perch. Brittet Savoriu alone could describe the superlative delicacy of these Ortolans here this month—they are the last refinements of human food—the fragrance exhaled when on the fire brings tears of expectant enjoyment to the direct eye. . . . The delicate crisp perch left nothing to be desired of fish. I will not attempt to speak of all the beauty of the marsh. At sunset the glassy water turns to bright gold, as if the sand of Pactolus lay beneath. So all these things and more are here always, but not a matter of record. Look out for those people who are marked "did not shoot." They may get the biggest bag after all.

A pleasant sentiment. Mr. Gunn did not shoot every day, but he clearly appreciated those culinary and aesthetic gifts of the marsh beyond dabblers. Today, the perch and frogs are still legal. Most hunters would never dream of taking a coot (mud hen), legal or illegal—a French taste like muskrat, requiring onions. Migratory shorebirds are illegal. I go to Mouillée for the shorebirds. Not that I have anything against ducks, but as a birder I am not allowed for good reason to walk the dikes during the hunting season.

BIRDING POINTE MOUILLÉE

Birders like me imagine Mouillée as a birding area. We really know that it's a reclaimed state-run gun club. In years when rainfall is below average, some very good expanses of mudflat habitat may be sustained for shorebirds, but one senses that this is not a high priority. There is always some area for shorebirds at Mouillée; however, many of the impoundments are flooded all summer in preparation for ducks. In years with no drawdown, shorebird enthusiasts may as well try other areas, but one can always go out to Mouillée to enjoy hundreds of great blue herons and great egrets, a few caspian terns, and even white pelicans.

It takes fifty minutes to drive from Ann Arbor to Mouillée, and I experience little nostalgia. I don't imagine that I was a member of the Shooting Club in any past life. Here we are, after all. I've got my cup of road coffee, a sandwich, some bottled water, my spotting scope, my binoculars, a bird book, maybe my dog, Sadie, and plenty of memories. I know what I'll see, I know what I might see, and I can fantasize about what I've never seen—a large-billed tern. Right. I pull into the small lot next to an industrial yellow crossing gate, grab my gear, and walk on out. The sun's still orange and the air still cool. The only landmark is the Fermi cooling tower, looming to the south.

If Sadie is along, it's okay. Birders as a rule hate dogs, forgetting that hunters have always used dogs not only to retrieve ducks but to spot and flush rails. Sadie's life list is rather extensive for a town dog, but she never bothers the wildlife much. Although she's a beagle/lab mix, she disdains water and has never swum a stroke, so she just walks and runs the dikes, like me. Her favorite thing about Mouillée is rolling on dead carp. After I take a shorebirding trip with her, the Dog-O-Mat can count on my business.

I typically walk the long dike along the Huron River out to the Banana and then circle back around, taking one of several cross dikes to return to my car. For the first half mile, it's mostly plantings for geese in the Nelson Unit south of the dike, no birds to speak of, but the north side is riverbank, now altered with gravel fill but still interesting. Least sandpipers commonly feed among the rocks in July and August, and there will be herring and ring-billed gulls aloft, as well as caspian terns, flashing their thick red bills. Not too far out is a small remnant natural point to the north, mostly flooded and filled with old logs, where one or two immature black-crowned night herons inevitably will be hunched at dawn.

In the Long Pond Unit to the southeast, flocks of herons and egrets will be feeding and taking wing, maybe an American bittern, and some shorebirds: plovers and peeps on the flats, greater and lesser yellowlegs in the shallows. Many visual treats here and also the stimulating squarks and rhrnxes of larger marsh birds, the pit-pit-pits of the yellowlegs, and much much more. The air smells heavy, rank with mud, vegetation, dead carp, and unknown chemicals.

Out almost two miles, the best birding is in the Vermet Unit, west of the Banana. It's a huge impoundment, and if flats are present it will host hundreds of short-billed dowitchers in July, returning from their tundra breeding habitat, as well as numerous greater and lesser yellowlegs. In August, the long-billed dowitchers arrive, joined perhaps by red knots, phalaropes, godwits, and Baird's and white-rumped sandpipers, as well as rarer species. Aside from avocets and willets, I have twice seen curlew sandpipers in this area—a major rarity anywhere in the United States.

By now the temperature will be climbing close to the humidity level, and the best habitat is past. I walk slower, admiring the dragonflies. I eat my sandwich, drink water steadily, and look around from time to time. Black-bellied plovers calling somewhere. My scope is beginning to weigh on my shoulder. By now it's mostly phragmites and loosestrife. I focus on my car, a mile away.

OBSESSION AND PLEASURE

People typically watch birds either with intent to kill and eat them or with delight, respect, and even worship. These impulses are perfectly compatible, historically and psychologically. Now that almost none of us need to hunt for subsistence, we tend to watch birds for pleasure. We put up our feeders, stop at the local pond to look at the ducks, want to see an eagle, or thrill to the dawn flights of white ibis in the Everglades. Sheer pleasure. It also calms the frontal lobe.

But the hunting impulse continues, not only among sportsmen and sportswomen but with some birders. I should know. I am a collector of birds, and I put my sightings in the *Record Book* (of the American Birding Association). As of this writing, I have seen more bird species in North America than anyone else, 851. In order to accomplish this strange feat I have sometimes flown off to chase rare birds with my frequent flyer miles and have spent more than a year of my life on Attu Island, Alaska. Birding at this level is a psychological disease, I'm sure, but I like where it takes me. I like the sense of possibility, the actuality of seeing a new bird (a "lifer"), and the sustained present moment of simply looking, seeing, and remembering. In 1991 I did a Shorebird Big Year, managing to see 86 species of shorebirds that year—a record—and during the summer I spent many days at Mouillée, recording:

American avocet
Semipalmated plover
Killdeer
Black-bellied plover
American golden plover
Marbled godwit
Hudsonian godwit
Willet
Greater yellowlegs
Lesser yellowlegs

Spotted sandpiper
Wilson's phalarope
Short-billed dowitcher
Long-billed dowitcher
Stilt sandpiper
Common snipe
Red knot
Dunlin
Sanderling
Curlew sandpiper
Semipalmated sandpiper
Western sandpiper
Least sandpiper
White-rumped sandpiper
Baird's sandpiper
Pectoral sandpiper

None of these was a life bird. Most could have been seen just as easily elsewhere. But it was a great summer for shorebirds at Mouillée, with a complete drawdown in the Vermet Unit. I was out there so often that I got the odd sense that I was reconnecting with individual birds; maybe . . . but certainly with particular flocks. That little group of lesser yellowlegs would be in the same shallow spot day after day, their number gradually increasing. Three red knots continued for ten days, then abruptly departed.

How to explain my love of the birds and my love of the experience of them? How to explain the sweet juncture of obsession and pleasure? Here is a poem I wrote to try to understand it.

A Mystery
Beyond that indigo. Beyond the power
Of the Peregrine, the Gyr. Beyond

The difficulty and accomplishment
In finding them: the night-walking,
Miles of listening in spartina marsh
The first full moon of summer
To find Black Rails. To do this as if
In combat, half-mystified
For years. Then to see one.

They prepossess us with their otherness,
Whether planned as ritual dawn observance
Or as astonishing as Arizona hailstorms—
It rests in them, beyond our effort

Reaching them: the otherness
Of wings and nest-weaving, the grace
That holds them hidden, still
So easily mortal.

They live beyond our circle of desire,
A thrush, horizon-braiding shearwaters,
A crane in mist, red eyeshine:
Sometimes an unremembered afterimage.
The thing we seek flies elsewhere,
Remains as music, a dark silence,
Becomes water, branches, open sky.

We live alone in us. We look around.
We focus on what often fears us close.
We choose as home an empty unfamiliar.
We learn to know what isn't understood.

THE SHOREBIRDS

A few of them breed in the high Arctic, stop at a place like Pointe Mouillée, and then migrate straight to South America. They may fly as high as twenty-five thousand feet. They need to eat well first, consuming vast quantities of worms and crustaceans and larvae. Some shorebirds breed in the boreal forests and don't migrate so far. Both yellowleg species, which we associate with mudflats here, nest in the tops of spruces. A few shorebirds actually breed in Michigan: killdeer, common snipe, woodcock, upland sandpipers, and piping plovers. They migrate within the United States. As a rule, shorebirds make themselves cryptic, by Darwinian design. Their russets and browns and blacks and tans fit their breeding habitats perfectly, and these colors shift in molt to blend with their transitional situations: shores and mudflats, equally muted, in migration and winter.

The calls of shorebirds, clear whistled or strident, tend to be single or repetitive, on one pitch. Unlike woodland birds, shorebirds mean to be heard across uninterrupted expanses. Shorebirds don't sing melodies. Many of their vocalizations are alarm calls.

At Mouillée or in any other good habitat, shorebirds tend to associate with their own kind. Partly that's due to habitat requirements: the tiny "peeps" congregate on solid mud; the long-legged yellowlegs feed in shallow water; Killdeer specialize in insects, so they are usually found in dry areas, but the dowitchers dig into soft mud like sewing machines. The longer the legs, the deeper the water; the longer the bill, the deeper the reach. Species association is also an aid to safety. Pointe Mouillée is an excellent spot to observe peregrine falcons and merlins, both of which enjoy a partial diet of shorebirds. The shorebirds, however, have an uncanny and instantaneous response to an approaching falcon. While they are feeding in loose association, each bird wanders his or her own way, feeding, feeding, walking, feeding, walking, in a chaos of random individual activity. Yet the flock takes wing like a school of fish, as if one organism, bunching, twisting, turning, veering—and veering fast. The peregrine is faster, but it wants an individual target. The shorebird flock becomes white then dark as it turns again and again in the sunlight. This is amazing for us to see, the dazzling synchronicity of the flock, but it must be disorienting for the peregrine. Was I chasing this one or that one? Oh, never mind. Maybe that mallard over there?

I began birding in graduate school, as a means of coping with the stress of writing my dissertation on *Piers Plowman* and late medieval Lives of Christ. I would walk in the woods with my daughter Amy in her Gerry Carrier and would watch breeding warblers and, once, breeding great horned owls. One of Amy's first words was *pheasant.* It was a relief to get away from the library, and it still is. That's when I became a birder. I started keeping a list of sightings, and then I actually started driving to various places in New Jersey to see birds I hadn't yet seen. That was the beginning of the obsession.

The fascination started much earlier. I remember walking out across the Parker River mudflats with my father, when I was six. This was near Newburyport, Massachusetts. He was studying the ecological relationship between clams and green crabs and would take me with him from time to time out to his study plots. He would dig up square yards of mud, counting and measuring clams and crabs and no doubt doing much else beyond my comprehension. I had my own pail and shovel, to dig my own clams, but since I didn't like clams I always threw them back. The walk across the mudflats was hard going. Step by step, it was sink, pull, sink, pull, sink, pull, sink, pull. It seemed to me that my dad's boots sank a lot deeper than mine, and even though he was bigger and stronger I was thinking that I was lucky that my boots didn't sink so deep. Then I saw the shorebirds. I asked my dad how come they could walk on the mud and we couldn't. He said, "They're lighter, and they have long toes. And wings if they need them."

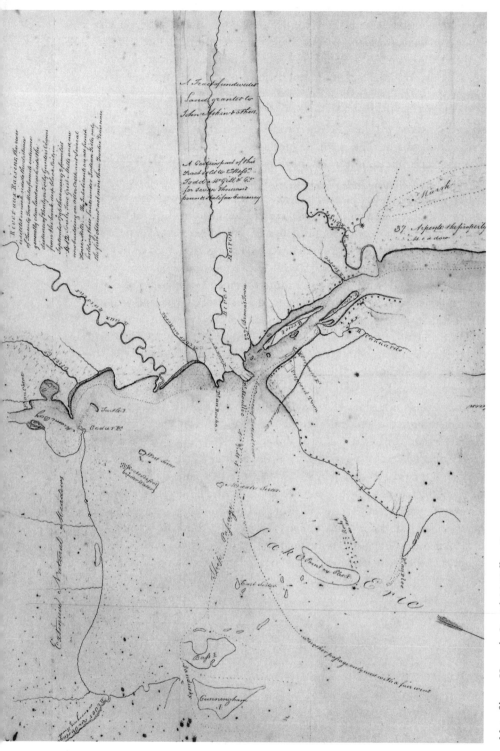

Map of lower Huron by Patrick McNiff, 1796

River Huron is eight miles north of Rocky river, and twelve south of the river Ecorce, and empties itself into the lake Erie, about four miles north [sic] of Detroit or the strait. With respect to soil, there is a great degree of similarity throughout this part of the country, dark, or rather, black, light, and wherever, with few exceptions, it has been cultivated productive.

In these respects none are superior to the lands on this river. They consist of extensive prairies, covered so closely with hazel and other shrubberies, as to afford a pleasant shade to the delighted traveller, who cannot but take an agreeable interest in the beautiful sceneries by which he is surrounded.

The river, though narrow, is navigable twenty miles for boats, and has a deep and gentle current. There is but one claim, which arises under an Indian deed, dated in the year 1794, purporting to be a conveyance to Gabriel Godfroy, of four thousand five hundred acres of land, upon which tract he has placed a tenant, who lives near the river as a ferryman. The deed is signed by one chief only, and that without a witness. To a title the claimant can have no pretensions.

—Report of C. Jouett, Indian agent at Detroit, 1803

The Board took into consideration the claim of Gabriel Godfroy . . . under the date of 29th November, 1805.

This tract is situate on river Huron, of lake Erie, and contains, by estimation, three hundred arpents, it being six arpents in front by fifty in depth, bounded in front by said river Huron, and on every other side by the United States' lands.

Whereupon, Joseph Porlier Benac was brought forth as a witness in behalf of the claimant, who being duly sworn, deposed and said, that, previous to the 1st July, 1796, Jean Batiste Sanscrainte was in possession and occupancy of the premises, and continued so until he sold to the claimant, who has kept on the same a man named Babaud, as a ferryman, and who cultivated about one arpent as a garden; and from that time to this date the claimant has constantly kept a tenant, who has attended the ferry, and has cultivated part of the premises: a house is erected thereon.

And therefore it doth appear to the commissioners that the claimant is entitled to the above described tract of land, and that he have a certificate thereof.

—American State Papers 16 (Public Lands)

A. L. BECKER

Learning to Punt

THIS IS A STORY ABOUT the first time I nearly died, that sharpest memory, and the revival of fainter memories evoked when, in Keith Taylor's canoe, we paddled down the Huron from Flat Rock on a day when the river was thick with walleyes running. I could see them from the bow, just below the surface. We were paddling downstream, on a cold gray Erie day, toward Pointe Mouillée at the mouth of the river. When the rain got heavy, we sheltered under a railway trestle, a mile or so above the place where the Old Dixie Highway crosses the river—once called Godfroy's Ferry: across Hull's Trace, the Military Road, the Turnpike, the Indian Trail down the west end of Lake Erie, a pathway that must be as old as the first people, the paleohunters three millennia ago.

That old, old roadway must be there, partly, because the lake is often just too wild to cross in a canoe and that shoreline path is the shortest way round the west end, to warmer winters.

And because of the marshes—the lake perch, migrating ducks, wild rice, bullfrogs, bulrushes, shelter from storms, and, for a long time, fur of the beaver.

And it was important, too, that the Huron River is part of the canoe route to Lake Michigan and the West, along lakes and creeks often named Portage.

I told Keith a few small fragments of memories about my grandfather's hunting camp on the edge of the marsh at Pointe Mouillée, at the mouth of the river. A freight train going north passed above us and shook down stones. We saw two eagles. He said, write about it.

I don't remember any eagles at all when I was a kid. I do remember duck hawks skimming the tops of the cattails in the early 1940s. I was around ten.

Most of the Pointe Mouillée of the early 1940s is gone now. The marsh has been rebuilt from the dregs of the Detroit River. The storms and the cyclic rising and falling of Erie—the "Panther" in Wendat speech— devoured the marsh, though now it all may be reviving, with a new shoal to protect it—and a toxic aura, some people who live there say. I can not find the spot where my grandfather's camp was. I have tried hard, in a canoe and hip boots, but the old high ground is changed, not just the wetland. The ducks are still there, in clouds, on the spring and fall migrations.

When I was in the fourth grade in Monroe, J. S. Gray, the editor of the *Monroe Evening News,* visited our class and showed us his old maps of Monroe County in the seventeenth and eighteenth centuries. His son, Whitmore, was in the class too. Some of the maps are originals, some large photostats he made of maps in Washington. *Photostat* was a new word, and J. S. Gray printed it out on the blackboard and we copied it. It's one of the few words I can remember when I got.

J. S. Gray took the maps from tubes and rolled them out on the teacher's desk, one by one. He did not tack them to the wall. He held down the curling corners with books. We gathered around. He pointed to Monroe, on the oldest maps named Frenchtown, at the mouth of the River Raisin; the beaches we knew; the Old Dixie Highway; Pt. aux Roche (Stony Point); R. aux Signe (Swan Creek); and R. aux hurons (the Huron River), the northern boundary of Monroe county.

J. S. Gray's maps are still on the walls of the Monroe Historical Society Archives, held up under glass. If you look at them, be sure to ask for J. S. Gray's commentary.

But the oldest map I've seen of the mouth of the Huron is at the Clements Library in Ann Arbor—a copy of a 1731 French map by Henri-Louis Deschamps de Boishebert (1679–1736), and there, among a sparsity of markings, are R. aux hurons and Lapointe Mouiliee. It marks the stockaded village des hurons to the north and, to the south, R. au Signe (Swan Creek). It's a beautiful map, signed like a painting.

The Jesuits had already learned to speak the languages there.

The native people did not call themselves Hurons—they were, by then, Wendat, spelled also *Wyandot* or *Wyandotte.* The word *Huron* is related to Old French *hure* (bristling hair).

The Wendat village near the mouth of the Huron was later called Brownstown, after the village leader, Adam Brown, named in Wendat Tahunehametee, said to have been captured as a child during the French and Indian wars—a white Indian, who spoke English, and he had a foster son, William Walker, later an interpreter in the U.S. Indian Department. There is a long history for the Wendats, early converts of the Blackrobes, said to be the oldest tribe by the other tribes. The Wendat were the skilled translators into and out of the languages of the other tribes—the Ojibway, the Shawnee, the Potawatomi, the Ottawa, and the Iroquois. In that village by the R. aux hurons, the tribes met and became an alliance under the leadership of Tecumseh—on the losing side in the War of 1812.

We learned about the War of 1812 in the eighth grade. We worked all year on our own historical maps crayoned onto rolls of brown butcher paper. Most of local history is the War of 1812.

In the late 1790s, after the treaty of Greenville, when the land was "bought" from the tribes, Peter McNiff made another very engaging map (No. 2 in the J.S. Gray Collection in Monroe). It calls itself "A Rough Sketch of Part of Wayne County Territory of the United States North West of River Ohio 2 Miles to the Inch."

Of the Huron River, above Pointe Mouillée (spelled here *Moullie*), is written: "Navicable for boats upward of 100 miles"—and then there is an odd symbol, a little like two eyes and a nose looking out over a wall—and then, after this odd punctuation, the writing continues:

". . . For large canoes to its source where there is a portage of 6.4 gunter's chains leading into the Grand River that empties into Lake Michigan."

It says, "Deep black soil."

"Timber Ash, Oak, Maple, and black Walnut."

And it says, "The river a very rapid stream, clear sand bottom, never overflows its banks."

Abandoned Indian villages are noted up on the River Saline: "In various places along this branch large quantities of salt are made by the natives."

On later maps the names are translated, and Pointe Mouillée is "Swampy Point." That's the usual translation, but is it right? Mouillée can also mean an "anchorage"—protected water, deep enough behind the shoal for a large boat seeking refuge from one of the storms churned up on the big shallow lake.

From 1810, prior to the War of 1812, there is the French Claims Map, an American map showing the holdings of French families—the Canadians. The river is called here the River Huron of Erie, for there was another Huron River at the south end of Lake Huron, now called the Clinton River. There is one French claim on the River Huron of Erie, the ribbon farm of Gabriel Godfroy, a long narrow strip of land running back a few miles from the river to the high ground. Godfroy owned the ferry.

On July 4, 1812, they say you could see from Brownstown—just about where Keith and I took refuge under the trestle, out over the Pointe Mouillée cattails—the three masts and square sails of the British warship *Queen Charlotte*. It was anchored off the point to observe the men in General Hull's army building a makeshift corduroy bridge over the river, trying to get the guns and the supply wagons quickly up to Fort Detroit.

Some people I know seem never to have heard of the War of 1812. That was unbelievable to a kid from Monroe.

Commodore Oliver Hazard Perry captured the *Queen Charlotte* on September 10, 1813, with his famous big flag on which was written, "Don't Give

Up the Ship." After the victory, he sent his famous message to General William Henry Harrison: "We have met the enemy and they are ours; two ships, two brigs, one schooner and a sloop." That pretty much ended the war. What we have in memory is mainly Pogo's copy change: " . . . and they are us."

My favorite map in the J.S. Gray Collection is the 1814 map by Col. John Anderson. Gray calls it "scrupulously exact." It's big, in two sections. It shows the northwest end of Lake Erie, a perspective from the treacherous waters over which the flow of settlers then began after the War of 1812, on large wooden boats coming from Buffalo and, more slowly, through the swamps and up the Military Road, Hull's Trace, surveyed by using the tall steeple of St Mary's church in Frenchtown as the reference point. It is marked in rich detail, all about the battles along the road.

When I was a lad (I was ten, a "lad" according to the convention of *Boy's Life*), my grandfather leased an old hunting camp from a very old Frenchtown family, the Reaumes, who owned land west of the Pointe Mouillée Shooting Club.

The latter, the Pointe Mouillée Shooting Club, was a refuge for men of great wealth. A local historian wrote: "Besides a punter for each gunner the company employs a head keeper and underkeepers, with a competent chef housekeeper and sufficient servants."

My grandfather was not one of those men, though he surely wanted to be, nor was he one of those who served them or cooked for them. He was a first-generation American in the wave of Scandinavian and German Lutherans who came half a century after the English, several centuries after the French, and all the millennia after the native peoples. He was Aksel, and his friends were Jules and Otto. Aksel had a lumberyard; Jules a bookstore; and Otto a greenhouse, where I worked after school planting thousands of flats of tomatoes for World War II victory gardens. Aksel, Jules, and Otto each brought their sons and their grandsons to the hunting camp. It was a totally male place, dominated by male habits.

Otto "did not shoot," as they put it. He did not have a gun. He cooked and cut firewood and planted apple trees and a pole bean garden, even roses by the door where the spaniels slept. In the greenhouse he was strict with me, but at the hunting camp he was the jokester—small, quick, white hair, talking all the time, half in German, making jokes by putting bullfrogs down your shirt and setting off wild shouting contests. I took it in, that that could be done there. They never spoke of wives, sisters, or any women at all, never joked about sex. Or if they did, it was not in English, and if they swore it was not in English.

One Friday night, after dark, I went bullfrogging with my father and Young Reaume. Like all the marsh people then, like all the places on the landscape, Young Reaume had a French name, but the men just called him Young Reaume. He worked for them and for others who hunted regularly there.

We were in my father's duckboat, one of seven he built weekends in the garage. The lumber was odd-shaped rejects from Aksel's lumberyard. The lad built tree houses with his free boards; the father, who had first choice, built duckboats.

A duckboat is like a canoe with a flat bottom, for moving in very shallow water or over the boggy layers of marsh. This particular one was about fifteen feet long, with a partially decked bow, stern, and sides, pointed at both ends and pushed along with an eight-foot punting oar of ash or maple.

Young Reaume stood up like a gondolier and punted the boat along, pushing against the soft floor of the marsh. My father was sitting in the middle holding a long frog spear, a trident; and I was stretched out over the decking of the bow moving here and there a heavy jacklight—a kerosene lantern with a bulls-eye lens, set in a swiveling iron cradle. Young Reaume was sixteen or so, punting; I was only ten and doing a boy's job, shining the light in the frogs' eyes and holding them dazzled and unmoving until my father could spear them. I liked having a job and being there, but I would rather be punting or spearing. I wearied of shining the frogs, and the hot smell of the jacklight, but my father was stern, and one of the requisite habits for being there was not to complain. Even on his dying day my father said to me, once again, Duck hunters don't complain.

My father tossed the dying speared frogs into a bucket. No one spoke much, so as not to spook the frogs. It comes back, unexpected, that my father wore a tan fedora turned up in front, Young Reaume a black knit wool cap, and I a lined leather pilot's helmet with the ear flaps snapped up over the top. I wore it for the Duration.

I wanted to punt. I wanted to stand up in rubber boots turned down at the top. I wanted to smoke cigarettes like Young Reaume in the center groove of his lower lip while he used both hands to push the punting oar.

When the bucket was full and my arms were shaking from holding the jacklight so long, so uncomplainingly, they punted back to the camp, through the narrow gullies of the dark marsh, walled in on both sides by cattails, bulrushes, and the other thick marsh flora, as dense as a jungle. The smell was thick, too: dead frogs, rotting vegetation, kerosene, fish, mud, and very old water-soaked logs. The sump-pumping sound of the bittern fit the place. I could not believe it was a bird. My father called it shide-poke. Young Reaume said the bittern was good luck for the hunters.

Otto cut the legs off the bullfrogs and fried them in perch batter. I got to drink a small glass of beer and quickly fell asleep so soundly I had to be carried to the double feather bed in the cold room where I lay in my underwear beside my father.

The next day, Saturday, was another wet and gray lake Erie day, a good day for ducks they said, one after the other. I succeeded in begging off from sitting still in a small duck blind with my father and grandfather and uncle and the wet spaniels. I stayed back and followed Otto around, until Young Reaume came up one of the channels in his own punt and nodded that I should come with him. Otto said Yes, Okay, unbidden.

We went through the narrow channels of the marsh and not out into the bay where the men were shooting over their decoys. I was seated in the center, Young Reaume standing in back of me with the long oar. We went in silence. When I spoke out, Where . . . , Young Reaume shook his head and wiggled his cigarette from side to side.

The Gun Club was deserted, the gray-green cabins stove-in by fallen cottonwoods and elms, the porches wrecked by waves. Tree limbs all over everywhere. There was nothing man made that was new and fresh anywhere.

Young Reaume told me his father worked there, before, and so did he, and his grandfather's father owned the high ground out there. Nobody owned the whole marsh, Young Reaume said, as if he expected argument. I knew the tone of voice but not why anyone should own the whole thing.

We were passing along the back of the cabins, the landward side of the barrier island, the shoal at the mouth of the R. aux hurons that protected the marsh. The wrecked cabins faced the open lake that had pounded them in these years like a *Queen Charlotte* broadside. Behind the houses were some small gardens, with poles for beans and tomatoes. And behind each cabin was a wooden boathouse and a rampway to slide the punts down into the canal. Young Reaume showed me the pens where the live decoys used to be kept until a few years before. Catch a bunch of mallards in a net, then tie a rock like an anchor to one of their legs, then put them out all day and at night gather them back to the pen. I thought about the ducks but kept quiet. When the ducks were worn out being decoys they'd eat them, Young Reaume said.

I'll show you something else, he said. He quickened the punting, paddling with the long oar around the shoal and out into open water. We went out from the sheltered marsh into the waves of Lake Erie, cold looking even in sunlight. Young Reaume quartered the waves around the river mouth to what he called Deadman Point, the cigarette still hanging there, rounding his vowels, pointing here and there. He never touched it.

Dead people come down the Huron, from a long way, he said, pronouncing it like "your own." When he gestured he punted with one arm, pushing the oar with his shoulder and using his hand halfway down it as a fulcrum. Once he even stood on one leg and pushed the bottom of the oar hard with his heel.

Dead people come down the Huron, down a long way, and they fetch up here.

We pushed up on a small patch of stony beach and got out into the tangles of live and dead trees on which bodies could fetch up. We both looked around but didn't find anyone. I did find a brass belt buckle in the sand, and Young Reaume found a beautiful wet black arrowhead at the waterline.

The waves were getting steeper on Erie, so we didn't stay longer. It looked scary, but Young Reaume surfed the punt back into the shelter of the marsh.

You try it.

I got up too fast, and the shallow boat tilted. Young Reaume leaned and balanced it.

I soon found my feet, and Young Reaume stood behind me, helping me balance, and then handed me the long oar. I put it in the water and pulled it like a canoe paddle, holding the upper arm steady and pulling with the lower.

The boat swerved.

No, no, no. The other way. Take and push the top hand, hold firm the lower hand. Push. Bring it back. Turn. Top hand. Good. Again push. Bring. Push.

Yes . . . But too long pushes. Take short pushes. You get worn out with long pushes. Easy short pushes. Easy to keep doing it for a long time. Keep it sliding along.

Young Reaume sat down. It was hard to sustain a straight line, hard not to swerve and lurch standing in the shallow boat, but I went slowly along.

When we got back I was punting, and there was Otto to cheer us in. Then came the men, Aksel and Jules, my father and Uncle Jack, carrying their ducks, and they got cheered in, too.

There were a few mud hens, which Otto and Young Reaume said they liked and my grandfather Aksel said he didn't, and they went off into German, French, and Danish in a mock argument. I liked it—and also when Otto told them about my punting. Then everyone cleaned their ducks together, and told how they shot them, and where on their bodies they hit them, and what different ones had in their crops, and what kinds they were. They retold the hunting all evening.

I first learned ducks from inside out.

Then Otto cooked the ducks and mud hen, wrapped in strips of bacon and stuffed with onions to keep them from drying out. We ate the roast ducks, still full of pellets of bird shot that had to be spit out on the plate, Pling. That went out of control a few times, too.

Canvasback were best, and they contested the claims of who shot them, using the entry location of bird shot for evidence. Lots of canvasback, with canned white potatoes warmed up, and canned peas, and canned peach halves. White bread and butter. Homemade jam. Candy bars. Pipes.

I tried to tell about Deadman's Point, but there was way too much noise. I just listened and fell asleep listening. Someone carried me to the feather bed.

All of this was just one weekend. On Friday night, frogging; on Saturday, going to Deadman's Point and learning to punt; and on Sunday, making a tree house and looking over the cattails.

It was easier that morning to get out of going to the blind. The smallest shotgun was too heavy, and I could not take the kick. No fun. I just stayed behind. You couldn't even play with the dogs in the blind. You distract hunting dogs by playing with them, another one of the bottom-line things said there.

I read old hunting magazines, unsold from the rack at Jules's bookstore, and found *Boy's Life*. I sharpened a pencil and drew for a time, copying pictures of animals, guns, marsh birds, a very realistic bittern. I tried to throw my jackknife so it would stick in a tree, learned how bad the balance of it was for that. Even standing on a chair I could not see out beyond the cattails that surrounded the camp.

I could hear plenty—shotgun blasts, sounds of different kinds of ducks—whistlers and quackers. And then the bombing practice out on the lake. I climbed a tree, got halfway up, and couldn't reach the next highest limb, so I climbed down and asked Otto for boards I could have and a hammer and nails. Otto said, Look in the shed, and did not ask why I wanted them. I took some two-by-four ends and nailed them like ladder steps up the tree. It was slow and tiring getting the nails through the two-by-fours, but they went easily into the living elm. I put steps where the branches gave no footing, high enough so I could see easily over the cattails, and there I nailed up a longer piece across two limbs and made a seat where I could look out on the lake.

Perfect. I could see now the Grumman Navy Trainers from Grosse Isle dive-bombing targets towed on rafts out on the big lake.

[219]

It was a little windy, a little wet. I tried to draw the tops of the cattails, as a ground for the pictures of planes, but couldn't make it look right and gave up. There was no time for each cattail. I tried to draw diving planes. Better, but how could you draw them going so fast? Soft speed lines behind them made them look on fire. I tore pages off the newsprint tablet and dropped them. The planes swooped and rose again with a far-off roar, then circled back and did it again, dropping what looked like white paint or bird poop on the towed barge.

The dogs came back first and smelled at the newsprint and looked up and barked a little, then ran back on the path to the hunters, who were carrying in more ducks and dragging duckboats up onto the dry land. I kept still, a funny, scary hide-and-seek. I couldn't be sure it would be a game to them. I looked down. My father put two fingers in his mouth and made the sharp high whistle he used for calling the dogs and me. They came wagging their behinds and tail stubs. I kept quiet, pushing the game. Why did they dock the tails of the spaniels?

Until a dog put his front legs on the elm tree, looked up at me like a treed possum, and gave me away, so I shouted, I'm here. Everyone looked up. I

Shooting from a duckboat

pointed out at the lake and said, The whole marsh . . . the whole marsh . . . the whole marsh.

Better get down. Aksel's voice, with the Danish r—Betto get town.

Without intending to I fell back off my perch and down through the tree, headfirst, bumping branches, trying to grab one, breaking them, until I fetched up by one leg, upside down, in the lowest crotch, just a boy's body length from the ground. My leather hat fell off, and a dog grabbed it. I didn't hurt much, but it was overwhelmingly humiliating.

I couldn't get my foot free of the elm crotch. Dogs barked. Everyone stared, until Otto came over and helped me free my ankle and, with a hand on my back from Otto, I flipped over and landed on my feet, a good back somersault.

Aksel laughed first and repeated my name with Danish vowels and r's.

My father said, You should see him get out of bed in the morning. A kind of praise. The kind of thing a father—not a mother—might say about a lad in *Boy's Life*.

I found my feet for a time. Or as it says on a map, I learned to know the habits of that quarter and what could be done there. When I was in college, learning about Buddhism and ahimsa, the lake rose and washed away the shoal and drowned out most of the Mouillée marshes. I can't find the place where my grandfather's hunting camp used to be, off Reaume Road, which is off the Old Dixie. Hunting will be prohibited soon at Pointe Mouillée. If you go there you can see to the south, year-round, the massive concrete funnels of Fermi II standing over the rebuilt marsh—but still lots and lots of migrating ducks and shorebirds and now some families of eagles. I've seen them eating fish way out on the ice.

KEITH TAYLOR

The End of the River

EVEN THOUGH WE HID from the March storm in our canoe, floating beneath a railway trestle for an hour or more, Pete and I were still soaked. A strong wind came from the west, pushing us more quickly toward Lake Erie even as it sent chills up my already cold back.

For years I had wanted to enter one of the Great Lakes in the same way the early explorers would have entered them—from the perspective of a canoe emerging from a sheltered stream. I had thought I would most likely experience it through the rocks along Lake Superior or between sand dunes and summer tourists along Lake Michigan. Perhaps it was most appropriate that I should see it first from the Huron, passing through the marshes of Lake Erie with the contradictions of our river all around me. Migrating ducks, geese, and tundra swans filled the air above us in numbers large enough to distract us from the signs of industrialism: the artificially straightened banks of the river; drainage pipes leaking something into the brown water; smokestacks to the north; the cooling towers of a nuclear power plant off to the south.

After the last turn and beyond the last bridge, we could see the Detroit River through the few little barrier islands on the left. It was so large we couldn't distinguish it from the lake. Past the dikes of Pointe Mouillée to the right, Lake Erie stretched to the horizon, gray beneath the low sky. While we approached it, the clouds broke behind us to the west, and the setting sun shot out its orange light, changing the color of the lake. Now we saw whitecaps riding blue water. Beyond the water—only the rippled edge of the horizon line, blue-grey lapping against clouds.

The river widened, and the current all but disappeared. The wind behind us had died. We paddled along the south bank, past an automobile junkyard and broken pieces of concrete, toward the dike and the protected marshes.

Suddenly, as if we had crossed a line that had the fixed and rigid edges of a line on a map, everything changed at once. The wind came up again, but this time almost in a swirl, as if it wanted to pull us out into Lake Erie. And a current caught the canoe, not a gentle current carrying us along with it but something bigger and more urgent, carrying us off to places we didn't want to go.

"Work a little harder," Pete called back to me, "or we'll end up in Canada."

And we dug deeper into the water, trying to paddle ourselves to the edge and the safety of our car. Lake Erie had us. The Huron River was gone.

Contributors

Charles Baxter is the author of *First Light, Shadow Play, Harmony of the World, Through the Safety Net, A Relative Stranger, Believers* and a book of essays entitled *Burning Down the House*. His most recent novel is *The Feast of Love*. He has been honored with an Academy Award in Literature from the American Academy of Arts and Letters.

A. L. Becker is a retired professor of linguistics at the University of Michigan who spent most of his academic life working with the languages and literatures of Southeast Asia. His most recent book is *Beyond Translation: Essays toward a Modern Philology* (University of Michigan Press).

William Brudon is Associate Emeritus Professor of Medical Illustration and Art at the University of Michigan.

Katherine Clahassey is senior graphic artist in the Museum of Anthropology at the University of Michigan.

Nicholas Delbanco is the Robert Frost Collegiate Professor of English at the University of Michigan, where he also directs the Hopwood Awards Program. The author of seventeen previous works of fiction and nonfiction, he recently published a collection of essays, *The Lost Suitcase: Reflections on the Literary Life*.

Julie Ellison, professor of English at the University of Michigan and director of *Imagining America: Artists and Scholars in Public Life,* has published poetry in a number of journals. She is the author of three books of literary criticism. The most recent, *Cato's Tears and the Making of Anglo-American Emotion,* was published in 1999 by the University of Chicago Press.

Alice Fulton's most recent books are *Feeling as a Foreign Language: The Good Strangeness of Poetry* (Graywolf) and *Sensual Math* (W. W. Norton). She was awarded a fellowship from the John D. and Catherine T. MacArthur Foundation and has also received a Guggenheim Fellowship and an Ingram Merrill Award. She is professor of English at the University of Michigan.

Linda Gregerson is the author of two collections of poetry, most recently *The Woman Who Died in Her Sleep* (Houghton Mifflin), and of *The Reformation of the Subject: Spenser, Milton, and the English Reformation Epic*. The University of Michigan Press will publish her collection of essays on contemporary American poetry.

Bob Hicok's *Plus Shipping* was released by BOA Editions in 1998. *The Legend of Light* won the 1995 Felix Pollak Prize and was an ALA Notable Book of the Year. An NEA Fellow for 1999, Hicok has had poems appear in *Best American Poetry 1997* and *1999* and *The Pushcart Prize Anthology XXIV*.

Craig Holden is the author of three novels: *The River Sorrow, The Last Sanctuary,* and *Four Corners of Night.* He lives with his family outside Dexter, Michigan.

Laura Kasischke is the author of four books of poems and two novels: *Suspicious River* and *White Bird in a Blizzard.* She teaches at Washtenaw Community College and lives outside Chelsea, Michigan.

Janet Kauffman is the author of five books of fiction: *Places in the World a Woman Could Walk, Obscene Gestures for Women, Collaborators, A Body in Four Parts,* and, most recently, *Characters on the Loose* (Graywolf Press). She is professor of English at Eastern Michigan University.

Michael A. Kielb is a coauthor of *The Birds of Washtenaw County, Michigan* (University of Michigan Press) and of *The Birds of Michigan* (Indiana University Press). He lectures in biology at Eastern Michigan University and Washtenaw Community College.

John Knott is professor of English at the University of Michigan. He has published three books of literary criticism on English Renaissance literature and recently edited Judge Noah Cheever's *Pleasant Walks and Drives about Ann Arbor.* He is coeditor, with Robert Grese, of a forthcoming special issue of the *Michigan Quarterly Review, Reimagining Place.*

Stephen Leggett published five chapbooks of poetry during the 1970s and 1980s. More recently, with his band, the Buzzrats, he has released two CDs, *A Tiny Speck in a Ruthless Universe* and *Cartoon Twilight.* He lives outside Belleville, Michigan, in Wayne County.

Thomas Lynch is the author of three collections of poetry, most recently *Still Life in Milford* (W. W. Norton). His collection of essays, *The Undertaking: Life Studies from the Dismal Trade,* was a finalist for the National Book Award and won the American Book Award. A second collection of essays, *Bodies in Motion and at Rest,* will be published by W. W. Norton in 2000. He lives in Milford in Oakland County just a block up from the Huron River.

Ann Mikolowski's work is in the permanent collections of the Detroit Institute of Arts and the University of Michigan Museum of Art as well as in several prominent private collections. She illustrated many books published by the small presses and for thirty years was copublisher of the Alternative Press. She finished the drawing for this book shortly before her death in August 1999.

Ken Mikolowski has published three books of poems, most recently *Big Enigmas* (Past Tents Press). He has taught writing for many years at the Residential College of the University of Michigan. For even longer he and his wife, Ann, worked as publishers/editors/printers of the Alternative Press.

Daniel Minock is the author of the award-winning *Thistle Journal and Other Essays,* and his work has appeared in *Country Journal, Sierra, Snowy Egret,* and many other periodicals. He teaches at Washtenaw Community College and lives just outside Kensington Metropark in Livingston County.

Tish O'Dowd is the author of the novel *Floaters.* As a student at the University of Michigan she won many writing awards and has remained there teaching undergraduate fiction writing. She spends her year in Ann Arbor and on the coast of Maine.

John M. O'Shea is professor of anthropology and curator of Great Lakes archaeology in the Museum of Anthropology at the University of Michigan. He has published books on the Omaha Indians and on early Bronze Age society in eastern Europe. He studies the organization of Native American society immediately prior to European contact and has done extensive fieldwork in northeastern lower Michigan.

Tom Pohrt is a self-taught artist whose books include the best-selling *Crow and Weasel* (written by Barry Lopez) and his own *Coyote Goes Walking* and *Having a Wonderful Time.* He lives in Ann Arbor.

Paul Rentschler is an aquatic biologist. He served as executive director for the Huron River Watershed Council from 1989 to 1998 and is currently the council's watershed science coordinator. He lives in Ann Arbor with his wife, Lois, and his sons, Samuel and Josiah.

Carl R Sams II is an internationally known nature photographer who lives in Milford, Michigan, and has done much of his work in the Kensington area. With his wife, Jean Stoick, he has published *Images of the Wild* and a recent children's book, *Stranger in the Woods.* Magazines in which Carl Sams's images have appeared include *Audubon, National Geographic, National Wildlife, terre sauvage,* and *Arione.*

Paul Seelbach is a research ecologist with the Michigan Department of Natural Resources and an adjunct assistant professor in the School of Natural Resources and Environment of the University of Michigan. He studies stream hydrology, habitat conditions, and fish communities throughout Michigan.

Macklin Smith is a member of the English Department at the University of Michigan whose specialty is medieval literature. In addition to his academic publications, he has published a number of poems and articles on birding. As of this printing he has seen more species of North American birds than anyone else.

Jay Stielstra has written several musicals, including *North Country Opera, Tittabawassee Jane,* and *Old Man in Love.* In addition he has written far too many songs to actually count. Currently he is living outside Manchester, Michigan.

David Stringer is the author of a collection of poems, *The Beast Speaks,* and is a former winner of a Hopwood Award in poetry. Until his retirement, he taught high school in Ann Arbor. He now works as a freelance writer. He has lived for many years on Superior Pond along the Huron River.

Keith Taylor has published several small press collections of poetry and one of very short stories. He has received grants from the National Endowment for the Arts and from the Michigan Council for the Arts and Cultural Affairs. For most of the last two decades, he worked as a bookseller in Ann Arbor. Now he teaches part-time at the University of Michigan.

Richard Tillinghast is the author of several collections of poetry, most recently *Today in the Cafe Trieste,* published in Ireland by Salmon Press. He is also the author of *Robert Lowell's Life and Work: Damaged Grandeur,* published as part of the Poets on Poetry series by the University of Michigan Press. His travel articles and book reviews appear regularly in the *New York Times* and many other publications. He is professor of English at the University of Michigan.

Pamela Reed Toner has lived most of her life in Michigan. For a number of years she taught English to middle and high school students, and she now spends most of her time with her three children. This is her first publication.

Gerald P. Wykes is curator and supervising interpreter of the Lake Erie Marshlands Museum and Nature Center. He has been an interpreter for the Huron-Clinton Metroparks for twenty years and is also a freelance artist and illustrator. He lives in Monroe, Michigan.

Illustration Credits